# Saving The Dragons

## Catriona MacRury

To Katy,
Enjoy the read!

Sláinte
Cat

Irish House/5th St. Publishing

2016

First Printing: 2016

ISBN: 13:978-0692609491
ISBN-10:0692609490

Irish House/5th St. Publishing

Author Website: www.macruryonline.com

Author Email: Cat@macruryonline.com or macruryonline@yahoo.com

Please note: No dragons, gnarts, dogs or horses were injured during the making of this adventure.

Content Disclaimer: If by chance you should come across any misspelled words, punctuation errors or sentences that simply don't make sense *the leprechauns did it.*

# Acknowledgements

My niece, *Natalie Biernacki* and nephew, *Colter Strautman*.
Who gave me the idea to write this adventure.

My trusted and talented Freeland Critique Group:
*Jerry Mercer, Wynn Allen, Garr Kuhl, Doris Berg,*
*Kathleen Moorelock & Teresa MacElhinny*

Editor: *Steve Conifer*

Proofreaders: *Edna Van Noort & Shelly Ewing*

Spanish Translations: *Joaquin Garcia*

French & Italian Translations: *Gigi Ghislandi*

Cover & Map Designs: *DHM Designs, Donna Harriman-Murillo*

I'd like to thank the kind folks in *Cashel Ireland* and *Conwy, Wales*, who always make me feel so comfortable and welcome on my visits while writing.

*Joan Saben*, my long suffering traveling companion who put up with my short-cuts (*which were always longer*) missing the last ferry back to Dublin (*are you sure there is not another one?*) and the list goes on. Thank you my dear friend and fellow explorer of the Headless Chicken Guide Service

*Michael & Jenny Golding,* your endless encouragement has meant so much to me.

Last but not least *Miss Kaylee Golding* for being such a bright little light in my life and who spent hours looking over my shoulder as I typed, even though she was not old enough to read.

# Dedication

To Dad and Mom
**Dick & Ollie Strautman**
And my siblings
**Karen King Biernacki** and **Eric Strautman**

*Thank you. Without your love, support and patience, I would not have been able to bring Tharill's adventures to life.*

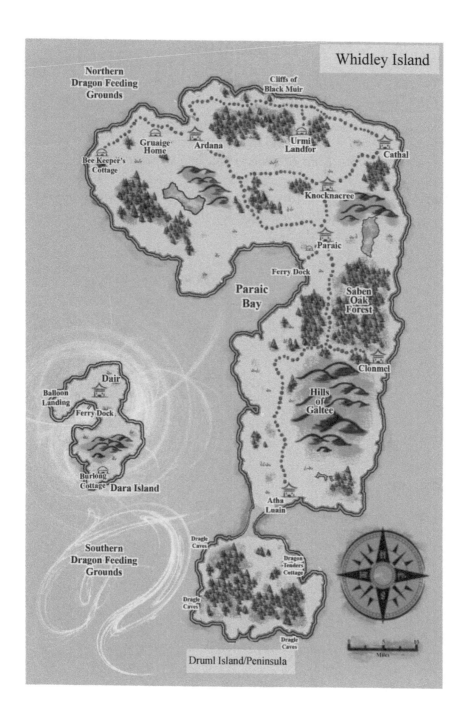

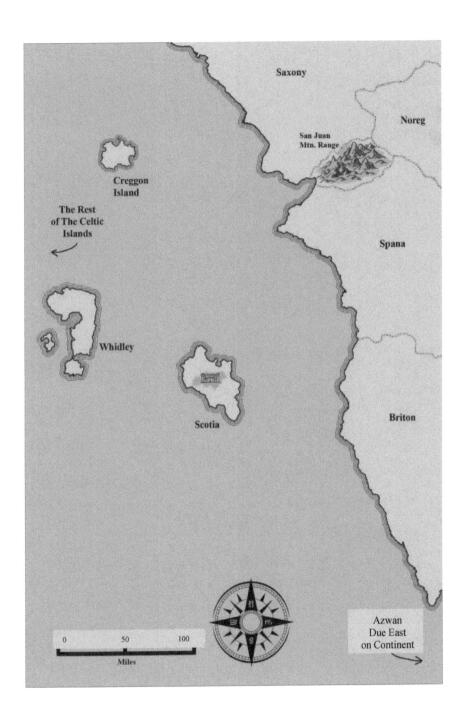

Catriona MacRury

# CHAPTER #1

## *DRAGONS BEFORE BREAKFAST*

Tharill Gruaige looked up to see a smattering of puffy white clouds lazily floating across the sky. The grass felt cool and damp under his bare feet as he walked toward the well with an empty bucket in hand. It was early morning, his favorite time of day. The dawn mist over the bay was slowly dissipating. Taking in a deep breath, he smelled salt air mixed with the aroma of eggs and gnart-bacon cooking in his uncle's cottage from where he had just come.

Placing the bucket on the hook and lowering it into the well, he waited a few moments while it filled with water. Had it really been a year since his father sailed away on just such a fine, clear morning as today, never to be seen again? Tharill's bright, olive-green eyes began to water so he shook the painful thoughts from his mind. A mild breeze tousled his shoulder length curly red hair giving him a disheveled appearance which matched his emotions for a moment.

Returning to the task of fetching water, the handle creaked with each rotation as the rope slowly brought the bucket up out of the darkness, water sloshing over the sides. His mind wandered between thoughts of the up-coming archery tournament and the fish that needed to be smoked for market.

A rushing sound from behind caught Tharill's attention. His eyes widened, the hair on the back of his neck pricked up, and his hand froze on the crank handle. Only one creature alive made that deep *whoosh-swish-whoosh* sound. It was the sound of a large dragon in flight.

Instinctively, Tharill ducked, turning loose the crank handle. The weight of the bucket plunging back down the well, caused the crank to spin out of control, striking Tharill's hand before he could get it out of the way. "Ouch!" He yelped collapsing his six-foot frame down to the ground next to the shelter of the well.

Tharill sat motionless, his back pressed against the cold stones of the well, cradling his injured hand in the crux of his arm. A momentary blast of air swept about him as a large dragon passed overhead, barely clearing the top of the well's little pitched roof. Tharill could almost reach out and touch the bright yellow stripe that ran from the animal's chin to its chest. The silver-blue underbelly looked like it would be soft to the touch. All four clawed feet were clinched close and tight to the bull dragon's body, some thirty-feet in length with a wing span of slightly over that, from tip to tip.

Something dangled from the dragon's tail, catching Tharill's eye. *A small tangle of vines, maybe?* In an instant the dragon was past, leaving only a faint musky aroma and one startled eighteen year old youth, in its wake.

Tharill cautiously stood up and watched as the dragon continued on its way west. *Out to sea to find his dragle,* he supposed.

"Are you okay?" Tharill's uncle Rist yelled, running from the small white-washed cottage they lived in.

"Yes, yes. Just shaken a bit, that's all."

"You are white as a snowberry, my lad! Look, your hand is bleeding." Rist examined Tharill's scraped and bleeding knuckles. "I can't believe how low that dragon was flying."

"And from the east! Why would a dragon be flying from inland instead of up the coastline this time of year?" Tharill puzzled, wincing as he inspected his wounded knuckle.

Maura, Rist's wife had been watching from the doorway of their home. "Oh, Tharill you're hurt!" she cried, noticing Tharill's knuckles as he and his uncle returned to the cottage. "Come sit at the table and I will tend to you." She pulled a chair away from the table and motioned for him to sit.

"I'll go back for the water," said Rist, patting his nephew on the shoulder.

Tharill sat down at the table where three plates had been set for breakfast. He looked over at the covered cast iron skillet on the cooking hearth, his stomach growling.

Maura applied a poultice to the lad's bleeding knuckles, wrapped them with a cloth bandage, and then proceeded to serve breakfast. Tharill ate heartily.

"He must not be hurt too bad!" Rist laughed, returning with the bucket of water. "He still has his appetite."

"It's not usual for dragons to fly over our property," Tharill commented through a mouthful of eggs.

"Aye," Rist replied. "Of course, it is common to see entire dragles in the bay, as it is a known dragon fishing grounds. But, they always fly up along the coast from Druml. Not from inland, not like the dragon this morning.

"We had that dragling fly over two summers ago," Maura reminded her husband.

"True, but draglings are bound to get lost or separated from their dragles from time to time," he said.

"That was no dragling," Tharill said. "His wingspan was well over thirty-feet."

"I saw that," Rist agreed. "It was a bull-dragon, for sure."

"Seems to me it was also flying unusually low," Maura said.

11

"You're telling me!" Tharill laughed. "I could have grabbed a claw and caught a ride!"

"That surely would have been a sight to behold, indeed." Maura giggled. "Could you tell which dragon it was?"

"It might have been Volcae. I think I saw one foot with only three claws," Tharill said.

"How old is Volcae?" Maura asked. "Maybe his sight or sense of direction is starting to go."

"He must be well over 100 years by now," Rist replied, "I'd have to check the Dragle records down in Druml, to be sure."

"Firemoon Tide is only three weeks away. Could he have shed some eyelid scales already, causing him to have vision problems?" Maura asked.

"I don't think so, but you never know," Rist answered.

"By the way, you'll need to go gnart hunting soon, as this is the last of the bacon and we only have two hams left in the smokehouse," Maura said.

"Great! I could use the practice before the archery competition at the Scotia Faire. I don't want to be bested by Prince Van Slauthe again," Tharill said.

"Oh, that's right," Rist said with a chuckle. "He beat you in long-bow and tied with Rory in mounted short-bow at the Faire, last year."

"He does have a good eye for distance. I'll give His Princeliness that much," Tharill grumbled.

"Let's eat up, lad. We have a long day's work ahead of us," Rist said with a wink and smile at Maura. "Those nets won't repair themselves."

Tharill put his fork down and gazed out the window. Rist noticed a sudden change in Tharill's features, a sadness had come over the lad.

"It is a year this week," Tharill said without looking away from the window.

Maura glanced at Rist and then looked down at her plate.

"Your father is not dead, Tharill. He is only lost," Rist insisted. Tharill slowly turned his head and looked at his uncle.

Rist noticed a tear on his nephew's cheek. "He is my twin, I would know if he was dead."

Tharill wiped the tears away with the back of his hand and said, "Yes, Uncle. I believe you."

"Come on, now. Let's get those nets from the boat and onto the mending racks," Rist said and shoving the last piece of gnart bacon into his mouth, he got to his feet.

Tharill and his uncle spent most of the day repairing nets for the next day's fishing. It would be their last fishing trip before market. They would be busy the rest of the week smoking the fish and preparing for market.

Just before teatime, Tharill noticed his brother, Rory walking up the road from the bay. Tharill waved and walked down the hill to meet his brother. Rory was sixteen, two years younger than Tharill. Both lads were tall and lean, but whereas Rory had inherited their mother's curly red hair, Tharill's hair was a deep auburn, typical of their father's side of the family. They both had the trademark olive-green eyes of the native Whidlians.

Whidley natives came in many different sizes, shapes, and hair colors, but they all had the same olive-green eyes. Even off-island women who married Whidley men would see their own eyes turn olive-green after giving birth to their first child. The eyes revealed an acquired immunity to the island's peculiar *Sleeping Sickness*, an immunity native islanders were born with.

"What's up, dung-nugget?" Rory shouted as Tharill began to trot down the steep path.

"Your breath, gnart-fart!" Tharill yelled back.

The two embraced and then clapped each other on the back. "How was the fishing?" Tharill asked. Rory had spent the last two days working on a neighbor's fishing boat.

"It was good, but an odd thing happened this morning," Rory answered as they walked up the hill.

"Whatcha mean?" Tharill inquired.

"The dragons," Rory replied.

Tharill stopped mid-stride. "What about the dragons?"

Rory stopped, too, and scratched his head. "Well, we reached our fishing grounds just after first light and there were dragons already feeding in the area. I'd say there were about eleven, including the draglings. We moved a little farther south to give them plenty of room. "We were busy setting net when Volcae – well, I think it was Volcae, anyway – he flew right over our heads towards his dragle. And I mean *right* over the top of us. I swear I saw one of his wings slap water after he passed. Then several of the dragons started roaring and squawking at each other – you know, the way they do when they're all worked up over something."

"Then what happened?" Tharill asked.

"They flew out to sea." Rory gestured to the west with his hand.

"Out to sea? Not south toward Druml?" Tharill asked in surprise.

Rory shook his head. "Out to sea and out of sight, due west."

As they approached the mending racks draped with netting, Rist greeted Rory with a hand shake. Maura waved her hellos from the cottage doorway, where she was sweeping. Without being asked, Rory started to help with the mending and Tharill picked up where he'd left off.

"By the way," Rory said, pointing to Tharill's hand, "what's up with your hand? Hurt yourself scratching your butt?"

Tharill playfully punched his brother in the shoulder. "It was the dragon's fault!" he began to explain.

"We had some excitement here this morning!" Rist joined in. "Your older brother tried to hitch a ride on a low-flying dragon and scraped up his knuckles instead."

Maura walked over with the milk pail in her hand. Holding out the empty pail to Tharill she said, "Please be a dear and bring Chloe in. It's time for her milking."

"You lads go ahead. I'll finish up here," Rist said.

"I'll get her rope from the shed," Rory offered, and Tharill tossed him the bucket to leave in the milking shed.

"I'll get the barnyard gate!" Tharill said.

Tharill waited for Rory at the gate. When Rory reached it they stood for a moment exchanging looks. "Race ya!" Both yelled simultaneously. They took off, like dragons-after-dark, almost elbow to elbow, at a full run up the winding path towards the pasture gate. Laughing, calling out insults back and forth, they made a very noisy pair. They startled a small blue-tailed fox sniffing at cow dung in the middle of the path. The fox gave a quick yelp and jumped into the brush.

As they rounded the last curve before the pasture gate Tharill had a slight lead. Without warning he slid to a stop. Rory barely missed slamming into his back. Whirling around and past Tharill like a fire-rat, he gasped, "What the dragons-breath? Are you trying to kill me?"

But Tharill didn't answer. He just stood there looking into the meadow beyond. Half-winded, Rory bent over and rested his hands on his knees, trying to catch his breath. He turned his head to follow his brother's gaze, and what he saw made no sense. Rory slowly stood up straight. There in the middle of Chloe's pasture sat a mid-sized island transport balloon and no Chloe in sight.

The transport was grounded and it was obvious that the balloon had collided with something. Its starboard sail was damaged. Rigging and shredded canvas hung from the broken spar.

Tharill could see at least three men working in the rigging on the damaged sail. There was also what appeared to be another spar lying on the ground next to the transport.

"That's a first," Rory said.

"What's a transport doing this far north?"

"Not a clue." Rory stepped closer to the pasture wall. "This day is becoming more interesting by the minute. What's next, ice worms in July?"

Climbing over the low stone wall, Tharill and Rory headed in the direction of the transport at a cautious pace. They could see a tall man clad in black pants, beige tunic and a double wrapped red sash with tassels that dangled past one knee pacing back and forth by the transport.

The lads were halfway across the meadow when the man with the red sash noticed them. He walked briskly towards them, hands swinging at his sides with each enormous stride.

"Bugger off, lads!" he shouted. "This is none of your concern. Bugger off!"

Tharill and Rory stopped. A deep crimson rose from Rory's neck and flashed up his face. "Bugger off?" he echoed, and lunged forward with a power-filled stride.

"Oh, no! Rory!" Tharill cried out. "Wait!" He hurried to catch up to his hot-tempered brother.

"Bugger off?" Rory shouted again. "You, sir, are on Gruaige property and I am Rory Gruaige!" he continued yelling as they advanced toward each other.

Tharill could now see this man was not only tall but well-muscled with thick arms, a broad chest, and powerful legs – the same legs that were, at this moment, quickly moving on a collision course with Rory.

They were less than ten feet away from each other when another man, wearing what appeared to be a transport captain's uniform came running from the balloon, yelling in a loud, anxious voice: "I'll handle this, my lord. I'll handle this!"

The man with the red sash stopped. Rory did not. He strode to within a few feet of the unknown man and looked up into the stranger's cold, violet/blue eyes.

"I ask again, who are you, sir?" Rory demanded. The man, undaunted, silently met Rory's eyes with a chilling, iron stare.

Tharill put his hand on Rory's shoulder and said, "Rory, calm down." Rory stood his ground, Tharill again pleaded, "Calm down, Here comes someone who will tell us what is going on, I am sure."

The uniformed man from the transport caught up with them. "I am... Captain Moseby... of the Celtic... Moon... Transport Company," he managed to puff out between gasps of air. Then he extended his hand and stepped between Rory and the man

16

with the stone-eyed stare. Moseby stood slightly bent over for a moment, trying to catch his breath.

"You say this is your family's property?" Moseby asked, once he'd finally begun breathing normally again. The man with the red sash stood silent.

Tharill reached in front of Rory, who was still locked in an intense stare with the stranger, and shook the Captain's hand. "I'm Tharill Gruaige. This is my brother, Rory. I see you've damaged your transport." Tharill pointed at the shredded sail.

"Yes, we caught a bad wind and had a bit of a 'Paddy-Jack' with a rather tall tree." Moseby chuckled, his face reddening. But Tharill felt the look of embarrassment and sheepish tone seemed somewhat feigned.

Still not saying a word, the man with the red sash turned and walked back towards the transport. The remaining three stood silent for a few moments, as if waiting for the man to go beyond earshot. Tharill kept his eye on Rory, who was still glaring at the man.

"What are you doing this far north in a balloon transport, and who was that man?" Rory barked.

Cautious of Rory's apparent anger, Moseby stepped back a pace and answered, "I am truly sorry for landing on your property. He had no right to speak to you that way. He hired me for a day tour of Whidley and is very unhappy about the way it has gone."

"Let's just find Chloe and head back before it gets dark," Tharill told his brother.

"Chloe?" the Captain asked.

"She's my uncle's milk cow," Tharill replied. "That's what brought us this way in the first place. This is her pasture."

"Sorry again. I believe our landing spooked her. I saw a black and white cow run into the trees over there," Moseby said pointing in the direction of a stand of trees.

Rory glowed at Moseby, spat on the ground, and walked off in the direction of the trees.

"My brother is a little hot-headed these days," Tharill said, watching as Rory stormed off.

"Again, I am very sorry. We should have the repairs completed shortly and be on our way soon." Moseby unstrapped a purse from his belt, pulled out two large gold coins, and offered them to Tharill. "Here is a gold willet each. Take them for your trouble."

Tharill eyed the coins and said, "No, that is not necessary." He had seen plenty of copper willet coins and on occasion even a silver willet piece but never a gold one. Moseby placed both coins in Tharill's uninjured hand and closed it around them.

"We may have scared your poor cow to the point she will not give milk for a day or two. These coins will hopefully make up for any loss your family will suffer for it," Moseby insisted. "I beg of you not to say anything about what you saw here today. You would not want me to lose my Captain's license over a silly tree, would you? Would you?" The Captain said, attempting a levity of tone that obviously belied his nervousness.

Tharill turned at the sound of a bell tinkling in the distance. Chloe's bell.

"You wouldn't want me to lose my license, would you?" the Captain repeated. "My customer is already furious with me. He is sure to complain to my company."

"You have a point. Chloe may not give milk for a while," Tharill said. "Good luck on your repair." Tharill turned and walked in the direction Rory had gone with the coins cold and heavy in his hand.

Returning to the transport, Captain Moseby approached the man with the red sash, who stood watching as the repairs were carried out by the crew.

"What did you think you were doing, confronting those two locals?" the Captain barked, unable to keep the reproach from his voice. "I told you to leave any dealings with the Whidlians to me."

In a low, heavily accented voice, the man with the sash answered, "That insolent, young, red-headed sot is lucky I didn't kill him." His tone icy and menacing.

"This is not good, not good at all," Moseby said, shaking his head. "The King will not be pleased, not pleased at all that you were seen by those two lads."

The man with the red sash narrowed his piercing violet/blue eyes at Moseby, "We would not have encountered any locals if your men had not been so careless with the dragon this morning," he said and brushed past the captain.

# CHAPTER #2

## *POISONED*

Chloe's bell clinked as Tharill and Rory walked down the pathway back toward the cottage. The sun was setting and the light beginning to fade, replaced with the growing shadows of the tree lined path. "What did you make of all that?" Rory asked.

Tharill shrugged. "I don't know, but something doesn't feel right about the whole thing." Tossing the coins to Rory he said, "Take a look at these gold pieces the captain gave me."

"Holy dragons breath!" Rory shifted them from palm to palm, feeling the weight of the gold.

"I would not have even considered taking them, but Uncle Rist and Aunt Maura really need the money. We have less fish than usual to sell at the upcoming market."

"What did you make of the *stare-down* king?" Rory smirked. "He tried to intimidate me. Not bloody likely. What a dung-nugget!"

"That dung-nugget seemed like a battle-seasoned soldier, and maybe commander of some sort. I don't care what he was wearing. I think he was in charge, not Captain Moseby."

"You really need to keep your temper in check, Rory. That whole situation could have turned ugly fast."

"Red Sash did not say a word," Rory said. "You notice that? I wonder what he was hiding."

"I wonder what both were hiding." Tharill stopped abruptly and pointed at something on the side of the path. "What is that?"

Rory walked over to what appeared to be a long stick and picked it up. Turning it over in his hands, he inspected the ends. "I think it is a piece of a broken arrow. And hollow, too."

"I've never seen an arrow that large." Tharill pulled on Chloe's rope to get her to follow. She appeared to be set on going straight to the barn without any detours.

"Ouch!" Rory yelped, dropping the stick. "I stabbed myself."

"You what?" Tharill laughed. "How in dragons-breath did you manage to do that?"

"It's not funny. It hurts and I'm bleeding!" Rory barked in anger and then laughed at himself in spite of the pain. "I tripped over an exposed tree root and I stuck myself in the forearm like a gnart-head."

"Here, let me see your combat wound, little brother," Tharill said.

Rory held out his arm as blood trickled down it.

"It's not too deep," Tharill said, inspecting the wound, "but what is this green slime-looking stuff?"

"I think it came from the arrow," Rory said.

"That can't be good." Tharill tone's was serious. He picked up the broken arrow shaft and green fluid dripped from the hollow shaft. He carefully sat the arrow down so as not to get any of the liquid on himself. Tharill unwrapped the bandage from his own hand and tore off a clean section to apply to Rory's arm. He also carefully wiped the green stuff away from the wound with some leaves then tossed them out of the way.

"I don't feel very well," Rory said.

Tharill's heart leaped at the sight of Rory's paling face. "Come on, we had better hurry home. I'll come back with a bucket or something for this arrow shaft."

With Chloe's rope still held tight in Tharill's uninjured hand, the two brothers began walking quickly down the path. As the barn came into sight Tharill stopped and turned to look at Rory. Putting his half-bandaged hand on Rory's shoulder, he was stunned at the heat he felt emanating from his brother's body. Startled, Tharill pulled his hand away.

"Rory, you're burning up!" he said, a growing concern shadowing his face.

"I feel really bad." Rory spoke softly but kept walking.

Tharill could see sweat dripping from Rory's forehead, his gait unsteady. They slowed their pace and continued down the path in silence. The cool evening air was filled with the sounds of chirping crickets and croaking frogs all around them.

Rory began to falter. Tharill tried to catch his brother before he fell, but could not. He could only watch as Rory's head bounced on the hard-packed path when he hit the ground.

"Rory! Rory!" Tharill's panic-stricken voice was loud and pleading. Tharill shook Rory several times, but to no avail. Rory Gruaige lay on the path, still and unconscious. Tharill leaned over his younger brother as an owl hooted in the distance. Chloe, now loosed from Tharill's grip, trotted along the path to the barn, her bell tinkling as she went.

Tharill struggled to pick Rory up, but his limp body was more than he could manage on his own.

"I'll be right back, Rory. I'll be *right* back," He whispered, gently laying Rory back on the ground.

He ran as fast as he could. His lungs stung with each breath. By the time he reached the cottage and flung open the front door he was gasping for air.

Rist lunged from his chair at the sound of the door slamming against the wall. "What? What is it?" He yelled.

"Rory!" was all Tharill could gasp out, and with the next breath, "Come!" He motioned for them to follow and ran back out into the night. Rist and Maura rushed out of the cottage. Maura ran barefooted, her skirts hiked to her knees as she ran.

The three raced through the night, Rist and Maura unaware of what lay ahead of them, Tharill not knowing if his younger brother would still be alive when they reached him.

Rory was still alive, but he lay motionless, his breathing a shallow wheeze. Maura kneeled beside Rory checking him for other injuries. His head had a bump on it from striking the ground, but she detected no broken bones.

"What happened?" Rist asked in a calm, steady voice, although at that moment he felt anything but calm or steady.

"Rory accidently poked himself with the end of that broken arrow," Tharill said, pointing at the large arrow lying on the side of the path. "It's hollow with some kind of green fluid inside."

"He is burning up," Maura said. "We must get him to a medico quickly."

"Take his legs, Tharill," Rist said. "I'll wrap my arms around his chest." The thought of when Rory was small enough to ride on his shoulders crossed his mind only to be instantly pushed aside by the weight of Rory's now unconscious body.

"We'll need that arrow as well. It may have some kind of poison in it," Maura said.

"I'll come back for it after we get Rory home," Tharill said.

With Rory held tight between Rist and Tharill, they matched their strides in an attempt to keep the lad from being jostled too much. Their pace was brisk and the distance covered quickly.

"Watch his head, now. Watch his head," Maura said as Rist and Tharill carried Rory through the cottage doorway.

Maura rushed into the room Rory and Tharill shared and threw back the blankets on Rory's bed. "Lay him down gently. Gently now," She said. "Then get me a bucket of cold water, quick as you can, Rist."

Tharill removed his brother's shoes and Maura took off his sweat-soaked shirt.

"I am going back for the arrow," Tharill said.

"Use a pair of your uncle's gnart-hide gloves to pick it up with, and take a piece of oil-cloth to wrap it in."

Rist returned with the bucket of water, set it on the table for Maura. "I'm going to take Bull to fetch the medico from town," Rist said over his shoulder as he went back out the front door. Bull was Rory's pride and joy: a very large, coal-black, high-spirited horse that possessed the same temperament as its namesake.

As Tharill ran along the path back towards Chloe's pasture he could feel his heart pounding in his chest. His lungs ached as he breathed in the cool night air, but he did not slow his pace. Thoughts and memories of Rory raced through his mind. *Fight little brother, fight to live.*

Although the moon was not full, it was very bright and Tharill had no trouble seeing where he was going. He heard a *whooshing* sound come from above the trees to his right. *The balloon transport, fixed and leaving,* he thought.

Tharill stopped where Rory had fallen and looked around for the arrow. It was nowhere to be found. *Am I in the right place?* He walked a little farther up the path and then turned around, scanning both sides for the arrow as he retraced his footsteps.

He spotted the handful of leaves he'd used to wipe the green liquid off Rory's arm. *I know this was the right place, but where is the arrow?* Using his gloved hand, Tharill wrapped the leaves in the oil-cloth and started back for the cottage.

He returned to find Bull standing in the front yard dripping with sweat from his quick run to town and back. Tharill burst through the cottage door. "The arrow was not there!" he exclaimed.

"What do you mean?" Rist asked, stunned.

"It was gone. The only sign I found that anything had actually happened in that spot was the leaves I used to wipe Rory's arm," Tharill said, holding out the oil-cloth. "I wrapped the leaves up in the cloth."

"There is no time to waste!" Maura yelled from the room Rory lay in.

"Help me hitch Bull up to the cart," Rist said, walking out the front door.

"Isn't the medico coming?" Tharill asked, panic giving his voice a higher pitch than normal.

"No, she is in Cathal on an emergency."

"We are taking him all the way to Cathal tonight?" Tharill said incredulously. "That will take hours!"

"No, we are taking him to Urmi."

"That crazy old druid?" Tharill screeched. "This is my brother, not an injured bird or dog!"

"Tharill!" Rist put his hand on his frightened nephew's shoulder and said, "We don't have time for this. Hitch up the cart."

Tharill stood in the doorway and watched as Maura dabbed Rory's forehead with a cold wet cloth. As she worked she hummed softly. Tharill recognized the tune as one of Rory's favorites. It was a slow, soothing, Celtic song.

"The cart is ready, aunt," Tharill said in a choked voice.

Bull stood by the front door harnessed to the cart, restless and ready to go. He dug at the dirt with one hoof, but did not move backward or forward.

"Easy, Bull. Easy now," Tharill said when he returned to the horse and rubbed its neck. Bull shook his large head and locks of his long black mane flopped from side to side.

Tharill heard the cottage door open. Rist came out carrying Rory wrapped in a blanket, followed by Maura holding a basket. Maura climbed in the cart as Rist and Tharill carefully lifted Rory into the back of the cart resting his head on her lap. Tharill sat next to Rist, who took up the reins.

Bull was a big and powerful horse. He knew the road down to the village very well and moved easily through the curves, pulling the cart with ease.

They made their way through the village and continued to the rough seaside road. There they turned north up the coast. It was low tide and the air smelled of salt and seaweed. The moon's reflection shimmered in tidal pools along the beach and across the large body of water.

Rory groaned when the cart hit a dip in the road, jostling its occupants. Tharill held on tight to the seat and side rail. He would rather have been on the floor of the cart beside Maura and Rory. The cart was bouncing and moving so fast he felt he might be thrown from it at any moment.

The cart turned inland at a fork and started up a steep incline. Bull pulled hard against the harness, his pace slowing and his breathing increasing to snorts.

The shoreline fell away to cliffs. The fragrance of lilac and Saben oak filled Tharill's lungs. He breathed in deeply. An almost tranquil feeling overtook him and his fears abated. They were now traveling through the Anum Cara forest, home to Druid Urmi Landfor.

Rory stirred under his blanket, taking in a long deep breath. *Thank Spirit,* Maura sighed in relief.

The cart slowed as they approached a small thatch-roofed cottage fronted by herb gardens on both sides of a little stone footpath.

Urmi stood at the gate dressed in woolen pants, a green tunic, and covered by a loose tan robe cinched in the middle with a silver buckle on a leather belt. He was short and rather rotund with a kindly face and soft manner.

"I had a feeling you'd be coming to see me," he said, moving closer to the cart. "Bring him inside and lay him on the bed."

Rist and Tharill carried Rory past the herb gardens and into the cottage. Maura followed close behind, her basket in hand.

They followed Urmi past his meal preparation area and into a side room. "Put him on the bed," he said. Rist and Tharill lay Rory's limp body down. Tharill's face was ashen as he looked down at his usually vibrant and cheerful brother.

"All will be well," Urmi said in a soft, soothing voice, then placed his hand on Tharill's shoulder.

Tharill felt a rush of warmth spring from the touch and run through his body. He gasped lightly in surprise. In the blink of an eye everything seemed fresher and lighter. He also felt hungry, very hungry, as though he'd not eaten all day or for the entire week.

"I'd better see to Bull," Tharill said.

"The barn is out back. Take him there," Urmi said. "There is a bowl of berries and a mug of milk waiting for you in the barn," Urmi added and shut the door behind Tharill.

Tharill took Bull to the old, partially dilapidated barn. He unhitched, brushed, watered, and then fed the horse. The fruit and milk were sitting on a small table along with a piece of buttered bread. Tharill ate heartily and drank the milk in big gulps. He was amazed at how incredibly good the food tasted even though it was such a simple meal.

*What a strange day it has been*, Tharill thought as drowsiness overcame him. He sat down on a pile of hay and without another thought toppled over, fast asleep.

Inside the cottage a warm fire burned in the hearth. Maura recalled the familiar aromas she had grown up with as a child of Druidic parents. She could smell thyme, garlic, lavender, and bay leaf in combination as well as individually.

The room where Rory lay had one shelved wall filled with bottles of assorted size and shape. As well as crocks, boxes, and jars. Various animal hides lay on the floor and drying plants hung from the rafters.

Maura took the bandage from Rory's arm and showed the injury to Urmi. "Tharill said that Rory accidently stuck himself with a broken arrow."

"I see." Urmi examined the arm. "The gash is not red or weeping any fluid. It appears to be a simple puncture wound. If there had been poison on the arrow, the wound area would be inflamed." He bent closer to Rory, looking at a greenish stain by the abrasion. "What is this?"

"Tharill said the arrow was hollow and had green liquid in it," Maura said. "Some of it was on Rory's arm, so Tharill wiped it off. I have the leaves he used to remove the fluid with." She removed the oil-cloth from her basket and unrolled it to reveal three large red leaves with a small amount of green stuff on them.

Urmi smelled the liquid as he held the leaves close to the lamp to get a better look. "I believe this is from the *einshlafen* plant but it is found only in the San Juan Mountain Range."

"Where is that?" Maura questioned.

"It is the disputed border lands between Saxony and Spana," Urmi said, pursing his lips, displeasure creased his brow.

Rist, who had been sitting quietly on a chair by the only window in the room, got to his feet. "I don't understand. What is this inch-laven plant?"

"Einshlafen," Urmi corrected him.

"I don't give a gnarts-ass what it is called or where it came from! What in dragon's breath has it done to our nephew?" Rist barked.

"Calm yourself, Rist. It is used to induce sleep. A drop will put a full grown man into a deep sleep for hours." Urmi put his hand on Maura's trembling arm.

"Rory is young and strong," he assured both of them. "Hand me my dragon cloak, Maura. We will sweat the fevering potion out of him."

She looked about her and saw it hanging on a hook across the room. "I'll get it," Rist said. He removed it from the hook and handed it to Maura.

The heavy garment was made of several layers of yellow neck scales from an adult dragon, sewn onto a spun-banin wool backing. The scales were rough to the touch. Maura's mother had one just like it. Dragon cloaks like this were usually hundreds of years old and passed down from one druid generation to the next.

Maura and Urmi spread the heavy wrap over Rory. It was very large and covered the lad from head to foot. Urmi positioned the hood over Rory's face.

"As he sweats the Einshlafen potion out we must continuously moisten his lips and wash his face with peppermint water." Urmi pointed at the wall of shelves and said, "There is crushed peppermint in that large red jar and clean rags on the shelf below."

Urmi left the room for a bucket of water, followed by Rist. "I'll get the water," Rist offered.

"No, Rist. I can manage." Urmi replied with a smile.

"I've got to do something or I will go mad," Rist argued.

"Go outside and walk through the garden. You will feel better. I've left a bowl of fruit and a goblet of wine on the meditating bench," Urmi said. As if in afterthought he added, "You know where the bench is."

"I am not hungry and I don't want to leave Maura and Rory. They might need me." Rist objected.

"They need you to be strong and well rested. Go now and eat what I have put out for you," Urmi encouraged Rist with a nod and smile.

Rist left the cottage and stood in the herb garden for a moment. He looked into the clear night and gazed at the bright expansion of twinkling stars. The air was filled with a soothing mixture of herb and flower fragrances.

*I actually have no idea where Urmi's meditating bench is,* he thought aloud, looking past the garden gate. He walked a few steps past the gate, wondering which way to go.

His attention was drawn to the sound of wind chimes tinkling in the distance. It sounded like the chimes were made of shells. *That's odd. I don't feel a breeze.*

Curious, he followed the sound. *No, they sound more like stones, or maybe shells and stones together.* In his mind he found himself picturing what the chimes looked like.

He followed a small path into an oak grove. The trees were very large, knotted and hundreds of years old. The sound of the chimes stopped once he reached a comfortable looking bench situated under one of the large oak trees. Upon the seat was a serving tray covered with a cloth. Rist removed the cloth to find a bowl of mixed berries and a goblet of wine.

*I take-it this is Urmi's meditating bench.* He tasted the wine. It was sweet and extremely refreshing.

Once seated upon the bench, he grabbed a handful of berries and tossed them one by one into his mouth. In the distance he could hear the sounds of a brook or a stream. He felt relaxed and calm. Again, he heard the light tinkle of wind chimes, this time directly above him. He looked up to see several chimes of assorted sizes and shapes. They were made with combinations of shells, stones, wood, bones, and feathers. There were also a few little glass baubles filled with either water or sand.

Rist lost track of time as he sat. He felt calm, in a trance-like state of mind, his thoughts filled with pleasant memories, happiness, and nothing else.

Rory lay on the bed sweating and shivering at the same time. Maura dabbed at his pale face with the cold wet rag and dripped peppermint water between his parted lips. He began to mumble something and she leaned closer to hear what he was saying.

"What is it, dear?" She asked.

"Father?" Rory murmured.

Maura could not hold back the tears any longer and she sunk to her knees sobbing.

# CHAPTER #3

## *URMI LANDFOR*

Tharill woke to the feel of a warm sensation on his cheek. Blinking his eyes from bright light, he realized the sun was shining on him through an open door. For a moment Tharill was confused about his location and how he got there.

Although unsure of his surroundings, Tharill felt strong, well rested and a bit hungry. Standing up he saw Bull poke his enormous head out of a stall. At once his mind cleared. *We're at Urmi's.* The memory of Rory's sudden illness rushed into his mind and immediately he wanted to check on his brother's condition.

He stood up and headed for the door. Behind him Bull whinnied. "Don't fret, Bull, I'll be back in a few minutes to feed you," Tharill promised over his shoulder, walking outside.

Bull whinnied again and struck the stall door loudly with a front hoof. The horse's continued protest forced Tharill to return to the barn.

"Hold your horses, horse!" he shouted, grabbing a pitchfork. Bull snorted, and then bobbed his head up and down. Tharill fondly recalled how Rory pampered and adored the horse.

31

He was sure Rory would want him to take care of Bull before leaving the barn.

He tossed a forkful of hay to Bull and returned the pitchfork to its hook. As he started to leave the barn he was overcome with the creepy sensation of being watched, if not judged as well. He turned to see a cow, three goats, five sheep, and a donkey staring at him. "Oh, give me a break!" he groaned. "I don't have time for all this." The animals stood in big-eyed silence. A feather dropping could have echoed in the stillness.

"Gnart farts!" he snapped. Pitchfork in hand once again, he tossed hay to all of the animals.

"Everybody happy?" he asked slapping his hands together. "May I serve anyone else?" The only reply was the sound of contented animals munching on their breakfast.

"Well then, I'll be off!" Tharill re-hung the fork and flicked a farewell salute at the barn inhabitants. He picked up the empty bowl and mug from the table and took them with him, closing the old barn door as he departed.

The morning was bright, not a cloud in the sky. Cool air was filled with fragrances of wild lavender and mint, which grew around Urmi's cottage and along the fence of the herb garden.

When Tharill entered the cottage he was met by Urmi, who took the bowl and mug from him. "Thank you for feeding my animals," he said with a wink.

*How does he do that? How does he know I fed them?* But, Tharill already knew the answer. It was just who Urmi was. It was the old Druids' way, simply natural for Urmi but astounding and mysterious to common folk.

"How is Rory?" Tharill asked with concern

"Resting comfortably and growing stronger with each breath. The worst is over and now he just sleeps a natural sleep."

"What do you mean *natural* sleep?"

"I believe the green fluid you wiped from Rory's arm was from the einshlafen plant. It is used in sleeping potions. Some of it must have entered the wound."

"That large broken arrow was hollow and the stuff dripped from it freely," Tharill noted.

"Too bad you could not have brought the arrow with you."

"It wasn't where I left it on the path. I am sure someone must have picked it up. The only other people around were from a downed balloon transport and there was definitely something unsavory going on with that lot."

At that thought, Tharill snapped his fingers in recollection and shoved his hand into his trouser pocket, pulling out the gold willets.

The front door swung open and Rist walked in. His hair was tousled and the shadow of a beard on his jaw.

"How is Rory?" he asked, looking into Urmi's dark green eyes, not sure what to expect.

"He is resting and doing much better," Urmi answered.

"And Maura, where is she?"

"Resting as well. She was up all night at Rory's side."

"I fell asleep after drinking the wine you left for me. Did you put something in it?" Rist's question sounded more like an accusation than a true query.

Tharill raised an eyebrow at the comment.

"No." Urmi laughed. "You just needed the rest, as did Tharill. Come, my friends. Let us eat the meal I have prepared."

Tharill instantly noticed how the enticing aroma of food teased at his nostrils, causing his belly to rumble. He put the coins on the table and seated himself.

Urmi placed three food-filled plates on the table, along with mugs of tea. "We will let Maura and Rory rest for now," he said, pulling a chair to the table for himself.

"Where did you come across those?" Rist asked, seating himself and pointing to the gold coins.

"In all the commotion, I completely forgot about them until now," Tharill answered. "Rory and I found a downed balloon transport in Chloe's pasture."

"What?" Rist reproached his nephew. "When did this happen?"

"Last night," Tharill responded, his face growing sullen. "When we went to fetch Chloe for milking."

Rist sighed, changing his tone, "What kind of balloon transport?"

"A small inner-island ship with studding sails. The captain said that they had clipped a tree and were repairing a broken spar."

"And who gave you the gold willits?" Rist asked, examining each one closely.

"The Captain. He said his name was Moseby of the Celtic Moon Transport Co. Have you ever heard of him?" Tharill asked.

"Yes, and I do not like what I've heard," Rist answered thin lipped. "Why did he say he was flying this far north?"

"Showing a non-islander the area, or so he said. As for the non-islander, he was a strange bird, a very strange bird indeed. He was dressed in a beige tunic and black pants with a long tasseled red sash." Tharill shook his head, "He appeared to have an air of authority, about him."

"What do you mean by 'air of authority'?" Maura asked, entering the room.

Rist stood and kissed his wife. Urmi made room for Maura at the table and brought her a plate of food along with a mug of tea. "I can't quite put my finger on it, Aunt. But, you could tell by his manner that he was used to commanding men." Tharill answered.

Maura brightened and changed the subject, "I've pulled the cloak off Rory. He is sleeping and breathing easy. The *sweat* is complete." All nodded their heads in approval and sounds of cheer echoed in the room with sighs of relief and best wishes.

"Very good," Urmi said, his face bright with a toothy grin. "I will check on him shortly. Hopefully he will be able to go home today. I know you must leave for the Dara Market soon and have a lot of fish to make ready."

Picking up one of the gold coins, Maura said, "Why did the Captain give you these?"

"He asked me not to tell anyone about his ship going down. At first I refused to take the coins. But he insisted, saying it would make *him* feel better, as Chloe had been frightened away when the ship hit the ground."

"I see," Maura said, skeptically.

"He said his customer was already mad about it and he also didn't want his boss to find out that he had flown into a tree."

"That is very interesting," Rist said, with a tone implying disgust. "Considering Moseby is the sole owner of that shabby little one-balloon transport company."

"Tharill, what damage was done to the transport?" Urmi asked.

"The spar on a studding sail was definitely snapped in two, the sail cloth shredded, and the rigging was all a-hoo."

"Did you see the tree the ship struck?" Rist continued to question.

"No, but I didn't think to look for it."

"Were there any broken branches or tree limbs lying around the area that appeared to be newly damaged?" Rist asked giving Urmi a sidelong glance.

"No, I didn't see anything like that, either. The pasture was empty except for the ship and Chloe hiding in a stand of trees." Tharill abruptly struck his fist on the table, startling all, and yelped, "That's it! That's it!" A brilliant energy flashed through Tharill as the events of the day fell into perspective for him.

"Do tell, my lad," Urmi prodded.

"The whole day makes sense now. Well, at least I think it does." Tharill beamed with excitement and turned his attention to Urmi.

"This morning Volcae flew unusually low over Uncle's place and he had something dangling from his tail. I originally thought it was a vine or some other piece of vegetation, but it could have been a piece of rope."

"That is very interesting," Urmi replied.

"The *so-called* tree they tangled with may very well have been Volcae instead," Rist surmised.

"I saw no sign of dragon-blow damage," Tharill said, almost as a question rather than a statement.

"There wouldn't be, if they came at him from above. Volcae would have to arch his neck to blow flame. Dragons don't fly up-side-down as far as I know," Rist added in jest.

"Tell me more about the broken arrow," Urmi said.

"It was larger than any arrow I'd ever seen, more like a spear in size. By the width of the piece Rory found, I'd guess the arrow might be four to five feet in length."

"Maybe it was a spear," Rist offered.

"No, I could see a groove in the arrow from the flight track of a bow."

Urmi inquired, "What do you mean by, flight track of a bow?"

"It is where the arrow rubs against the bow when ejected by the drawstring. It leaves a small heat mark from the friction on one side of the arrow."

"I see," said Urmi nodding his head

"But I don't know of any bow that could handle such a large arrow, or any man that could pull it if there were."

"What about a mechanical cross-bow?" Rist questioned and took another sip of his tea.

"Of course, you are right, a large battle cross-bow could. It could be mounted to the frame of the ship," Tharill said, then shook his head. "Cross-bows shoot bolts, not arrows."

"Did you see anything that could shoot an arrow that size on the transport?" Maura inquired.

"No, but there was a large tarp covering something on the bow of the ship," Tharill offered. "They made sure we got no closer to the ship than they wanted us to be."

"Is there any way to match an arrow to the bow it was shot from?" Urmi asked.

"Yes, each bow has its own unique flight track groove, so no two bows would leave the same track marks," Tharill said. "But, I don't know if you can compare flight tracks on cross-bows."

"Well, it is good to know and may be useful in the near future," Urmi said.

"How so?" Maura asked, her heels clicking on the floor as she walk to the whistling kettle to retrieve it.

Urmi tapped his chin and said, "The einshlafen potion was very condensed and luckily we sweated enough out of Rory that it didn't kill him. But, it could have. I believe that arrow may have been meant for Volcae. It might have bounced off him and broken apart or missed him entirely, shattering when it hit the ground."

"Dragon hunting has been banned for over forty years! Who would do such a fool thing?" Rist was incensed by the notion and held out his mug to be refilled with tea.

"Hello?" The faint voice of Rory Grauige could be heard from within his room. All froze and looked in that direction and the voice sounded again, "Hello? Where am I? Tharill?"

Tharill jumped from his seat knocking the chair over and hurried into his brother's room and found Rory had propped himself up on one elbow. The tousle haired lad was looking about in wide-eyed apprehension and genuine curiosity.

"How ya doing, gnart-fart?" Tharill quipped, ecstatic to see the rosy color back in Rory cheeks.

"Able to kick your dung-nugget butt." Rory smiled with relief at the site of his brother.

"That's my little brother!" Tharill chortled and embraced Rory in an almost crushing bear hug. A tear trickled down Tharill's face before he could wipe it away.

"I'm okay," Rory assured his brother and pulled away to regain his breath.

"Hungry?" Maura asked poking her head past the half opened door.

"Starving!"

"You sit right there and I'll bring you some food," She clucked.

Urmi sat down on the bed next to Rory. "Hello, lad."

"Hi, Urmi. How did I get here?"

"We brought you. What won't you do to get out of milking?" Tharill chuckled in nervous relief. "That arrow you impaled yourself with had a potion in it. It knocked yer dirk in the dirt. Do you remember anything?"

"I think I heard you guys talking about that arrow," Rory frowned with sketchy recollection.

"No, the arrow was gone when I returned."

"I couldn't move or even open my eyes when I fell. I am sure I heard voices I did not recognize talking about the arrow and something was said about me, too. But, I could only lie there. I was so sleepy and I could not stay awake."

Rist and Tharill looked at Urmi for an answer. "The potion could very well paralyze before total consciousness was lost," Urmi hypothesized.

"What did they say?" Maura asked, and shooed the others away from the bed so she could set the tray of hot food and mug of tea on Rory's lap.

"Something about the rest of the arrow," He said and gobbled up a piece of gnart bacon. "I can't recall exactly what was said. But, I do know they wanted to find the other parts of it."

Urmi signaled Maura and Rist to follow him out of the room. "We will let you eat and talk with your brother, my lad." Urmi patted Rory on the shoulder before leaving.

Seated at the table once again, Urmi began, "If you can stay one more night to let him rest that would be good. But, if you do need to get back tonight, just take it slow."

"I think we should spend the night," Maura said looking at Rist who nodded in agreement.

"Good, it is settled then," Urmi said with a smile. He enjoyed their company very much. "Now, to this arrow business, it is important to locate any part of that arrow. It would be helpful to bring it to the next Dragon Council meeting."

"As soon as we get home, I will send Tharill out to look for it," Rist said.

"Send Rory too, unless you need him to help you make ready the market fish," Urmi said.

"Should he not rest for a day or two after we return home?" Maura queried, concern etching her brow.

"No, by all means put him to work. The harder the labor, the better and have him drink plenty of snowberry juice and peppermint tea. It will aid in cleansing his body of any residue left from the einshlafen potion."

When breakfast was finished and the washing up complete, Maura suggested Rory take a hot bath in Urmi's trough outside. After a little coaxing from his brother with an offer to throw him in clothes and all, Rory conceded. The lads then set about empting the cold water out of the wooden, rectangle watering trough while Maura heated pots of water over the kitchen hearth fire. She also prepared the makings for some polices Urmi needed for a local man suffering from an infected rope burn, which he intended to see the next day.

After Rory's refreshing wash was over the two lads went for a walk, picked more fresh peppermint and took turns currying Bull, as Rory was still just a bit on the weak side. Then they spent the rest of the day relaxing and playing game after game of ficheall, Tharill's favorite board game.

Meanwhile Rist ventured out in the pasture and spent his morning fixing fences. After the noon meal he played a game of ficheall with Tharill. As Rory was chomping at the bit to ply his skill against Tharill again, Rist gave up his seat after only one intense and ponderous filled game.

"If there was a ficheall competition in the Celtic Islands, my lad, you could be sure to do well," Rist marveled and patted his nephew on the shoulder before heading back outside to see what other chores he could do for Urmi.

After dinner they enjoyed an evening of singing old Gaelic songs and listening to Urmi play melodies on his crwth. Sounds of music and joy flowed through and out of the cozy room.

Four miles to the south of Urmi's cottage, a dragoness faltered in flight, gasping for air as blood dripped from the gaping wound in her neck. Her small dragling flew at her side, furiously flapping his little wings in an attempt to keep up with her.

Suddenly the dragoness' chest was pierced by a large arrow. She dropped from the sky, tumbling through tree branches and crashing to the ground. Her dragling landed by her body, squawking in horror and trembling with fear at the sight of his lifeless mother. Defenseless, he crawled under one of her extended wings.

# CHAPTER #4
## Part 1

### *BOULDERS ON THE BEACH*

Urmi felt an uneasiness building within himself. He wasn't sure why; after all, it had been a pleasant evening spent in song and merriment with his visitors, and Rory was mending at a brisk pace. As he closed the bedroom window he thought he heard the rumble of thunder in the distance. Urmi reopened the window and sniffed the air. *It doesn't smell like rain.* He frowned and peered up into the night sky. *No clouds, either.*

A chill trickled down his spine. He shivered, even though it was warm in his room. Urmi pulled back the blankets and crawled into his bed with a clear mind but uneasy heart. His emotions shifted between mad, scared, hurt, and confused. Urmi did not push the feelings aside but embraced each one as he began to drift off to sleep.

When Urmi opened his eyes he was startled to find he was no longer in his soft, warm bed, but standing in a dark grey fog. "Hello?" he said. "Is anyone there?" Only his voice echoed back. He could feel soft, moist sand under his bare feet. He could also hear waves lapping at a shoreline nearby; the air smelled of salt and rain. He thought he heard voices somewhere in the fog beyond and began to walk in that direction, the sand now wet against his feet.

Each step was slow and labored. His legs felt heavy and ached as if he'd been walking for miles. The voices grew louder. He could hear men talking, but did not understand the words. *An unfamiliar language.* He stopped to listen.

*Should I approach them or skirt around that area? Maybe they are fishermen having run aground in the dense fog. That would make sense.*

"Hello?" he called again, walking toward the voices. The fog swirled around his feet with every step. "Hello?" There was no answer.

The sound of rushing footsteps pricked his ears. Then the rattle of metal and squeak of leather caused him to turn away and start running. An arrow pierced the air close to him, then another and another. Urmi bobbed and weaved as he ran, attempting to escape the onslaught of arrows zipping by, all around him.

He stumbled and fell down a steep, sandy drop off, rolling head over feet and then sidelong. He tumbled and bounced again and again. Holding out his hands, he tried to slow his fall without success. Each roll sent choking sand into Urmi's nose and mouth.

The old druid hit the bottom of the ravine with a thud. Though he had stopped tumbling, his head still spun. He blew air through his sand-clogged nostrils. His teeth were caked with sand and felt gritty. Through stinging, sand-scratched eyes he looked about. He could see only sand and the dense fog all around. Urmi did not stand; he was not sure if he could. The sound of trickling water caught his attention. He decided to follow the sound, knowing he needed to wash the sand from his eyes and mouth, even if it proved to be saltwater. That would better than no water at all.

Urmi struggled to stand. Apprehensive of falling again, he walked slumped over, carefully checking each step lest the ground give way under his feet. Then he decided to get down on all fours and began to crawl. The sound of the water grew louder and the fog more dense. Now he could hear bubbling water very close by now. *A small spring? That would be much better than saltwater. I will be able to drink as well as wash my eyes.*

He crawled to the edge of a little pool of water. Lying on his belly, he dipped his hands into the cool, fresh water and splashed it on his face. Blinking his eyes at the slight red tint of the water, he wondered at its color. *Minerals from the ground?* He tasted it. *It doesn't taste brackish.* It was slightly sweet, like plum juice. Urmi cupped his hands and drank in large gulps with each handful.

Dipping his head into the water, he was delighted to discover it felt fresh and clean. He opened his eyes, washing the remaining sand out of them. Although his vision was blurred by the water, something at the bottom of the spring caught his eye. Something shiny. He raised his head from the water and shook the wet hair from his face.

Using the sleeve of his shirt, he dried his sore red eyes. *What is that?* He looked back into the water and strained to see the bottom. The water now murky from his movements, silt swirling up from where he had dunked his head.

What had he seen? Was it a coin? If it was, then it was larger than any coin he knew of. *A silver medallion or pendant, perhaps?* That would be the right size and shape. He plunged a hand down as far as he could reach and walked his fingers across the bottom, feeling rocks, waterlogged sticks, and mud. He was about to give up when his hand touched something cold and flat. He groped further finding the object was also round and smooth, maybe five inches across. Grabbing hold, Urmi pulled on it but it wouldn't budge. *It must be wedged in place.*

Urmi worked his fingers under the object to give him some leverage. When it finally gave way, he lost his balance and struggled not to fall into the water.

As the shiny object cleared the water he could clearly see the duel dragons engraved on it. *Yes, it is a medallion!* Excitement raced through his mind at the splendor and detail of the gold smith's interpretation of the dragons and their journey knots. *I know this crest! It is the crest of the Alchemist Yggdrasil of Uppsala!*

Startled from his joy by the *zip* of an arrow just before it hit the sand by him, Urmi flinched and lost his grip on the medallion, sending it gliding down into the water. Another arrow whizzed by. Urmi tottered to his feet, jumped over the water, and hit the ground running - albeit more of a stagger than a run.

He heard men shouting behind him as more arrows flew past. The fog appeared to be darker and thicker off to his left, so he headed in that direction, running blindly as fast as he could. *If I fall, I fall.* His pursuers would be just as blind in the thick fog.

Running into the dark grey-black fog, he began to cough. This was not fog, he realized now, but a thick layer of smoke. He ran through it holding his breath, hoping it would clear, his eyes already red and teary, stinging with pain.

Dropping onto his belly, he found a thin ribbon of clean air between the sand and the smoke; he gasped for air just inches above the sand. He lay in the shelter of the thick smoke, trying to breathe as quietly as possible. Urmi could hear shouting and coughing behind him. He could still not make out the language as they grew closer. He did not move. *They'll have to step on me to find me,* he told himself.

Urmi felt a light breeze as the smoke continued to roll over, around, and past him. The sound of the voices, now within a few paces, turned into echoes of loud choking and hacking-coughs. He belly-crawled crosswise to the breeze; he went a short distance and then lay quietly, listening. Urmi could tell he was slowly moving away from where the men had looked for him. The noise of the struggling searchers grew faint and then died out completely, Urmi crawled on.

He was exhausted and hungry by the time he cleared the smoke. Finally able to stand and take deep breaths, Urmi was happy to be out of the smoke but dismayed that the dark grey fog had still not dissipated. He had gone from one form of darkness to another. *At least the air is breathable in the fog,* he thought.

He looked around, wondering which way to go. There was no breeze in the fog, and it was thick, like moss covering a rock. *It looks the same in every direction, grey and cold.* With his hands on his hips, he stared down at his feet for a long while in contemplation.

A large dark bird flew close to his head, startling him from his thoughts. Ducking, he dropped to one knee. Another large bird flew over. *Gulls?* He stood brushed the sand off his clothes. Examining the earth beneath him, he noticed the sand had a burgundy tint to it. He scooped up a handful and examined it. It was wet and dripped a thick red liquid. *Smells like rotten fish heads. Where there are fish heads, there are fishermen!* The thought revived his energy and cheer. He heard more birds in the distance. *Yes, seagulls!*

Urmi stood and walked toward the bird sounds with a sense of relief and excitement. He picked up his pace and heard the sound of soft waves rolling onto a shoreline. The bickering bird noises grew louder and closer. From behind, a large bird flew past him, then another and another. *These aren't seagulls.* His heart raced and he was gripped by a sudden feeling of dread.

More birds flew into the fog before him and he carefully padded in the same direction. The sound of the waves increased and appeared to be lapping against several large boulders on the shoreline ahead. As Urmi strained to see the large, motionless, aberrations through the dense fog, his body shivered, uncontrollably. The sound of the birds became almost deafening.

Urmi hesitated and turned around, thinking he should go back. *But to where and what?* He had no idea where he was or how he'd come to be here. Something in him told him to go forward;

there would be no turning back, now or ever. Step by step, the boulders became more visible and the birds' screeching almost unbearable. Urmi gasped in horror, his body jolted by shock. Hundreds of birds were flying chaotically about, some circling above what he now knew were not boulders at all.

There on the blood-red beach were the carcasses of several large dragons. They lay belly-up, deep gashes in their chests. Vultures tore at the flesh. The smell of death and terror was all around him. Urmi sank to his knees, retching in disgust and horror. He vomited only bile, his head spinning, the shrieking of vultures piercing his eardrums like needles. He cried out with pain, a pain that came from within his soul, a pain without measure.

Urmi woke with what felt to be a heavy pressure weighing down on his chest. He seemed paralyzed for a moment, able only to open his eyes. *Calm thyself. Surround thyself with light.* He lay quiet for several minutes feeling ill as if a cold wind was blowing through him. Through him and into his very being.

The two-year-old dragling cried out as men pulled its twelve-foot-long body away from its dead mother, by the tail. The dragling tried to blow-flame to defend itself, but other men quickly tied a rope around its mouth and head. They then dragged the terrified creature into a wooden and metal cage. Once it was securely inside the cage a man slid the door panel into place, leaving the trembling dragling in complete and nearly suffocating darkness.

# CHAPTER #4
# Part 2

## *HOMEWARD BOUND*

Shortly before dawn a mother squirrel chattered merrily to her little family outside Urmi's window. He lie quiet in his warm bed and listened to the sounds of morning. He considered his dream. *It must have been a warning. But, of things to come or a foreseeable future that may still be averted?* He closed his eye and rubbed his face. *The medallion appeared to be Yggdrasil. What would that wretched man have to do with the death of many dragons?* Urmi sighed, got out of bed, dressed and ventured from his room. "Yes, a new day," Urmi muttered to himself, the door thudding shut behind him. "And this new day comes with an added sense of awareness."

Maura was dressed and waiting when the somber druid entered the main room. "Good morning, my dear," his smile thin and forced. "How was your rest?"

"It was fine. And yours?" She answered and noticed his sad expression. They stopped at the door and Maura shrugged on a shawl to fend off the morning chill. "Well?" She prodded but he did not respond and so they walked on in silence.

When Urmi did decide to speak there was a slight tremor in his voice. "My slumber was troubled," he began. Then said, "Watch your step, here," and he took her by the hand where the path began to snake its way down the cliff side and led her the rest of the way to the shoreline.

Maura waited a few strides before asking, "In what way?"

Urmi hesitated, "A thunder which was not thunder and a dream that begged of reality."

"Do you desire to talk about it?" She encouraged and stepped cautiously around a fallen tree branch.

"I believe the dream needs to soak up a bit more light," Urmi frowned. "If that is possible before I can fully appreciate its meaning." He stopped for a moment and looked at her, sadness washing over his face and out through his soul. Picking up the pace again, they walked on in silence down to the beach. There they opened their arms and voices to welcome in the new day, a long practiced druidic ritual for both.

On their way back to the cottage, Maura approached Urmi about his dream again, "Were my lads in your dream?" Lines of worry creased her normally joyful face. "I have a sense of impending peril for Tharill and Rory. I would rather they did not go to the Faire this season. But, I also know that I can't shield them from everything, although I wish I could."

"Come," Urmi encouraged, we'll talk over a nice pot of tea." At the cottage they did just that and with mugs of tea in hand Urmi led the way back outside. "Let's sit in the garden and enjoy our tea in the fresh air. Rist will line the lads out in what needs to be done to prepare for your trip home." The two friends walked to a bench by the side of the cottage and settled in. "I dreamt of being chased, shot at with arrows and then finding many dead dragons,"

Maura gasped, "No! Where? Arrows?" Her tea spilled over the edge of her mug and splashed onto her dress. Urmi got to his feet and hurried to fetch a towel. "Thank you," she wiped at the stain not shifting her gaze from Urmi. "Arrows?" She repeated anxiety clear in her tone.

"I don't know if the arrows are connected to Rory and Tharill," he picked up her mug and handed it back to her. "It may simply be a sign of something deadly and silent in the wind to be aware of."

"But the lads are going to the archery competition on Scotia in less than a week," Maura fretted, white knuckling her mug. Urmi laid a reassuring hand on her shoulder and both sat down on the bench again.

He shook his head in thought, "No I believe the arrows were weapons of silence, not to draw attention to their misdeeds." The tea had cooled and Urmi grimaced at its taste. I saw an amulet that I am sure belongs to Yggdrasil of Uppsala. Maura cocked her head and looked away in thought appearing to recall if the name was known to her. "He is the Alchemist that was exiled from Cymru over forty years ago for experimenting on ice worms trying to make a very powerful gunpowder."

"Ice worms?" Maura laughed. "What do ice worms have to do with gunpowder?"

Urmi poured the rest of his tea out, as did Maura. "Ice worms naturally produce an aggregation pheromone called Nitrophenol."

"I didn't know you studied alchemy," she grinned and patted him on the back. "You old dragon, where did you study that?"

"In my travels as an apprentice bard, my teacher took me to the strange and wondrous lands in the Far East. We stayed there for close to six years and he sent me to several teachers of varying knowledge and disciplines," he recalled with perceptible fondness. "Yes, I learned many festinating things while I was there."

The sound of Bull's hooves and the cart wheels rattling along the driveway between the barn and cottage drew Urmi and

Maura's attention. "Well my dear, it is in great happiness I send you home with a healthy nephew and sadness by your departing so soon."

"I will bring several jars of my snowberry jam when I come next time," Maura promised. "Is there anything I can bring you from the Dara market?"

"Thank you, but I may take the ferry over for the day on my way to Atha Luain in the next few days."

"Are you going to the dragon caves to check on the dragles?" Maura asked.

"That is my intention," Urmi replied his brow knitted in deep thought. "I feel as though I should go to the Dragon Council Meeting, as well."

By mid-morning the Gruaige family had said their good-byes to Urmi and were ready to make the trip home. Rory appeared to be happy back at the rein and Bull responded eagerly. The horse knew he was headed home and kept a quick, easy pace all the way back. There was not much conversation for the first few miles each person lost in individual thoughts. The day was bright, with a few clouds speckling the sky. A cool breeze was blowing inland from the sea.

"I'll have my snowberry preserves ready for market in the next two days," Maura said. "When do you plan to leave for market?"

"Within the next four to five days," Rist answered. "That will give us a day to get there and another day to get set up."

"Are we going to fish tomorrow?" Tharill asked.

"No, we will go with what fish we have ready."

"Uncle, I am sorry to have caused you to lose these past two days of fishing," Rory said.

"Lad, you are worth more to me than any amount of money the extra fish would have brought," Rist said. "Besides, we have the two gold willits given to Tharill."

"You do not plan on spending those, do you?" Maura barked, which startled Rist.

"Why not?" he said.

"We don't know anything about where they came from."

"Well, we know where they are going and that is more important."

"I guess you are right."

Bull's sudden leap to the left side of the road was so violent and abrupt it almost toppled the cart's occupants.

"Easy now, easy boy, easy..." Rory cooed at the horse with a gentle voice while maintaining a strong grip on the reins. He brought Bull to a standstill and jumped out to make sure the horse was not injured in some way.

All of them turned at the sound of a loud screeching in the distance. Bull reared up, pulling away from Rory who did not let go of the horse.

"What in dragon's breath is that?" Maura cried out.

"A wounded animal of some kind?" Rist said.

"It sounds like a dragling to me," Tharill said.

They stood quietly and listened for the sound again, but it did not come. After a few minutes they all piled back into the cart and a more settled Bull continued them on their journey.

The Grauige family arrived home in the early afternoon. Rist went directly to the smoking shed and Maura to the kitchen where her snowberry preserves sat ready to be packed for market.

Tharill and Rory grabbed their bows, quivers, a velum target and returned to Chloe's pasture. Although they searched diligently for well over an hour there was no trace of the broken arrow or that a downed balloon transport had ever been there. Tharill and Rory turned their attention to archery practice for the rest of the day not leaving the pasture until late afternoon. They walked down the familiar path back to the cottage, each caught up in their own thoughts.

Rory broke the silence, "Tharill, could you kill a man?"

Tharill stopped midstride shocked at the nature of the question.

"Come again?"

"I mean, could you aim an arrow, pistol or rifle at a man with the intent of killing him?"

"Well," Tharill considered and started to walk again, "if my life or that of a family member was in danger, I think I would not have a choice. Why do you ask?"

"I am thinking of joining the Celtic Islands Gardaí." Rory said, looking for his brother's reaction.

"Have you talked to Uncle Rist about it?" Tharill said, a quizzical expression crossed his face.

"No, you are the first person I've told." Rory said, apprehension in his voice.

"Hence the question about me being able to kill someone, if it came down to it?" Tharill surmised. "Then the answer would be, yes. But, it's not about what I would or wouldn't do. It's about what you would do," Tharill offered. "May I ask how this decision came about?"

"Lieutenant O'Rourke of the Gardaí approached me last year during the Island Faire after I won the Mounted Short-bow division. He asked me if I would be interested in joining the Celtic Island Gardaí. They were looking for new trainees and had a very active archery club that I might be interested in."

"Why didn't you tell me back then?" Tharill asked a ting of hurt in his voice.

"Everyone has me already pegged to follow in Grandfather's footsteps as the next Druml Dragon Tender."

"We all thought you wanted to be a Dragon Tender. That is all you ever talked about as a kid."

"Father wanted me to be the Dragon Tender and I wanted to please him. He is not here anymore-" Rory's voice choked at the words and he lowered his head.

Tharill stopped and patted his brother on the shoulder, "Father wanted you to become the man you want to be. Mother and Father both only wanted you to be happy at whatever you decided to do as an adult."

"I don't remember Mother at all," Rory cut in.

"She made Father and I promise to raise you the way she wanted you raised and I hoped we have done that." Tharill said and shifted his gaze to the sky. "And Rist, Maura and I have tried to carry on without Father."

"Do you think she and Father would approve of me going into the Garda?" Rory asked.

"If that is what you truly desire, then yes." Tharill lingered a moment and then asked, "when are you going to tell Uncle Rist and Aunt Maura?"

"After I talk more with Lieutenant O'Rourke. He will be attending the Highland Faire again this year." Rory gazed at his brother with deep affection and added, "Your support on this means more than I can say, Tharill."

"You got it, little brother," Tharill said. "Not meaning to change the subject, but are you up to competing in the Mounted Short-bow again this year?"

"Do gnarts fart in the woods?" Rory chided, his eyes bright with joy.

"Do dragons have bad breath?" Tharill joked and knuckled his younger brother on the head.

"But all joking aside, you'll need to get Bull on this week's cargo ship to Scotia."

Rory snapped his fingers in recollection, "Oh, that's right! I'll talk to uncle Rist about it tonight."

"As for myself, I am looking forward to knocking that snooty Prince Rutgar Van Slauthe's dirk-in-the-dirt at long-bow this year." Tharill said through twisted lips. "I should have beaten him last year. I was just off that day."

Rory rolled his eyes, "Really? What about the year before?" He laughed.

"Don't make me hurt you little brother, don't make me do it!"

The dusk passed into evening and the evening into a comfortable gathering around the hearth before bedtime.

"Go ahead and take Bull to the Paraic-Dara Ferry tomorrow. I've made arrangements for him to travel with Aodh McCrudden's horses," Rist said stirring the coals of the fire.

"Thank you, Uncle Rist." Rory said.

"I don't think that is wise!" Maura objected. "He is just now on the mend from the poison arrow."

"I am truly well, aunt." Rory said with a wink of his eye.

"We will leave the day after and meet up with Rory in Paraic. Malacai O'Murchu's son Colin is already there and has a room at Sullivan's Boarding House," Rist said to Maura.

"No, absolutely not!" Maura's anger flared. "That place has a bad reputation and is across the street from the Fin-n-Fiddle which has an even worse reputation."

"Maybe I should take Bull instead of Rory." Tharill offered.

"Oh, no you don't!" Rory objected. "I want to inspect the hold before Bull is loaded. I'm not going to send him off willy-nilly in some ship I've never seen."

"Of course that is why you want to go," Tharill said a hint of sarcasm in his tone.

Rist held up his hand and said, "Maura, Rory will be fine. Tharill, I need you here to help me load the cart for market."

Directing his attention to Rory, Rist said, "I trust you not to cast a blemish on the Gruaige family name the one night you are on your own in Paraic. Do I make myself clear?"

Rory smiled, "I promise," and raised his eyebrows at his brother.

Sleep that night was difficult for Rory. He would lie down and then something would prick his mind causing him to get out of bed and re-check his baggage for possible forgotten items. When he did finally sleep it was a restless slumber and at first light he was out of bed and out the door.

Curro Delagarza inspected the large cross-bow apparatus mounted on the bow of Moseby's balloon transport. "Tomorrow will be our last chance to harvest a thorax from an adult bull dragon. Don't mess this up!" Delagarza warned Moseby.

Moseby only grunted in response and then flung the tarp back over the weapon.

# CHAPTER #5

## *YOU CAN LEAD A HORSE TO WATER*

Bull was fed, saddled and ready to go shortly after breakfast. The morning was overcast, a chill in the air.

"Rory, do you have everything you need for both the market and the Highland Faire?" Maura asked. "Remember you and Tharill leave the day after Market closes for the Faire. You will not be coming back here but go straight to Scotia."

"Yes, I'll take my short-bow with me, now. My cross-bow and clothes will be going on the cart with Tharill and Uncle."

Rory hugged his aunt and shook hands with Tharill and his uncle before mounting Bull. Rist handed him several silver willets. "This is for your part of the room and Bull's shipping expenses."

"Thank you uncle Rist."

Bull snorted and began to paw at the ground.

"Easy now, easy boy." Rory cooed to his horse rubbing the animals' neck with a gloved hand.

"Remember to get a receipt from the ship's captain for Bull's passage and keep. I don't want them to hit you with another bill when the horse arrives at Scotia." Rist said.

With all good-byes said, Rory turned the impatient horse toward the road to Paraic and set off at a comfortable canter.

Rory was making good time on his ride from his Aunt and Uncle's cottage in Ardana to Paraic. Bull could hold his steady and comfortable rocking-horse gallop without effort for several miles at a time. The cool misty morning looked to be leading into soft weather by afternoon so Rory let Bull continue at the more than brisk pace.

By midday, Rory began to feel hungry. Passing an inviting meadow he decided to break for a meal and let Bull rest and graze for a bit.

He took Bull's bridle off and hung it on the saddle. Then he dug through one of his saddlebags and found a chunk of cheese, slab of smoked gnart, butter and half a round of bread. *Oh, thank you Auntie Maura!*

Rory stepped over to a fallen tree and sat down while Bull began to graze. He was making himself a sandwich when the sound of riders approaching on the road caught his attention.

Two men wearing brightly embroidered vests over puffy sleeved tunics and billowing pants mounted on well-muscled albeit smallish grey horses passed the meadow without noticing Bull or Rory. The two men sounded to be arguing but Rory could not make out what they were saying.

Bull raised his head and whinnied at the passing horses. One of the horses whinnied back. The riders stopped, turned around in their saddles and said something to each other.

With a mouthful of cheese and bread, Rory smiled and waved hello.

The men turned their horses and approached Rory. "Greetings, friend," said one of the men, a turban covering what appeared to be a head of curly black hair.

"Gree..gree..," Rory gulped the remaining cheese in his mouth. "Greetings back," he said clearing his throat and with a sip of water from his flask. It was then Rory noticed that both men had short bows slung over their shoulders.

"I do beg your pardon, we have interrupted your noon meal," the second man apologized.

"No, it is quite alright," Rory said, wiping his knife on his pants and returned it to his belt. "Are you lost?"

"We are here to hunt wild gnart and are supposed to meet our guide at the Knocknacree cross roads," the first man said, "Have we passed it?"

"You are on the wrong road," Rory said. "This road takes you North West up Ardana way. Knocknacree is east of here. There is a turn off a mile or so back that will take you there. Look for the tree split by lightening and turn there."

"I was right, after all!" laughed the second man.

"You'll want to get a move on as dusk is the best time for gnart hunting and Knocknacree is a good six miles from here." Rory said walking over to get a better look at their bows.

"Nice short bow," Rory said pointing to first man's bow.

"Thank you, this is the first time I've had it out and am looking forward to trying it," first man replied, un-slinging the bow and handing down to Rory.

The second man dismounted his horse and introduced himself.

"I am Badar Al-Nassir and this is my brother Fozan."

Also dismounting his horse Fozan pointed to Bull and said, "You have a fine looking horse."

"Thank you, he is still a colt and has a way to come," Rory answered still examining the craftsmanship of the Fozan's bow. "This is a really well made bow and the art etchings on it are like none I've ever seen."

Fozan smiled and thanked Rory for the compliment as Rory handed the bow back to him.

Rory then turned his attention to the small dish-faced horses, "I've not seen horses like these before. What breed are they?"

"They are Azwani and like my brother and I, they are twins," Badar said.

Rory stepped back for a moment, looked from one horse to the other and then one man to the other. "Yes, yes! That is it!" he laughed, "I see it now. Are you staying on the island for the night?"

"Yes, we plan to return to Paraic after the hunt. We are staying at Sullivan's Boarding House." Badar replied.

"I am too!" Rory answered, thrilled. "Would you like to meet up after your hunt?"

"Yes," Badar answered. "Are you competing in the Scotia Faire?"

"Do gnarts have tusks?" Rory joked.

"I have been told they do," Fozan answered, puzzled by the question.

"Oh, it's a local joke!" Rory laughed. "Just ask for my room number at Sullivan's and come get me when you are ready."

As Badar and Fozan turned their horses back onto the road, Rory shouted after them. "Hold up there! I don't have anything else to do today but check in at Sullivan's and get Bull settled in for the night. How about I get you over to Knocknacree so as you can meet up with your hunting guide?"

"That would be most kind!" Badar said.

"We would enjoy your company on the hunt, too," Fozan added. "I would enjoy, of all things to watch your young stallion in action."

Rory whistled to Bull, who appeared to be reluctant to leave a very lush patch of grass he was grazing on. But, with a second whistle and "Bull! Come on boy!" from Rory the horse picked up his head and trotted over to where he stood.

Within minutes the three newly found friends were galloping in the direction of Knocknacree.

Their guide, Michael McGee, was waiting at the cross roads where they had agreed to meet. "I was about to give up on you," Michael said, mounting his horse. "But, here you are and with one of the Grauige lads to boot. Are you hunting with us today, Rory?"

"Yes, I'd like to tally along if it is all right with you."

"Happy to have you!" Michael answered. "You can help me flush if you and Bull are up to the task."

"We are up for the task!" Rory answered. Bull was already pawing at the ground in anticipation of what was to come.

"Your horse seems to know we are about to go on a hunt." Fozan said.

"Yes, I do believe he does! My brother and uncles hunted in this very area in June and brought home three good size gnarts." Tharill answered.

"Well, let us find more good sized boars today!" Michael said and kicked his horse into motion, leading the way off the road and down a narrow path edged by tall saben-oak trees and thick leafy bushes. The riders followed single file for about ten minutes until the path gave way to a long tapered clearing. Michael dismounted and kneeled down looking at some marks in the soil.

"It looks to be a large boar gnart leading three or four sows," Michael said and pointed in a southerly direction.

"How large do you think the boar is?" Rory asked.

"Well, the tracks are not that big. So, I would say this is a young boar."

"Then we need to keep looking?" Rory asked.

"Yes, I think we would be wasting our time tracking this herd," Michael answered and got back in his saddle.

Rory turned to Badar and Fozan, "The boar must weigh over three-hundred pounds to be harvested."

"Oh, I see," Badar said with an agreeing nod of his head.

"We have such rules for hunting big game in Azwan as well," Fozan offered.

The group traveled on for another 20 minutes before Michael saw more gnart tracks. Once again he dismounted and peered closely at the tracks, but this time he waved the others to come and look at the prints. "This is a big one!" he said with glee. "A real big one!"

Fozan, Badar and Rory kneeled by the gnart tracks staring at the size of them. "This is a four-hundred pounder, at least!" Rory cried the excitement in his voice carried over to the others who cheered in agreement.

Fozan slapped his brother on the back startling the horses. "Let the hunt begin!"

Badar and Fozan strung their bows and readied their arrow quivers for easy access. Bull picked up on Rory's excitement and started prancing in place. "Easy, boy," Rory whispered rubbing the horse's neck. The four rode forward, Michael and Rory spreading out to the sides of the clearing with Badar and Fozan riding down the middle. The Azwan mares also began to prance and snort with apprehension.

"There! There!" shouted Michael pointing at a large tusked beast running out from the cover of the brush several feet in front of him.

Badar was the closest to the area where the mighty beast ran from. Dropping his reins he kneed his horse into pursuit, pulled an arrow from his quiver, placed it, pulled the bow-string back and loosed the arrow. Within the blink of an eye he had another arrow poised and ready to release, which he did.

The first arrow whizzed past the boar as the animal darted to the left. The next arrow caught the animal in the flank causing the boar to tumble, head over feet. But, he did not stay down and the arrow broke when the animal fell.

Badar had another arrow in the bow and ready to go when the animal turned and charged at Badar's horse. The horse did not waver in her direction but put her head down opening her mouth and bearing her teeth. Badar loosed one arrow after another in quick succession striking the boar in the face and chest.

The boar struck the horse head-on ripping into the horses' chest with its tusks. The horse lost her footing and tumbled over the boar causing Badar to fly from the saddle landing head first onto the ground.

Fozan sunk three more arrows into the huge beast as it turned to gore the struggling horse again. Rory loosed an arrow that went into the raging boars' heart killing it dead before it hit the ground.

Fozan jumped from his horse and ran to Badar who was unconscious. Michael caught the wounded mare and began to examine her injuries. Rory dismounted Bull and poked at the four-hundred plus pound boar with his bow to make sure it was truly dead. It was.

Badar groaned and then opened his eyes. "Almas! Is Almas alright?"

"Michael is looking after her right now," Fozan answered. "But it is you, my brother, I am most concerned of. Can you turn your head?"

Fozan, still lying on his back, turned his head from left to right, held up his hands and moved his feet. "I don't think anything is broken," he said.

"Can you sit up?"

"Yes," Badar answered and slowly set up with the help of his brother.

"Here, take some water," Fozan suggested holding a water-bladder to Badar's lips.

"How is Almas?" Badar shouted past Fozan after taking a sip. "How is my brave lovely Diamond?"

"She has a large gash in her chest. It looks worse than it is deep." Michael yelled back. "Rory, get the salve from my saddle bag, would you?"

Rory left the boar and trotted to where the other three horses patiently stood awaiting their masters' return. He opened Michael's saddlebags and retrieved a jar of what appeared to be salve. There was also a large needle and thread in the bag.

"Do you need the needle as well?" Rory asked.

"No, stitches in chest wounds tend to just pull out. The ointment will do."

Almas stood quivering but not resisting Michael's touch. Rory held her reins, rubbing her shoulder and speaking softly to her while Michael applied the thick balm to her wounds.

Fozan helped Badar to his feet and they walked to where the injured horse was being treated. As they approached Almas whinnied to her master.

"This will stop the bleeding and quickly promote healthy flesh to grow," Michael assured Badar.

"How are you Badar?" Rory asked noticing Badar's shaky stride, even with the assistance of his brother.

"He was lucky!" Fozan chimed in. "He landed on his head!"

"That sounds like something my brother would say about me," Rory said with a grin.

"We now need to build a litter to haul the huge beast on," Michael said, when he finished tending to Alamas' wounds.

"You stay here with your brother and the horses," Rory said. "Michael and I can manage. We've constructed many litters and will make short work of it, returning quickly."

The four weary men and horses rode into Paraic late that evening. At the edge of town they parted with Michael who had hauled the boar behind his horse.

"I will take the carcass to the butcher and then head home," Michael said.

"Thank you, more than I can say for attending to my Almas," Badar said, shaking the man's hand from where he sat behind Rory on Bull.

"I've never seen a horse attack such a ferocious beast as a gnart that size," Michael said, shaking his head and viewing the mare with great admiration.

"She and her sister come from a long line of courageous horses, their bloodline going back over a hundred years. Such acts of bravery are in her nature. She would give her life for me," Badar said, glowing with pride as he gazed at his mare being lead by Fozan.

"I watched her gait closely on the way here and I am sure she will make a full recovery. Although, she will bear a scar across her chest for the rest of her life," Michael added.

"A scar she will display with pride!" Fozan said.

Rory, Badar and Fozan continued down the main street of Paraic passing the very noisy Fin-n-Fiddle Pub. Rory crooned his neck to look through the windows as he passed. Badar looked at his brother and smiled making an ale-mug tipping motion with his hand to his mouth.

They unsaddled their horses, rubbed them down and fed them at O'Neill's Stables. Rory noticed that several stalls had been tagged with Aodh McCrudden's shipping instructions for transporting the horses to Dara Island and then over to his ship at the Off-Islanders dock. Bull's stall had no such tag as Rory planned on taking him to Aodh's vessel himself on the first morning ferry.

The three walked together until they arrived at Sullivan's Boarding House. Rory stopped and said, "I think I will go over to the Fin-n-Fiddle for a pint. Would you like to come? I will buy!"

Badar shook his head and said, "Thank you but we do not partake of alcoholic spirits."

"But thank you for the offer," Fozan said.

"How about breakfast then?" Rory asked.

"That sounds very good. When will you rise?" Badar asked rubbing at his sore neck.

"Six AM. I must have Bull on the Seven-thirty ferry to Dara," Rory said. "I am taking him to Aodh McCrudden's livestock transport ship for the morning tide sailing."

At that they bid their farewells and went their separate ways, Badar and Fozan to their rooms and Rory to the pub.

Fozan and Badar had waited over thirty minutes in the boarding house's dining room for Rory when Fozan decided to go knock on Rory's door. Getting no response he rejoined his brother and ate breakfast.

"We must have misunderstood the time we were to meet Rory," Badar said.

"I don't believe we did," Fozan answered shaking his head.

"He must have taken an earlier ferry to Dara," Badar guessed.

"But, why didn't he leave a note or tell someone to notify us?"

"I guess we will find out when we see him at the Faire on Scotia," Badar said with a shrug of his shoulders.

When breakfast was finished the two brothers made their way to the butcher's shop to ask about their gnart.

"Fine animal!" the butcher said shaking Fozan's hand vigorously.

"Thank you," Fozan said, his face shining with pride.

"When will the carcass be ready for transport to our ship," Badar asked. "We would like to sail for Scotia today."

"Oh, I see…" the butcher said, rubbing his jaw. "I will get my lad right on it and have it barreled and salted by this afternoon. Will that work for you?"

Both brothers nodded in agreement asked the fee and paid the man. The butcher offered to cart the barrels over to Dara for them at no extra charge and the brothers left the shop very contented.

Their next stop was the stable to make sure the stable boy they had paid the day before had done a good job feeding and cleaning the two stalls. Badar examined Almas and was very pleased with how the wound had already begun to knit. He applied more of the balm as Michael had instructed and proceeded to brush the mare as she ate her grain.

"Badar!" Fozan shouted from somewhere down the row of stalls.

Badar poked his head out through the stall door, but did not see his brother. "Where are you?"

Fozan stepped out of a stall and waved Badar to come to him. When Badar got there he was amazed at what he saw.

"Rory?"

"Yes and I can't wake him!" Fozan said, panic in his voice.

"I will find a doctor!" Badar cried and ran from the stable.

Fozan grabbed a water bucket and went to the trough, filling it. He then threw the contents of the bucket over Rory's head as he sat slumped again the inside wall of Bull's stall. The water had no effect on the lad. *This is not from drink.* Fozan shook Rory and then slapped him. Nothing.

Within minutes Badar return with a black coated man in tow. "I have a doctor!" he shouted running into the barn.

The doctor kneeled down next to Rory, listened to his heart and took his pulse.

"What is it?" Fozan pushed for an answer.

"He has been drugged," the gray bearded doctor replied in a soft, but firm voice. "Was he at the Fin-n-Fiddle last night?"

"I think so," Fozan answered.

"He said he was going there for a drink," Badar added.

"I have seen just this thing many times this month," the doctor declared, his tone clearly agitated.

"What do you mean?" Fozan asked.

"Drugged and robbed," the doctor replied, shaking his head.

"Will he survive?" Badar asked, his face lined with concern.

"Yes," the doctor answered and dug through his bag for something. "I will give him some smelling salts under the nose and that should rouse him."

Rouse him it did. Rory Grauige's head jolted up as if his hair were lit a flame. His arms flailing about him, Rory gasped. "What, what is going on?"

"Be calm my lad. All will be right as rain. Now drink this," the doctor said holding a small brown bottle of liquid to Rory's lips. Rory obediently took a sip, gagged a bit and then rubbed his face with his hands.

"What time is it?" He asked, a sense urgency in his voice.

"It is close on half eight, in the morning," the doctor responded.

"Oh, no!" Rory cried. "I've missed McCrudden's sailing. How will I get Bull to the Faire?"

"I can't help you with that, I am afraid," the doctor said getting to his feet. Turning to Badar he handed the little bottle to him and said, "Make sure the lad takes a sip of this three times a day until it is all gone. That should be about five days. This will help get the poison out of his system."

"Poison?" Badar asked, walking the doctor out of the stables.

"I believe he was given a dose of enishlafen," the doctor said. "It is a type of sleeping potion. But, can easily be lethal. There has been a string of these types of robberies using the potion to knock the victim out. Every one of the cases I have dealt with has been connected to the Fin-n-Fiddle. Beware and tell your friend not to go back there."

Badar agreed and paid the doctor the small fee requested. When he returned to Bull's stall, Rory was on his feet. "I don't know what happened," Rory said. "I only had one drink."

"You were drugged," Badar said. "Here, the doctor wants you to take this three times a day until gone."

"What do you mean, drugged?" Rory asked.

"Check your pockets, do you have your money?" Badar responded. And Rory did search his pockets. All of his money was gone.

"My Aunt Maura is going to kill me!" Rory walked to a bench in the breezeway of the stable and sat down. "I've lost the money to ship Bull for the Faire. But, that ship has already sailed anyway."

"Fear not! My friend," Fozan said and put his hand on Rory's slumping shoulder. "We are bound for Scotia on the evening tide. We will be happy to offer you and your fine black horse passage there."

"Oh, thank you!" Rory replied straightening his posture a bit. "It will only be Bull, I am afraid. I have to help my brother and uncle at the market this week. We all plan to go together by transport balloon."

"We are happy to help in any way," Badar said, a reassuring smile on his face.

Captain Moseby stood silent on the deck of his transport balloon, his second in command next to him, watching the caged dragling being loaded on to a Noreg built schooner. "If the adult dragons find that boat, they'll kill everyone aboard and burn it to the water line," Moseby said.

"Aye, Cap," the second agreed. "I see Delagarza is not sailing with the dragling."

"He is not a stupid man," Moseby chuckled.

# CHAPTER #6

## *VOLCAES' FATE*

It was raining lightly when Rist and Tharill emerged from the smoke house that afternoon.

"Rory should be getting close to Paraic, by now." Rist said.

"I hope so. He didn't take his oilskin coat. He'll get soaked without it," Tharill said. "It always rains harder down Paraic way, than up here."

"What?" Rist snapped. "Maura asked him if he had everything. It was apparent this morning that it would rain at some point before the day's end. Did he think he would make it all the way to Paraic before it started?"

"I don't think he thought of it at all," Tharill laughed. "He was more than likely only considering how he would spend his time with Colin in Paraic tonight."

"We won't mention that to your Aunt Maura," Rist said, cringing at the thought of the two lads on their own in Paraic for the night.

"Who is that walking up the road?" Tharill asked pointing down the hill.

"You have a keen eye," Rist said. "I don't see anyone."

Rist picked up his pace to greet whoever was coming toward the cottage, Tharill by his side.

"Hello, Grauiges," the short squat man waved with one hand and clung to a long walking stick with the other. He was dressed head to foot in a long, bulky cloak of which the hood almost completely covered his face.

"Urmi," Rist yelled back. "Welcome, welcome."

"I did not recognize him in that long cloak." Tharill said.

"You may have the good sight my lad, but I have the better hearing. I would know that voice anywhere." Rist said.

The three shook hands and walked to the cottage together. Tharill relieved Urmi of a leather satchel he had slung over his shoulder noticing the intricate bead work on the front flap.

"Can you stay the night?" Rist asked.

"I would very much like to, but no, I must push on to Druml." Urmi said.

"In the rain?" Rist asked.

"I am well dry in my oil-skin cloak and I like walking in the rain. It helps to clear my mind when it is cluttered."

"Aunt Maura will not let you leave before she fills your belly with food and plies you with hot coffee to warm you." Tharill said.

"I welcome the break," Urmi said.

Maura did indeed make him eat and drink before she would let him leave that rainy afternoon. Rist also offered to carry him as far as Paraic in the cart the next day. But Urmi would not be dissuaded and continued his journey on foot after he finished eating.

The rain stopped by early evening and while sitting by the hearth that night Rist and Tharill finalized their plans for the next day.

"It will be a slow trip with Poorboy pulling the cart," Tharill said.

The old grey horse was getting up there in years and was soon due to be put out to pasture for good. But, as Bull had to be shipped to Scotia before Market, Poorboy would have to make one last trip to the Dara Market.

"We will leave early and take our time," Rist said. "There is no need to push the old guy."

True to his word, Rist got Tharill up before dawn to load the cart. Maura's snowberry jam jars were packed in crates and loaded first. Next the bundles of smoked fish were placed in the cart, then the tools and lastly personal items.

After breakfast and all good-byes said, Rist and Tharill climbed into the cart. With a tap from the reins and a resentful swish of his tail, Poorboy leaned into his harness. The cart creaked forward and they were off.

As the cart clattered along, Poorboy's hooves began a steady clop-clop-clop on the moist well packed road. Tharill found himself beginning to nod off even though the hard bench was not comfortable.

Tharill was startled from his slumber by the sound of trees crashing to the ground. Poorboy lunged forward and away from the sound.

Handing the reins of the panicking horse to Tharill, Rist jumped from the still moving cart and ran into the forest where the commotion had come from.

"What in dragon's breath?" Tharill yelped trying to comprehend what had just happened. "Settle down, settle down," he reassured the horse, "You're okay, Poorboy."

Tharill jumped from the cart and looped the reins around the cart rail. He rushed to the front of the horse and rubbed Poorboys' muzzle. "See, now you are fine," he whispered gently patting him on the neck.

"Tharill!" Rist yelled from the woods.

Tharill tied the horse's lead rope to a tree branch and jogged off in the direction his uncle's voice had come from. He found himself traversing through what appeared to be numerous, freshly fallen tree branches.

He spotted Rist crouching down looking at something on the ground.

"What is going on?" Tharill asked and saw the small dark puddle his uncle was staring at. "What is that?"

"Dragon's blood," he said straightening up while visually scanning the area. "Don't touch it. It will burn your skin."

"What is going on?' Tharill repeated.

"Come on, this way," he said following a trail of downed tree branches and blood puddles.

Tharill decided to hold his questions for later.

They made their way down a sloping hill carefully maneuvering between broken branches and freshly fallen trees. A faint sound wafted up the hill and grew louder as they trekked on.

*Wind rushing through of a cave?* Tharill stopped to listen better. *There is no wind.*

Rist and Tharill pushed past the remains of a large up rooted fern. From that vantage point they could see a wounded dragon. The large bull dragon lay shuddering with every gurgling breath. From its breast protruded a large arrow where blood gushed from the wound.

"No!" Rist choked out the word and walked closer to the dying animal.

"Is there anything we can do?" Tharill asked.

"I..I don't think so," Rist choked out the words and put a hand on the dragon's neck. The dragon's eyelids fluttered at his touch and then opened for a moment.

"Oh, Volcae, who did this to you?" Rist said gently stroking the magnificent creature's neck.

"This is horrible," Tharill said looking around as if to find an answer laying on the ground somewhere.

They stood quiet as Volcae took in his last breath and then shuddered into the final throes of death.

Tharill and Rist retreated from the scene unable to bear watching the process. The rain began to fall again, lightly tapping on the tree leaves before splashing to the ground. "I need to pull the arrow out and take it to the sheriff in Paraic." Rist said a stricken look on his face. "Hurry back to the cart and get my gloves."

Without saying a word, Tharill sprinted back through the woods towards the road where the cart was. He found Poorboy grazing on some long green grass next to the tree he was tethered to. The horse lifted his head and looked at Tharill for a moment and then went back to eating.

Tharill reached under the bench seat for his uncle's gloves but did not locate them. He walked to the back of the cart and found them there. He started to leave when he heard shouting from beyond a bend in the road. He stood quiet trying to understand what was being said.

Poorboy let out a loud whinny and another horse whinnied back. The shouts stopped and were replaced by the sound of pounding of hooves.

Tharill was about to move Poorboy and the cart off the road when Rist, now shirtless, appeared from the woods. He was running with his jacket slung over one shoulder and the arrow wrapped in his shirt.

"Let's go, let's go!" he yelled, stopping only long enough to slip the wrapped arrow into the back of the cart before jumping onto the seat.

Tharill climbed into the cart as Rist slapped the reins on the horse's back. The cart jolted forward and Tharill almost lost his grip on the seat back.

"Did you see who was on the road?" Tharill asked over the sound of Poorboy's hooves clambering on the wet road surface.

"There were four men speaking in a language I did not recognize," Rist said handing the reins to Tharill. "Take these for a minute."

Rist pulled on his jacket and then reached under the seat. He pulled out a small burlap sack from which he removed a pistol. He cocked the pistol, laid it on his lap and covered it with the burlap.

Rist took the reins back and slowed Poorboy to a walk. They traveled in silence for about two miles; the rain softly falling all around.

Tharill noticed something ahead on the road. As the cart drew closer he realized it was a leather satchel with bead work on the front. Rist was about to stop the cart when the sound of pounding hooves came from behind them.

"Steady, lad," Rist said and tapped the reins again to encourage Poorboy to pick up his gait to a trot.

Tharill stared at the satchel as they drove past it. "That looks like Urmi's!" he said.

"Stop! Stop!" someone yelled from behind them.

Rist did not pull up but he also did not ask Poorboy to pick-up the pace.

"Let us keep Volcae's fate to ourselves for now," Rist said.

The pounding hooves grew closer. "Stop I say!" The voice was now loud and angry. The echo of saddle leather slapping against the pursuing horse filled the air. "For dung's sake, Rist wait!"

Rist pulled the cart to a stop when he recognized his neighbor's voice. But he did not un-cock the pistol or put it back under the seat. Tharill looked past his uncle to see the beet-red face of Malacai O'Murchu astraddle a dripping wet and panting bay colored horse.

"Greetings Malacai what brings you out in such a rush?" Rist said, his voice smooth and unconcerned.

"I am ... so glad ... to catch you!" yelped the rotund man as he dismounted his exhausted horse.

"I can't say ... enough ... how glad ... I am to see you." Malacai repeated between gasps for air. Reaching his hand up to shake hands with Rist he added, "Greetings, Tharill."

"Malacai," Rist nodded his hello.

"That fool son of mine went off to market without the customer order list," Malacai griped pulling an envelope from under his jacket and handing it to Rist. "My wholesale customers will want their orders filled and ready to go as soon as Colin lands on Dara."

"Oh, I see," Rist said, "happy to help."

"Rory is already there, he can help Colin get the orders ready." Tharill tried to sound reassuring.

"I will make sure it gets done. Fear not my friend," Rist said patting Malacai on the shoulder.

"Thank you Rist," Malacai said. "And now, I must hurry back to my farm. One of my bee colonies has swarmed and I have not been able to find it. They have been acting very peculiar these past few days, very peculiar in deed."

"Malacai, did you happen to see anyone else on the road as you were coming this way?" Rist asked.

"Why... no one at all. Should I?"

"No, there was a satchel in the road back there. I wondered if you saw who dropped it."

"Oh, I saw no satchel, but then again I was in a hurry to catch you. I didn't want to ride all the way to Paraic."

Tharill straightened up as if to say something, but Rist gave him a quick glance. Tharill gave a weak smile and said, "Have a good ride back and hope you locate your bees soon."

"Thank you Tharill!" Malacai said remounting his slightly rested horse.

"Make sure my boy does not lose his head over all those pretty Dara girls. He will have given all of my honey away with only kisses as payment, if he had his way." Malacai sighed and turned his horse back toward Cathal.

Rist snapped the reins and with the clop of a hoof Poorboy once more leaned into his harness pulling the cart forward.

"I can understand Malacai not seeing the men on the road as they may very well have gone into the woods. But, there is no way he could have missed that leather satchel. It lay almost in the middle of the road. We had to drive around it so as not to drive over it," Tharill said, frustrated by Malacai's statement. "Maybe we should go back and pick it up. I am sure it was Urmi's."

"No we need to get out of this area and get that arrow to the sheriff in Paraic."

Rist taped the reins again and Poorboy broke into a steady trot.

Malacai stopped his horse, looked about, dismounted and picked up the satchel. Slinging it over his shoulder he got back on his horse and kicked the animal into a fast gallop.

Steve
Conifer /

Michael
Prescott

Amazon

of entries, the announcement of the prize, the cancellation or postponement of the game, the trip, or any trip related event, a winner's inability to participate, or any Sweepstakes-related materials. Sponsor reserves the right to conduct a background check of any and all records of potential winners, including, without limitation, civil and criminal court records and police reports, and entry in the Sweepstakes constitutes entrant's permission for Sponsor to conduct such background check, provided that, to the extent additional authorization is necessary under law, potential winners shall authorize such check. Sponsor reserves the right (at its sole discretion) to disqualify a potential winner based on the results of the background check or failure to properly authorize such check. Entry materials that have been tampered with or altered are void. Sponsor reserves the right, in its sole discretion, to cancel or suspend part or all of this Sweepstakes at any time without notice and for any reason including, if in the judges' opinion there is any suspected or actual evidence of electronic or non-electronic tampering with any portion of the Sweepstakes, or if virus, bugs, non-authorized human intervention or other causes corrupt or impair the administration, security, fairness, or integrity and proper play of the Sweepstakes. In the event of cancellation, Sponsor may void any entries it suspects are at issue and, at its discretion, if terminated, award prize in a random drawing from among all non-suspect, eligible entries received up to the date of cancellation. Sponsor reserves the right to disqualify entrants who violate these Official Rules or interfere with this Sweepstakes in any manner. If an entrant is disqualified, Sponsor reserves the right to terminate that entrant's eligibility to participate in the Sweepstakes. **Caution: Any attempt by an entrant or any other individual to damage or undermine the legitimate operation of the Sweepstakes may be in violation of criminal and civil laws and, should such an attempt be made, the Sponsor reserves the right to seek any and all remedies available from any such person to the fullest extent permitted by law, including criminal prosecution.** Sponsor's failure to enforce any term of these Official Rules shall not constitute a waiver of that or any other provision. Sponsor reserves the right to disqualify entrants who violate these Official Rules or interfere with this Sweepstakes in any manner. If an entrant is disqualified, Sponsor reserves the right to terminate that entrant's eligibility to participate in the Sweepstakes.

10. **DISPUTES:** Except where prohibited, all issues/questions concerning the construction, validity, interpretation, and enforceability of these Official Rules, or the rights and obligations of the entrant and Sponsor in connection with the Sweepstakes, shall be governed by, and construed in accordance with, the laws of the State of California, without giving effect to any choice of law or conflict of law rules (whether of the State of California or any other jurisdiction) that would cause the application of the laws of any jurisdiction other than the State of California. Jurisdiction and venue shall be solely within the State of California.

11. **ARBITRATION:** Except where prohibited by law, as a condition of participating in this Sweepstakes, participant agrees that (1) any and all disputes and causes of action arising out of or connected with this Sweepstakes, or any prizes awarded, shall be resolved individually, without resort to any form of class action, and exclusively by final and binding arbitration under the rules of the American Arbitration Association and held at the AAA regional office nearest the participant; (2) the Federal Arbitration Act shall govern the interpretation, enforcement and all proceedings at such arbitration; and (3) judgment upon such arbitration award may be entered in any court having jurisdiction. Under no circumstances will participant be permitted to obtain awards for, and participant hereby waives all rights to claim, punitive, incidental or consequential damages, or any other damages, including attorneys' fees, other than participant's actual out-of-pocket expenses (i.e., costs associated with participating in this Sweepstakes), and

# CHAPTER #7

## *THE GIRL IN TROUSERS*

Reesa woke to the inviting aroma of snowberry scones fresh out of the oven. She was not in her own bed, but in that of a rented cottage on Dara Island. Even though the bed was comfortable and warm, it was not hers. *There is just something about waking in your own bed that cannot be matched,* she mused. *Only gone a week and already homesick.*

She lay silent, eyes closed, taking in the sounds and smells around her. Her bedroom window was open and the fresh breeze smelled of saltwater and flowers. The songs of small birds were almost totally drowned out by the high-pitched screams of arguing seagulls.

She could also hear her mother and father talking in the other room. The three of them had arrived two days ago via Balloon Transport in the midst of a pouring rain. The flight had taken ten days to get here from their home in the far north of the Celtic Islands. The warm, sunny weather of Dara would be a welcome change, her parents had told her before departing. But sadly, the rain had not let up since their arrival.

Reesa's father, Professor Mortimar Burlong, the foremost authority in the field of Ignispirology, had published several papers and given many lectures on the subject. He was often accompanied by his wife and daughter in the course of his work.

His current project was to document the scale-shedding of the Whidley Island dragons which coincided with the Fire Moon Tide, due in late August.

"It is time to wake, sleepy-head."

Reesa opened her eyes with a start and saw her mother standing at the foot of her bed.

"Oh, sorry, dear. I didn't mean to startle you," her mother said, folding a blouse she had plucked from the floor.

"I was listening to the birds," Reesa said, sitting up.

"Breakfast is ready." Her mother set the folded garment on the bed and walked toward the door. "Please act like a lady and don't throw your clothes on the floor," she added over her shoulder.

Reesa pulled her favorite pair of trousers on and took a blue shirt from her wardrobe. It was very rare to see females in trousers and totally unheard of for young ladies of *Reesa's* social class and rank. She loved to accompany her father on his research trips. These trips took him to distant forests, mountains, and islands which required Reesa to be able to climb, crawl, wade through water, and hike great distances.

Her mother had grown tired of constantly repairing torn skirts and dresses years ago. She decided to make some pairs of durable trousers instead for her only child to wear on these outings.

Walking into the kitchen barefoot with uncombed hair, Reesa plopped herself, very un-lady-like, into a chair and grabbed a scone. Her mother turned from the cooking hearth and gasped at the sight of her daughter.

"Reesa! We've been here less than a day and you have already gone native!" Olive screeched, trying not to laugh. "Go fix your hair and put shoes on!"

"Look what you've done to my beautiful daughter, Mortimar!" she scolded her husband.

Professor Burlong, who was already sitting at the table, knew he was in deep dragon dung when his wife called him by his Christian name.

Reesa shoved a scone into her mouth and skipped out of the kitchen, heading back to her bedroom. She loved to tease her mother with such pranks.

The Professor shook his head, saying, "no, my dear Olive, she is very much her mother's daughter!" Their eyes met and exchanged unspoken words in the sort of communication that only twenty-five years of love, friendship, and marriage could make possible. Olive shrugged and rolled her eyes at her husband.

"She is sixteen now. It is time she started acting and dressing like a young lady her age," Olive insisted, setting three bowls on the table.

The Professor blew on his cup of hot tea and reached for a scone. "My dear Olive," he started but was cut short.

"Don't 'my dear Olive' me!" She snapped, a pot of porridge in one hand and a wooden spoon in the other. "She should be in finishing school with young ladies of her age and rank." The Professor's eyes grew wide at the sight of his wife pointing a dripping spoon at him.

He was about to answer when he heard a tiny, tense voice behind him. "Is that where you really want me? Sent away to a boarding school?" Reesa stood in the doorway. Her curly black hair, now neatly combed, braided, and held back with a blue ribbon the color of her tear-filled eyes.

"No, sweetheart, no!" her mother said, setting both pot and spoon down. She walked over to Reesa and hugged her. "We just want what is best for you and your future. That is all." Wiping a tear from Reesa's cheek with her apron she said, "Now there is no need for tears on such a sunny morning."

"Your mother's right. We want to do the right thing for you, sweetheart," the Professor added. "That's all. Your mother and I worry that dragging you along on my research trips will leave you at a disadvantage in society later on."

"Come sit and eat your breakfast. We will talk of this no

more this morning," her mother said, walking Reesa over to her chair at the table.

"What are your plans for today?" Olive asked her husband.

"The Dragon Council meets next week, I'd like to attend, if possible. So, I don't have much time to make ready for my lecture. Today, I will work on transferring many of my notes onto my new journal." The Professor raised his teacup in tribute to his daughter, who had given him the new set of large leather-bound journals for his last birthday.

"And what do you girls have planned for the day?" he asked.

"I am going to walk down the hill to the market for some fresh fruit and vegetables," Olive said, taking a sip of tea. "Would you like to come with me, Reesa?"

"I'd love to," Reesa said, a hint of cheerfulness returning to her voice. "It's a great day for walking. Do I have to wear a dress?"

"Please," her mother answered through narrowed eyes. "You can explore after we return."

The word "explore" always meant "okay to wear trousers." Other than in the company of her father during research, Reesa was not usually permitted to wear trousers outside the home and garden area.

Reesa's definition of "exploring" was more akin to that of an adventurous mountain goat than a cultured young lady of sixteen. But, for now she would return to her room and put on a dress to please her mother.

Within the hour the family of three was walking down the tree-lined path from their holiday cottage to the town below, where the market was bustling with activity. Shoppers were checking fruit at a stand. A lady in a lacey bright green dress and matching bonnet picked through ribbons that hung from a hook on a lace and linen cart. Booth Tenders called out their products and prices to passers-by while chickens clucked in cages.

The aroma of fresh baked snowberry pie caught the professor's attention. "How about some pie?" the professor asked, a twinkle in his sky blue eyes.

"We just had breakfast, Mortimar. Can we not walk about and work that off first?" Olive answered, shaking her head. "Land alive, my dear, how can you even think of food after the large breakfast you consumed less than an hour past?"

"There should always be room for pie in one's constitution." The professor chuckled as he proceeded with large strides in the direction of the aroma's source. Olive turned and grinned at her daughter. "Goodness sakes alive. That man eats like a longshoreman!" They stood there for a moment and watched the tall, rather rotund man make his way through the throng of shoppers scone in one hand, meat pie in the other and a bit of both bulging in his cheeks.

"Mother, I am not hungry. May I wander about and look for some new sketching pads? I only have one left and it is always better to have an extra one on hand," Reesa asked.

"Have you enough of the local currency?" her mother asked.

"Yes, I believe so. Where shall we meet and when?" Reesa asked.

After years of traveling with her parents on Professor Burlong's research expeditions, Reesa had learned the importance of establishing meeting places and times whenever they parted company.

Ten years earlier at a dig in El Qasr, the remains of what were believed to be the extinct Psobthis Dragon of Egypt had been discovered. As Mrs. Burlong was teaching in Britannia, the Professor had taken Reesa with him to Egypt. A miscommunication between the Professor and Reesa's nanny caused both nanny and Reesa to be left alone at a train station in Cairo for several heart-pounding hours. This resulted in two things: Mrs. Burlong's quitting her teaching position to accompany her husband, and a set rule on pre-arranged meeting places whenever the three were separated.

"Let's meet under the gazebo by the clock tower at 1 p.m. Will that give you enough time to look around, my dear?" Mrs.

Burlong asked.

"Plenty!"

Reesa clapped her hands together. A small purple velvet purse dangled from her wrist, and with wide eyes she looked about. *I do believe I saw a stationary purveyor's shop two lanes back.* Reesa enjoyed going to markets where ever she was. It was a good way to get the feel of the local life and meet interesting people.

The sound of laughter caught her attention as she walked past a booth selling snowberries. She noticed two lads about her same age joking around inside the booth while they worked. The sight saddened Reesa for a moment. Due to her father's constant travel schedule she rarely stayed in one place long enough to make good friends. She smiled at their happiness and walked on.

Reesa loved traveling with her father and found the study of dragons very interesting. She desired to follow in her father's footsteps as an Ignispirologist someday.

The sight of a window display filled with canvas, blank broadsheets, paint tubes, and other art supplies caught her eye and she stepped through the open doorway.

"Good morning, Miss! How may I help you?" came the voice of a slightly built man from behind the counter. His glasses were propped on a beak of a nose with intelligent brown eyes gazing through.

"Good morning, sir. I am in need of one or two sketch pads," she replied, looking past him at a huge painting of a stunningly beautiful blue-backed dragon with a large fish grasped in one claw.

Catching the direction of her fixed look, he stepped out of the way and said, "magnificent, isn't she?" He, too, was looking up at the painting.

"A Whidley dragon, I presume," Reesa said, admiring the brushstrokes that brought the creature to life, with the sun shining on its back and the water dripping from the claws.

"Yes, her name is Maudrus of the Ean Corcra Dragle."

"Who painted this?" Reesa asked without taking her eyes

from the painting.

"I did."

"Oh, congratulations! You have captured the moment in its entirety!" She went on marveling at the painting.

"Thank you very much." The small man blushed at the compliment.

"My name is Dogfael ap Gwynellyn, at your service." The small man bowed with a pleasant nod of his head.

"Reesa Burlong," she answered with an equal curtsy.

"Burlong? Are you related to Professor Burlong?" He brightened even more.

"Yes, he is my father. Do you know of him?" Reesa was genuinely surprised.

"Oh, yes! I met him close to fifteen years ago on Skellig Island." Dogfael leaned on the counter. "We were both attending the dragon council that year. I am the conservation agent for Whidley and Dara islands."

Reesa returned her attention to the painting, closely examining the signature. "Oh, it's you!" she exclaimed.

"Me?"

"We have several of your paintings at our home in Chester. I thought the style was familiar," Reesa said with pleasure.

"You are too kind, but thank you very much, I am sure," Dogfael replied. "Sketch pads, is it? Well, let us see what might fill your needs."

After Dogfael had shown Reesa several pads in a variety of sizes, she chose two. He wrapped them in paper for her and they said their good-byes.

She met her parents at the gazebo around 1 p.m., whereupon they decided to walk over to the ice cream parlor for some cool drinks to take the edge off the uncommonly warm day. They sat at an outside table in the shade of the table's umbrella. While they enjoyed their refreshing drinks, Reesa told her father about meeting Dogfael ap Gwynellyn while shopping for sketch pads.

"Oh, I must stop by to say hello while we are here," the

Professor said, excitement in his words. "I have not seen him in years! What an artist and as nice a fellow as you will ever meet! Yes, I must say hello and introduce you, my dear," he added, patting his wife's gloved hand.

"Those are his paintings hanging in the parlor," Reesa relayed to her mother.

"How happy I would be to meet such an artist," Olive said. "Is his shop close by?" she asked her daughter.

"Why, yes! It is only two blocks down the main lane."

"Well, then, shall we go pay Dogfael a visit today?" the Professor suggested.

"And ask him to dinner this week, we must," Olive replied.

Reesa frowned slightly, but said nothing and turned her attention to her soda.

"What is it, my dear?" her mother asked.

"I was hoping to spend the rest of the day exploring the dragon-watching locations. This is the first day it has not rained since we arrived."

"You must be due for a little 'trouser time,'" the Professor chuckled, exchanging looks with his wife, who nodded in agreement. "That will be fine, my dear." The Professor added, "We will expect to see you back at the cottage in time for dinner. Agreed?"

"Agreed!" Reesa said with delight, barely able to contain her excitement in a lady-like manner. She gulped down the rest of her soda, dabbed at the edges of her mouth with a napkin, and then got up from the table. She started to walk away, but returned to kiss both of her parents on the cheek.

"Love you!" she yelled over her shoulder as she gaily walked back up the lane to the holiday cottages. Reesa was already visualizing what she'd pack in her knapsack: pencils, charcoal for drawing, one small sketch pad and another large one, her pocket knife, eyeglass, bit of rope, and an apple for a snack.

Within minutes of entering her room she changed and came back out the front door, her lovely, braided curls now hidden under a tweed fisherman's hat. She had donned a blue shirt tucked into loose-fitting trousers held securely about her waist with a belt made from thick harness leather. With her knapsack slung over her shoulder and shirt sleeves rolled up to her elbows, Reesa Burlong trucked down the path behind the cottage, exploration on her mind.

The sloping, well-traveled path was muddy with rain water trickling down the center. Reesa's ankle-high, lace-up boots had been recently resoled and gripped well with each step. She admiringly reflected on the height and age of the trees that lined the path on both sides. *Some type of pine tree; I need to remember to ask father what they are.*

After hiking for a half mile or so she came across an overgrown trail. Pushing a leafy shrub out of the way, she glimpsed water beyond the trees. Leaving the main trail, she brushed past the vegetation and slogged her way down the winding trail. It ended at a precipice that overlooked the sea.

Reesa stood breathless, in awe of the majestic view in front of her. Clear blue skies above a rippling dark blue sea with small crests of white here and there. Beyond she could see the southeastern tip of Whidley Island, where the cliffs of Druml soared up seven hundred feet above the water in places. Right now it was a peninsula, but when the Firemoon Tide came it would be an island of its own.

*Druml Cliffs, home of the ancient dragon caves,* she thought to herself, *dating back to before records were kept. How splendid!* Reesa pulled her Metius eyeglass from her knapsack and held it to one eye. She could see the cliffs but not the caves from where she stood.

Closing the eyeglass she looked around for a better viewpoint. Spotting a rock outcropping a few feet past a large tree, she decided to try viewing the cliffs from there. She pulled the rope from her knapsack and shoved the eyeglass into her belt.

She carefully maneuvered around the pine tree, sliding a bit in the mud. Standing with her back against the tree, she pulled her eyeglass from her knapsack and looked through it. *I can almost see the dragle caves. Yes! There are the Ean Gorm and Ean Dubh dragle caves. But, I can't see the Ean Corcra dragle caves from here.*

Reesa leaned over the ledge, holding onto a branch of a smaller tree. She looked down at a sheer drop of more than five hundred feet to the rocks and water below. *Oh, my!* She took in a deep breath. Looking to her right she saw a more promising vantage point, although run-off water created a slight trickling waterfall. She would have to traverse the slick area to get to the edge.

With her rope slung over one shoulder and the eyeglass tucked safely away again, Reesa carefully crept through the undergrowth and mud to the waterfall's edge. Un-shouldering her braided rope, she tied one end around the base of a small pine tree and the other around her waist. She started to make her way through the mud and streaming water when the ground beneath her feet gave way and she tumbled after it. The rope made a *twang* sound as it snapped taut under her weight, the force slamming the girl against the side of the muddy cliff.

# CHAPTER #8

## *DARA MARKET*

"What do you mean, robbed?" The stout, six-foot six-inch tall and orange-red headed Colin O'Murchu asked pulling a chair close to Rory's bed to sit his bulky frame.

"Just what I said," Rory moaned from where he lay on the comfortable bed Colin had just helped him into. "Some gob-shite put something in my glass of stout when I was at the Fin-n-Fiddle, last night."

"I looked in the Fin-n-Fiddle for you," Colin frowned. "But, I didn't see you so I just came up to our room and read, figuring you'd be along in your own time."

"I wish I had come directly here," Rory said, grabbing a glass of water from the night table. "They took all of my money."

"What about Bull? How did you get him on old man McCrudden's tub? He has always demanded payment in full before he'd let any livestock set a hoof on that leaky scowl of his!"

"Oh, that is the least of my worries," Rory complained.

"Least? That should be at the top of your what-to-worry-about list!" Colin cried. "Aren't you going to compete in mounted short-bow at the Scotia Faire?"

"I've got transport for Bull with some new friends," Rory smiled at the thought. "He sails this afternoon with two brothers who are also going to compete at the Faire."

"I see," Colin said, nodding his head. "Lucky for you, they have a ship."

"My worry is what Uncle Rist and Tharill are going to say about me going to the Fin-n-Fiddle for a stout, being slipped a mickey and having all my money stolen. *That* is what is at the top of my *what-to-worry-about* list."

"Yes," Colin agreed. "That should be at the top of your list."

It was mid-day when Tharill and Rist pulled Poorboy to a stop in front of Sullivan's Boarding House. There were already several passengers, wagons and carts waiting for the next ferry.

"I am going to take this arrow to the sheriff's office, find Rory and then get our cart in queue for the ferry." Rist said reaching under the seat for the arrow and then jumping down from the cart.

"Will do," Tharill replied and noted how busy the main street was as he coaxed Poorboy a few more steps to a hitching rail.

Paraic, being the largest town on Whidley Island was the gathering point for all walks of commerce coming onto the island and exports going out. The Annual Dair Marketplace on Dara Island brought purveyors from all over the known world to trade, buy and sell their wares.

As many from other countries feared the Off-Islander Sleeping Sickness, the island of Dara would be as close as they would ever come to seeing the famed Whidley Island dragons, tasting the island's delicious snowberry preserves and smoked shamton fish.

Tharill jumped from the cart and tied Poorboy to the post. Spotting a trough and water bucket he decided to water and feed the tired old horse before they boarded the ferry.

"Tharill!" A voice from the steps of the boarding house shouted above the passersby and street traffic noise.

Tharill looked up to see the towering and bulky figure of Colin O'Murchu smiling down on him. "If you are looking for Rory, he is still in his room."

"Thanks. Would you tell him to get his gnart-arse down here?"

"Well, actually..." Colin said scratching at his round belly. "You better go talk to him before he sees his uncle."

"You are joking, right?" Tharill moaned. "Please tell me you are joking."

"Nope."

Tharill bounded up the boarding house steps two at a time. Colin moved aside to let him pass and then followed him in. "What room is he in?" Tharill called over his arched shoulder.

"Seven," Colin answered, following at a distance.

Rory tottered to his feet at the sound of the first pound on his room door. *Oh, dung-heap! I bet that is Tharill.* He just stood there for a moment considering his available escape routes if needed.

"Open up, you gnarts-arse!" Tharill ordered.

Rory slowly walked to the door and opened it. "What did you do?" Tharill demanded.

"How do you know I did anything?" Rory shot back, anger raged in his voice.

"Talk!"

"I didn't do anything! I was the one who had something done to!"

"What do you mean?" Tharill asked, one eye flinching as if taking Rory's measure of truthfulness.

"I went to the Fin-n-Fiddle for one pint," Rory said raising his hand to avert the objection he knew Tharill was about to voice. "I know. I know. I was not supposed to go. But, I truly just wanted to have one pint and listen to the music before turning in for the night."

"Well?" Tharill glared at his brother. "What happened?"

"He got robbed!" Colin chimed in.

"What?" Tharill said, astonishment clear in his voice as he stepped back to get another look at Rory. "Are you alright? Did they hurt you?"

"No, no!" Rory reassured. "I was drugged. Fozan and Badar found me in Bull's stall. They could not rouse me and sent for a doctor."

"What in dragons breath?" Tharill cried. "And you are sure you are all right? What did the doctor say? Here, sit down on the bed."

"The doctor said he thought it was in-shelf-on," Colin offered but hunched his shoulders as if unsure of how the word was pronounced.

"Einshlafen," Rory corrected.

"Again?" Tharill said shaking his head in disbelief.

"The doctor said that it had happened to others too," Rory said.

"Is it all right for you to travel today?" Tharill asked, concerned.

"Oh, I'm good," Rory answered with a reassuring smile.

"Where is Bull?"

"I met two Azwani brothers yesterday and went gnart hunting with them and Michael the Guide," Rory said, his face brightening at the change in subject.

"Azwani? All the way here from Azwan?" Tharill was intrigued.

"Badar and Fozan Al-Nassir," Rory said. "We had a great time hunting and they harvested a huge boar!"

"What were they hunting with?"

"The most beautiful short-bows I've ever seen," Rory said.

A knock sounded at the door and Colin opened it to find Rist holding a basket Maura had prepared for their noon meal. Rist looked at Colin, who was staring at the basket, "Anyone hungry?" Rist asked.

After listening to Rory's story of the prior evening's happenings and the meal was finished Rist announced, "Colin would you be so good as to leave us for now? We will join you outside shortly. I have a family matter to discuss with Tharill and Rory at the moment."

"Of course, would it be all right for me to take a couple of scones with me?" he answered.

"Help yourself lad," Rist said with a laugh as Colin had already had twice what he, Tharill and Rory had combined. Colin closed the door behind him as he left the room.

Looking directly at Rory, Rist said, "Volcae was shot dead with an einshlafen filled arrow yesterday."

Rory gasped and looked at Tharill. "Are you sure?"

"We came across him as he was taking his last breaths of life," Tharill said and put a hand on his brother's shoulder.

"What in the dragon's breath is going on? Is the whole world going crazy?" Rory said putting his hands on his head. "Why would anyone kill one of our dragons?" He shook his head in disbelief still cradling it in his hands.

"Your grand-father notified the sheriff that a dragoness and her dragling were missing from the Ean Dubh Dragle a few days ago," Rist added, despair in his voice.

"What did the sheriff say about the arrow?" Tharill asked his uncle.

"He is sending it to your grandfather to take to the Dragon Council Meeting on Scotia."

The sound of breaking glass came from the hall and Tharill opened the door to see what was going on. Standing in the hall was one Colin O'Murchu, his mouth full of scone, a broken glass at his feet and an astonished look on his face.

"What are you doing out here?" Tharill asked, an annoyed tone clear in his voice.

"Oh, dropped my glass of milk," Colin answered with a stupefied grin crossing his face.

"It doesn't matter," Rist said. "We need to be on our way to the ferry. It will be loading soon."

"Your ease-dropping is going to get you hurt someday, Colin." Tharill warned as he made his way down the hall.

Rory was the first to jump from the ferry onto the Dair town-dock. He knew the ferryman, Caleb and enjoyed helping him dock the boat. Caleb, a weathered, scruffy-bearded native of Whidley threw a mooring line to Rory. "Tie 'er fast, lad, while she's well-centered!"

Rory looped two half hitches on a mooring cleat, pulled them tight, and then looped two more. Watching, Caleb hollered, "Good job and thanks!" to Rory while he finished securing the ferry.

Tharill was standing by Poorboy, lead rope in hand and ready to disembark, when Rory returned. "The balloon transport is in," Rory said pointing to a huge balloon hovering over a landing platform in the distance.

"I bet it was packed with travelers coming to watch the dragons during the up-coming Firemoon Tide." Tharill said.

"Rory!" Rist yelled adding a quick whistle to make sure he got the lad's attention. "Let's get ready to go."

After the drawbridge was lowered into place, Caleb gave the *all clear* sign. Carts and people started to move forward. The old dock creaked under the weight of the loaded wagons, carts and hand pushed vending displays.

Although it had not rained this day the roads and footpaths were still muddy and slick. Poorboy struggled to get his footing when he stepped off of the wooden planks of the dock on to the ground.

"Easy now, Poorboy." Rist said in a low reassuring voice. "You're getting up there in age, old friend."

The road to the market was packed with vendors hurrying

to get to their stalls which slowed everyone down. Cart jams were abundant already and Rist sighed at the chaotic scene ahead of him.

"Tharill!" Rist shouted to be heard above the general noise. "I want you and Rory to run ahead and open the shutters and doors of the stalls. It would be nice to have them aired out a bit before we open."

Like Tharill's uncle, most merchants had been coming to the market for years, if not generations. The Gruaige family owned four well built wooden stalls.

Hearing what his uncle had said, Rory, who was riding with Colin on his cart replied, "we can do that. It beats waiting for these dung heaps to make up their minds about which way they are going."

"Great, thanks. I get to sit here all alone for who-knows how long before those eejits in front figure out which way they are going," Colin complained.

"So sorry. So long!" Rory laughed and leapt down from Colin's cart. At this Colin flipped Rory the 'dirty thumb' and said something crude.

Rist took the keys from his belt and handed them to Tharill who had returned to the cart after evaluating the traffic jam. "I'll be there as soon as I can." Rist frowned.

The two lads made their way through the morning crowds to the Gruaige stalls. All four stalls had been freshly painted earlier that year in a sunny yellow, with white trim, giving them a very modern and stylish look.

Tharill and Rory opened the doors and shutters on each stall. They inspected each one for roof leaks, rodents and signs of tampering. They found none. Two of the stalls were for vending, one for storage and the last stall had been set up as living quarters complete with cook stove, table and chairs, wash stand and hammocks.

The day was bright and early shoppers started making their way into market center. Tharill looked down the lane toward the ferry dock but did not see his uncle's cart. The lane was still congested with carts and wagons trying to go this way and that.

"Uncle Rist better get here soon. Folks are already out shopping," Rory said.

"It's a mess down there!" Tharill shouted, walking back to the stall. "I think I saw an overturned cart and that may be the paddy-jack behind the jam."

"Well, I guess we can get the signs out and prep the stalls for Uncle Rist's arrival, at least," Tharill said. "I was hoping to get the set up finished early so we could go hiking."

"Me too," Rory sighed. "Well, we might as well get at it! The sooner we get finished the sooner we can take off." Rory grabbed the *GRUAIGE SMOKED SHAMTON* sign and hung it on the hooks over the stall window. He stood back and admired it for a minute as he had painstakingly painted it himself.

They swept the floors and wiped down the shelves in both stalls. When the two youths had finished they stood back to admire their accomplishments and then sat down for a break.

"What are you two slackers doing, just sitting there growing moss?" Rist yelled from the cart, as it slowly made its way up the lane.

"It's about time!" Tharill hollered back.

"You stop at the pub for breakfast?" Rory added and winked to his brother.

"What a mess the dock road was," Rist shrugged. "I could use a nap with all the frustration I've built up. What do you say, you lads set the stall up and run it for your tired old uncle?" Tharill and Rory looked at each other, wide-eyed and mouths agape, as if to object.

Rist burst into a light hearted laugh. "What a sight you two make. Come on let's get the stalls set-up and open so you can go on your *much anticipated* hike."

"Works for me!" Rory exclaimed.

"Work, *works for you*?" Tharill teased. "That will be a first."

The next two hours were spent transferring pounds of smoked, salted and dried fish, along with cases of assorted snowberry products into the stalls and then onto the shelves.

The two sided *GRUAIGE SNOWBERRY SHOP* sign with white lettering on a royal blue background was hung over the door of the second stall. And as the morning waned customers began filling the stalls and making purchases. Rory and Tharill helped serve customers while Rist took Poorboy and the cart to the town stables.

During a lull in the business, Tharill left the *snowberry* stall to help Rory with the last of the large smoked shamton. Rory tossed ten pound sides of shamton to Tharill who hung each one on a hook. A very pretty girl with dark curly hair in a sky-blue dress walked by catching Tharill's eye. He stood for a moment mesmerized by her grace and beauty. Their eyes met for just an instant. Although, she seemed to look right through and past him, as if he was invisible.

Tharill blinked, his heart leapt and his head exploded in pain when a large smoked shamton slammed into the side of his face. He hit the ground with a heavy thud.

Tharill sat on the floor of the booth dazed. The side of his face a raspberry red and the large shamton lay in his lap like a sleeping child or fish, as the case may be.

Rory laughed. The girl appeared to take no notice and walked past.

"You are a royal gnarts-arse. You know that?" Tharill scolded through clinched teeth.

"Dibbs, if we see her again," Rory winked.

A stout woman poked her head through the stall window and asked, "Do you know where the purveyor of the snowberry stall is? I want to buy some preserves."

"I can help you, missus," Rory said choking back a laugh and giving Tharill the *dirty thumb* behind his back, as he walked out of the stall. Turning back to his brother, Rory added, "better get back to work, fish-face."

Rist returned to find both stalls well stocked and in good

order. "You lads did a good job getting the stalls set-up," Rist said with a nod of his head, "I can manage for awhile. Go ahead and take off for a bit."

"Thanks!" Rory said moving aside to let a customer browse through the jars of snowberry preserves.

Trotting next door Rory poked his head into the fish stall and said, "Uncle said we can go. Are you ready?"

"I only need to take these empty crates to the storage stall," Tharill replied and gestured toward two other empty crates for Rory to pick up. After putting the crates into the storage stall they began to walk up a side street as the main lane was still packed with vendors unloading carts and wagons. Walking up a parallel street lined with brightly painted two story houses and large shade trees, they made good time. It did not take long to reach the top of the street line where the town ended. There was only one road leading up the side of the hill from that point and it ended where a line of holiday cottages lay just past the hill's crest.

Tharill and Rory spotted two trails leading into the forest and stopped for a minute to decide which appeared to be the driest path. They had both hiked these trails before and knew that they ended at the cliff's which overlooked the dragon fishing grounds between Dara Island and where the dragon caves were located in the seaside cliffs of Druml.

"Gnart farts," Rory said, "it sure is muddy. What do you think?"

"Both trails are muddy, might as well take the shortest one," Tharill suggested. "Agreed?"

"Do gnarts have tusks?" Rory asked.

"Do dragons fart flames?" Tharill answered and he stepped onto the soggy ground of the narrow trail, Rory close on his heels.

Proceeding up their chosen path each found a good walking stick and trudged along the winding trail. The foliage was thick and the trees very tall on both sides of the trail. They could not see around any curves or beyond the edges of the trail itself.

After slogging uphill for close to an hour, the trail opened to a grand precipice that over looked the deep blue water between

Druml, the very southern tip of Whidley Island and Dara Island.

"Sweet Dragon's breath!" Tharill gasped, catching himself as he slid in the mud, toward the cliff's edge.

"Tharill!" Rory cried, catching Tharill's arm, "for dung's sake, watch your step!"

"It's slick as dragon's snot, right there!" Tharill said indicating the water run-off area he had just crossed. "Be careful!"

Walking close to the tree line, which was less than three feet to the cliff's sheer drop, they kept traversing on what was left of the washed-out path. Cornering a bend in the path something caught Tharill's attention.

"What's that?" Tharill pointed to a bundle setting next to a tree.

"I don't know."

"Let's check it out." Tharill said and walked on. Stopping in front of it he said, "It's a knapsack."

"Or day pack," Rory suggested. Picking it up he continued, "It's not wet, so it hasn't been here long."

Tharill put his finger to his lips, "did you hear that?"

Rory stood still, listening and then he said, "Yes! Yes! I hear it!" He turned and looked up the trail that followed the cliff's edge.

The barely auditable words of, "hh-elp, hh-ee-lp" could be faintly heard up the trail. Carefully making his way up the narrowing trail, Tharill spotted a taut rope tied to the base of a tree and slung down the face of the cliff. The call for help was louder and coming from somewhere down the side of the cliff.

"Hold on, we will pull you up!" Tharill yelled over the edge of the cliff, unable to see past the cliff's edge. Together they pulled the rope hand over fist until they caught sight of small muddy hands grabbing at the top of the cliff's edge.

"Keep pulling, we almost have him!" Tharill called over his shoulder to Rory. With two more good pulls a short extremely muddy boyish figure was heaved over the edge to safety.

"What in dragon's breath were you doing hanging off the side of this cliff?" Tharill scolded, "this is no place for children to be playing! Where are your parents?"

The small figure, *a boy between the ages of eleven and twelve*, Tharill guessed, just sat, eyes closed, cross-legged and shivering.

Taking pity on the boy, Rory said, "It's okay, you are safe now, lad." Taking his handkerchief from his back pocket Rory offered it to the boy. "Here, why don't you wipe some of that mud off of your face? There's a good lad."

The boy obediently took the handkerchief but did not do anything but hold it in his trembling hands. He didn't shift his gaze from the ground where he sat.

Rory stood back and with a questioning look in his eyes he said, "Tharill, I think…" but before Rory could finish his statement Tharill had lifted the boy up on to his feet.

"Okay, my lad!" He said with authority in his voice, "What is your name and where are your parents?"

"Tharill-" Rory tried to interrupt, but his brother was busy trying to untie the rope from around the boy's chest.

The slap was quick, too quick for Tharill to duck or get out of the way. Stunned by the blow he had just received to his face from the youth, Tharill stood silent with mouth agape for a moment. The youth's hat flung to the ground by the motion of the slap and revealed streams of long curly black hair bouncing about the youth's shoulders.

"You're a girl!" Tharill accused.

"Of course I'm a girl! You eejit!" Reesa Burlong shouted in return. She leaned over to pick up her hat, shaking bits of mud from her hair as she did.

"What were you doing hanging on the side of a cliff?" Tharill barked back.

"The ground gave way under me. If I hadn't tied off to that tree," she retorted, pointing at the large tree, "I'd have fallen to my death!"

"Smart thinking," Rory said, trying to calm the tension.

"You shouldn't have been so close to the edge to need tying off to begin with!" Tharill, blasted, adding, "And you being a girl!"

"Bugger off! Shite head!" Reesa returned.

"Bugger off? Shite head? What kind of language is that for a girl to use?" Tharill's anger was starting to show or was it embarrassment?

"My name is Rory Gruaige," Rory stuck out his hand at an attempt to defuse the situation.

Stuffing her curls back under her hat, Reesa replied, "I'm Reesa Burlong." Purposely not looking at Tharill she walked over to her knapsack and slung it over her shoulder.

Rory untied the rope from around the tree and coiled it for her. "Here is your rope," he said, handing it to her with an attempt at a smile only turning out to be an odd crooked grin.

The look caused Reesa to smile in return. Tharill said nothing, standing to the side out of the way.

"Do you want us to walk you home?" Rory asked with genuine concern in his voice. "It's no trouble, really. I think we have all had plenty of excitement for one day."

Reesa stood looking at both of them for a moment and said, "I'd like that, thanks," And then she started back down the path, staying close to the trees as she walked.

*Are you okay? Can we walk you home? It's no trouble, really.* Tharill mumbled to himself as he followed behind Reesa and Rory.

"What? Did you say something, Tharill?" Rory asked over his shoulder, not stopping.

"Uh no, Just talking to myself," he replied, trudging down the path with his head hung low and hands tucked in his jacket pockets.

*I bet you are,* Rory laughed under his breath. *I bet you are saying all kinds of things to yourself.* A huge smile and subdued snort of laughter burst from his lips.

And that is how the bonds of friendship first begin to knit; a chance encounter, a misstep in an unexpected direction, or other sudden spontaneous meeting. From that moment on something in Tharill would be different. Something he was unsure he was ready for.

# CHAPTER #9

## *BENDING THE BOW*

Curro Delagarza stood on a secluded beach located on the southwest tip of Whidley Island, inspecting a cage containing the captured dragling. "How old would you say it is?" he questioned Captain Moseby.

"Oh, at least two years, I'd say."

"I think he's bigger than Yggdrasil wanted," Delagarza said peering at the ten-foot long, five-foot at-the-shoulder tall beast, as it struggled to move in the cramped confines of the wood and metal built cage. "But, we will send him on to Creggan Island," he continued to consider the age of the dragon. "Are you sure he won't blow flame and burn your boat up?"

"As long as we keep him well muzzled, he can't get his mouth open," Moseby said, a slanted grin crossed his face. He poked at the dragling with a long gaff hook and the dragling growled in response. "We will have no trouble from him."

"Well then," Delagarza paused to take a last look at the sturdiness of the cage before turning to leave. "I am flying out on the morning balloon transport to Scotia Island before continuing on to Creggan. Make sure the other dragons you catch are smaller than this one. I don't want any trouble from these smelly creatures when we sail from Creggan to Spana." With that said, Delagarza turned and walked up the path where his horse awaited him.

Prince Rutgar Van Slauthe, lean and tall for his eighteen years of age, with a bow and quiver of arrows slung across his shoulder, strolled quietly through the festival grounds as dawn broke over the eastern mountains of Scotia Island. Following closely behind was a tall man with dark middle-eastern features. A stark contrast to the Prince's white-blonde shoulder length thinly-braided hair and fair Saxon complexion.

"Rastom," the Prince called.

"Your Highness?" the man was at his master's side within two strides.

"Wasn't this archery field somewhat smaller last year?"

"Yes, Sire. It appears they have removed several trees to widen the mounted competition field," Rastom Razmadze agreed scanning the area. They walked on studying the archery field layout.

Razmadze, a Mameluk born into the service of the Van Slauthe Royal family as was his father and his father before him, was clothed in the traditional Mameluk attire of white turban, loose billowing red trousers and an intricately embroidered green vest over a high collared tan tunic. His gold colored double-wrapped waist sash held a jewel-hilted scimitar, two flintlocks, each decorated with a brass crescent and star, along with a razor-sharp dagger in a bejeweled scabbard.

Rutgar stopped and looked back at his, always vigilant, body guard considering the man with genuine fondness. Being born into a Mameluk family was not being born into slavery but rather a time honored lineage. To become a Mameluk out of an established family line was rare indeed. Male children born into established Mameluk families were groomed for service almost from birth, honing their fighting and weapons skills with age. Rastom began attending royal functions with his father, whom was Mameluk to King Victor Van Slauthe, at the young age of four years. He began to learn the art of being vigilantly aware and assertive without being intrusive, all at the same time. Always, within an arm's reach of the king, but seamlessly blending in with the background. Rastom, his younger brother and any future male siblings would become the protectors of yet born princes and princess' of the Van Slauthe family.

"Sire," Razmadze said and gestured in the direction of a man approaching them from the archery registration tent. Rutgar turned and smiled at the man waving his hellos.

"Greetings, Prince Van Slauthe!" The kilt clad man announced with glee. "We are honored to have you compete in our humble competition again this year."

"Thank you, Mr. Wallace," Rutgar said and shook the man's extended hand. Wallace then nodded to Rastom who smiled and bowed slightly in recognition.

"Please, call me Christian," Wallace suggested.

"Very well, Christian," Rutgar agreed, pronouncing the word 'well' as 'vell' in his thick Saxon accent.

With a sweep of his hand, Wallace indicated that he would escort them to the archery tent. "The sign-up sheets are ready if you'd like to get started," he said and the three started toward the tent. "We will start at seven this morning with *targets for distance, mounted short-bow* and *rapid fire target.*" Suddenly stopping in his tracks, Wallace added with delight in his voice, "We also have six ladies in our *ladies division,* this year!"

"Outstanding! I do believe there were only four last year," Rutgar remarked, nodding his head in approval. "I would like my younger sister to compete next year if my father would be willing to grant her permission to attend. She is quite good for her young age of eleven."

Wallace and Rutgar continued to discuss the young princess' archery abilities as Rastom held the tent flap open for them.

Rory affectionately rubbed the muzzle of his well-muscled black horse who impatiently tapped his hoof against the stall door. "Easy Bull, breakfast is coming."

"Who, in their right mind would name a horse Bull?" queried a light-hearted female voice from the stable's front door.

Rory turned to find Reesa Burlong donning a bright yellow archery costume, bow and quiver slung over her shoulder. "Reesa!" Rory replied, not bothering to hide his excitement. "It is so good to see you!"

She walked past the stall doors of whinnying horses who were voicing their displeasure at not being fed yet this morning. "How did market go for you and your family?"

"We sold out, as usual," Rory replied and poured a scoop of grain into Bull's feedbag.

"I ask again, why name him Bull?" She enquired and gave the horse's neck a quick pat.

Rory laughed as he attached the bag to the horse's halter. "When he was a foal, he'd head butt me. I think he learned the bad habit from a milk-goat we kept in the pasture with him." He then grabbed a pitchfork and tossed some hay into the stall. "I'm glad you decided to compete in the lady's competition. I am sure you will enjoy it. My cousin Liffey O'Shannessey is competing again this year. You and she will get along very well, I am sure." Rory cocked his head, as if considering what to say next. Then added, "she is … adventurous … to say the least," he looked down, a wide grin blossomed across his reddening face.

Reesa smiled. "A close cousin," she suggested.

"Oh, no she is my grandfather's cousin's granddaughter," he replied, sheepishly.

Reesa removed the quiver and bow from her shoulder and leaned them against an unoccupied stall's door. "No, I mean, are you good friends?" she reiterated, a soft smile parted her lips.

An instant shade of crimson crossed Rory's cheeks and he looked away. "Yes, we are. We both share the love of archery and her grandfather is also the dragon Tender on her island."

"Really?" Reesa was very interested to hear that. "Then it is true that dragon keeping is passed down from one generation to the next?"

"Most of the time," Rory said and began to curry Bull as the horse munched contentedly on his oats.

"Father says that dragons can sense or smell Dragon Keepers when they are close and they would not ever hurt a dragon tender, no matter what. Is that correct?"

"It is," answered a voice from a side-door of the stables. Rory and Reesa peered into the light of the open door and saw the silhouette of Tharill Gruaige.

"Where have you been?" Rory quizzed. "Aunt Maura and I waited for you and Uncle Rist this morning. We finally just ate without you." Rory picked up a different brush and continued grooming his horse without looking back at Tharill, as Reesa stood silent.

"Good morning Miss Burlong," Tharill nodded his head in greeting as he approached them. "Uncle Rist wanted to make sure the arrow that killed Volcae made it to the Dragon Council meeting this morning.

"I thought he gave it to Garda O'Ceann in Paraic before we left for market." Rory said and paused what he was doing to question Tharill closer. "Did O'Ceann have trouble getting here with it?"

"Yes," Tharill said drawing Reesa's attention away from the horse she was petting. "He came across some late night intruders in his office and they attacked him."

Reesa gasped, putting her hand to her mouth. "Is he all right?"

"He was beat up pretty bad receiving two broken ribs and swollen eyes," Tharill said sympathetically. "But he is on the mend and they did not get the arrow which O'Ceann had already taken to the shipping office to be placed in the ships large lock-box." Rory started to say something but was cut short by Reesa.

"Wait, did you say Volcae was killed with an arrow? That can't be!" She was shocked. "My father would have told me," she said through tear filled eyes. "No, not Volcae. Why? Why would someone shoot him? And killed with an arrow?" She suddenly snapped at Tharill, "I don't believe you!" Tharill stepped back as it looked as though she might strike out at him.

"Reesa," Tharill said gently. "I am so sorry. I've seen the wonderful paintings you've done of him and his dragle. But, it is true. Your father has not been told yet. That is why he hasn't said anything to you."

"An arrow?" She shook her head.

"The arrow was as large as a spear and Uncle Rist thinks it had the same poison in it that almost killed Rory." He stepped closer to her and to his surprise she buried her head in his chest, sobbing without restraint. Tharill put his arms around her, in an attempt to comfort her.

Rory stood watching for a moment and then went to retrieve Bull's saddle and bridle. "So, where is the arrow now?" he asked over his shoulder and shook out Bull's saddle blanket.

Reesa pulled away and Tharill looked down at her watering eyes and pinched face. "Here," he said handing her his handkerchief. "Uncle Rist and O'Ceann have gone to find grandfather who will present the arrow to the king during the Dragon Council meeting."

"He was a spectacular looking dragon," Reesa said in quiet reflection. "I will miss drawing and painting him. His wing span was truly magnificent. What a joy to watch him glide over the water when he would hunt for fish," tears spilled from her eyes again. "I'm sorry, I should go and talk to my father." She turned to leave, but Tharill lightly caught her hand and she stopped, not turning around.

"Reesa," Tharill said softly. "Volcae has fathered at least one bull-dragling this year and he also has two adult daughters. He does live on. Not only in his offspring, but in your art."

"Thank you," she said and walked out of the stable still clutching the damp handkerchief.

'There you are! There you are!" Darby O'Shannessey Gruaige shouted in recognition of Garda Dahy O'Ceann. Darby, nephew of and assistant to Dragon Council member Fergal O'Shannessey Gruaige, had been tasked with a vital mission. But, time was running out to complete it and he was visibility distressed when he approached the Garda. "The council meeting is due to start within the next fifteen minutes and once the chamber doors are closed no one else is permitted in!" Darby yelled hurrying toward O'Ceann.

"Calm down Darby," Rist instructed. "We had our own problems just trying to get this arrow to Scotia Island." He motioned to Garda O'Ceann, "He was attacked in his own station house by men looking for the arrow."

It was then that Darby noticed the swollen eyes and bruising about O'Ceann's face. "I am so sorry Dahy," he relayed with genuine compassion. "Thank you both for everything you risked to bring the arrow to us. We must go to the castle now! We don't have a moment to waste. When the doors shut that is it!"

Rist took the arrow from O'Ceann and said, "Go rest now Dahy. We will take this up to the castle."

O'Ceann nodded, a look of gratitude and relief swept across his painfully swollen face. "I'll wait for you in the archery tent," he said and hobbled away in that direction.

"Hurry, hurry! We must go now!" Darby urged, Rist. And they both ran toward the castle, close to a mile away. Rist with the cloth wrapped arrow tucked securely under his arm kept a vigilant watch for anyone or thing that may appear to be out of place. When they reached the outer chamber, Darby took the arrow from Rist and hurried to the doors as they were closing.

Bull entered the field at a full gallop to a crowd of cheering bystanders. Rory dropped his reins, pulled an arrow over his shoulder and applied it to his bow. Kneeing his horse in the direction of the scattered targets he release arrow after arrow. Whipping between trees, over jumps and around obstacles, horse and rider functioned as one. At the end of the run, Rory picked up his reins and Bull slid to a complete stop. His back fetlocks digging into the ground as he did. In one fluid motion the big black stallion spun around and lunged into a gallop again.

Rory, again dropping the reins, turned sharply in his saddle to shoot at targets on the opposite side. This was the part of the competition Rory excelled at, as most competitors were right handed and did not do well aiming from the other side. Whereas he was left handed and these shots came easily for him. Bull's eye after bull's eye as the horse thundered through the course with such grace and power. The admiring crowd cheered the pair on and exploded into louder whoops and hollers when Rory brought Bull to another sliding stop and then spun the horse in dazzling tight circles.

Amid the cheers and praises entered the next contestant, Prince Rutgar Van Slauthe on a stunning dapple-grey stallion. The prince rode over to Rory to offer his complements on a round well shot. "Nicely done! Nicely Done!" the prince commended.

"Are all of your arrows hallmarked?" Rory shot back.

"Of course," Rutgar replied, confused and shocked at Rory's question. "Why wouldn't they be?"

"Play the innocent all you like! We know the truth!" Rory growled and cantered his horse off the field without another glance at the prince.

Prince Rutgar stared at Rory as he left the field, bewildered at Rory's brashness. They had always been competitive in nature but never coarse or rude toward each other, in any way. This exchange would be with Rutgar for the rest of the day and his ability to focus on the competition suffered from it costing him shots here would have normally found ease to make.

Over at the ladies competition Reesa Burling had just walked off the field after a round of well placed shots showed her marksmanship to be above average. She displayed a broad smile which appeared to make her face glow and blue eyes sparkle. Mrs. Burlong screeched in delight as she ran towards her daughter with the professor in tow. "Reesa, Reesa! I do believe you will win this round!" The ecstatic woman shrieked, forgetting all propriety by hopping up and down in her excitement.

"Well, I don't know about that, Mom," Reesa's face turned a warm shade of soft pink. "But, I did do well, didn't I?" She beamed and hugged both of her parents at the same time. The trio stood for a moment soaking up the mutually shared delight.

Reesa waved at her new friend to come join them. "Mother and father this is my new friend Miss Liffey O'Shannessey."

"Pleased to make your acquaintance," Mrs. Burlong greeted. Liffey nodded and said hello.

"We watched you compete," Mr. Burlong complemented. "Very impressive indeed!" Liffey smiled and thanked him, a blush of shyness crossed her cheeks.

"We are going to get cream sodas," Reesa said. "Please do come with us." Liffey nodded her head and the two began to walk toward the refreshment tent.

"She sure doesn't say much," Professor Burlong observed to his wife.

"Her aim on the archery field pretty much speaks volumes though," Olive replied with a wink and a squeeze of her husband's hand.

Christian Wallace was very pleased with the way the day was going. Folks from all of the islands and many from the continent had come to watch the competition and cheer on the best archers from their home towns, villages and islands. The contestants had almost doubled from last year now that the word was out on the continent of the skill level being displayed.

The trinket and food vendors waved at him as he walked by, showing their pleasure at the amount of willets being spent on their wares. *Yes, it is a very good turnout, indeed.* Christian smiled.

Then he stopped. Something had caught his eye as he walked by one of the trinket vendor's tent. He walked around back of the tent. "You are not of the King's guards! What is-," he began, but the words were cut short as was his life.

# CHAPTER #10

## *THE DRAGON COUNCIL MEETING*

Fergal Gruaige walked down the ancient hall in deep thought, looking more inward than in the direction he was going. His scrolls were tucked under his arm. His heart heavy, mind crowded and his body ached with apprehension. The news he must give the King during the Dragon Council meeting was dark and the outlook for the immediate future was not much brighter.

There was treachery in the air and Fergal was not looking forward to presenting his findings on who was behind such villainy and why it was now occurring in the normally peaceful Celtic Islands. If the evidence he had to present to King Fios was to be believed, what was to become of life as it was known and had been lived for over sixty years in the islands? Not to mention the fate of the dragons residing there.

It could mean only one thing, war. War with a larger, better trained and equipped enemy force than the Celtic Island realm could ever hope to muster in time to defend itself and protect the dragons.

"Are you okay?" came a small voice from beside Fergal.

Fergal blinked with a start, stopped walking and looked down.

"Milo," Fergal reached out with his free hand and touched the less than five foot tall man's shoulder. "How good to see you," and Fergal was genuinely pleased to see his old friend.

"You had the sullen look of a very worried man, walking with the weight of the world on your shoulders." Milo said and returned Fergal's gesture with a hand on his arm. "Are you unwell?"

"I am in good health, old friend," Fergal responded but, the lack of conviction betrayed his true state of mind. "I am heading to the Dragon Council to reveal my findings on the recent dragon slayings," he continued.

"I am also heading in that direction. May we walk together or do you need this time to prepare?" Milo asked.

"Glad to have your company, indeed. Please do let us walk together," Fergal smiled at Milo and with a hand gesture to continue, they proceeded to walk down the dimly lit corridor toward the council meeting hall on the far side of the castle.

"Would it be impertinent to ask if your findings have anything to do with King Van Slauthe?" Milo asked.

"Why do you ask?"

"It is not a secret that he has desires to expand his own kingdom. What a *coup d'état* it would be for him to add the Celtic Islands to his realm."

Fergal stopped and looked down into the elder man's bright green eyes. "Milo, I dread the thought of it, but that may very well be what he intends."

"We have fended off invaders before and we can do it again, my friend," Milo said.

"That was over 100 years ago and we could not have done it without our highly trained Archer Forces." Fergal, adjusted the scrolls under his arm and then added, "There are no real bowers now, except for those that compete for sport at the Scotia Faire. We can't count on prize seekers to repel invaders with trained forces. There is a very big difference between losing an arrow at a target and aiming at a living person to kill."

"I agree," said Milo, "but let us not judge this young generation too harshly. They have not yet been confronted with anything like what may soon be their reality. Plus, wars are fought with muskets and cannons these days, not bows and arrows."

"Then why kill a dragon with an arrow?" Fergal wondered.

"Because it can be lethal, as well as silent?" Milo suggested.

They walked in silence for a few minutes, passing through the long outer chamber corridor lined with the busts of past Dragon Council members. Fergal stopped again and drew in a deep breath before turning the last corner that led to the entry of the waiting hall. Milo stood in silence next to him, until Fergal was ready to continue.

When they turned the corner they were greeted with the sight of sunlight streaming through twenty-foot-tall stained glass windows casting prisms of rainbow colors which danced on the flagstone floor. They both smiled at the sight.

"The clouds have cleared and the sun shines once again," Milo said.

"Yes, Milo, sunny days always follow the dark rainy ones, don't they." Fergal said.

"You can't have one without the other," Milo agreed.

"I will try to keep that in mind as this whole situation of the dragon killings plays out."

They approached two huge closed doors bearing large brass pull rings. Footmen stood on either side of them. One of the footmen who held a ledger stepped forward and smiled, "Welcome my lords, your names please."

"Fergal O'Shannessey Gruaige of Whidley Island," Fergal said.

"Casswallawn Milo ap Muirig of Cymru," Milo replied when the footman glanced his way. After checking his list, the footman signaled for one of the doors to be opened. Both men were escorted into the waiting hall of the throne room and announced.

"Oh, could you check to see if my assistant, Darby O'Shannessey has arrived yet?" Fergal asked turning back to the footman with the list.

"No, I do not see a mark by his name, my lord." The footman replied after glancing at the names he had checked off.

"Thank you." Fergal said and he walked into the waiting hall, looking around as he did.

Milo's attention was caught by a heavy set man on a settee waving at him. Milo waved back and touched Fergal's arm saying, "I need to speak with Rhys ap Llwynwyn before we get started."

"Of course, I must find my assistant as well," Fergal said. "I will save you a seat." They shook hands and separated. Milo waved at Rhys and proceeded in his direction.

Fergal took a goblet of wine from a beverage tray and walked through the crowd of thirty plus council members. He acknowledged a number of colleagues as he passed by but did not stop to speak to any of them. He wanted to meet with Darby before the meeting started to discuss the evidence he was to present to King Fios Crann O'Darach.

The ornate throne room doors swung open to the sound of two highland pipers playing the O'Darach clan anthem. Their kilts with the Castle Guard tartan of black and green swung about their knees as they marched in step to the tune. The tall feathered bonnets upon their heads bore the regiment's trade-mark red hackles.

"My Lords, the King's Court is now open for your admittance. Please make your way to your seats. The King will be with you shortly." The loud announcement by Seamus MacDougal could just barely be heard over the high pitched pipes.

MacDougal, the King's Court Valet, banged the floor with a metal footed, long handled wooden scepter. Dressed in his clan tartan of red and black over sky-blue plaid kilt he looked every inch of his six-foot-six height. With a snow-fox hide sporran, jeweled sgian dubh in his belt and bone-handled dirk secured in his kilt hose, he was an intimidating sight to behold.

"This way my lords, this way now, you must come!" he

bellowed in an authoritative voice.

Fergal walked toward the open door way as directed, but did not enter and looked nervously about wondering where Darby was. *He has got to be here.* Fergal reassured himself. *I will wait by the door, until I can wait no longer.*

Darby had been Fergal's loyal assistant for more than four years now. He was very young for an assistant of a Dragon Council member but had proved a motivated, quick study who loved learning about dragon husbandry. Yet, he was more than an assistant or protégé, he was also of distant relation. Fergal trusted the young man of a mere twenty-two years of age with very important tasks and confidences, as well.

"Fergal! Are you coming?" Milo's voice echoed from the throne room.

Fergal looked into the open doorway to find Milo motioning him forward.

"Are you coming?" Milo repeated, "The doors will be closing any minute."

"Well." Fergal looked back over his shoulder again, "I cannot seem to locate Darby." A pang of worry stabbed at his chest. *It is not like Darby to be late to anything.* Fergal considered, *my report will be unacceptable without the evidence.*

"Come, come!" Milo insisted.

Fergal walked through the open throne room doors as the pipers marched to the other end of the room. The large oak doors were slowly eased forward by two footmen, once closed they would not be reopened for any reason until King Fios dismissed the council members.

"Wait,.. wait... wait for me to enter! I have ... important business ... with the crown!" gasped a running and nearly out of breath Darby O'Shannessey.

"Hold the doors," sounded the commanding voice of Seamus MacDougal. "My dear Mister O'Shannessey how kind of you to join us. Your master may regain his proper color once again."

"Thank you. Thank you, Seamus." Darby panted.

Darby shuffled past Seamus with a slight bow, his curly red locks dropping into his olive-green eyes. The large doors slammed shut behind him resounding above the voices of the now filled throne room. Those in the assembly began to take their seats.

Fergal spotted his assistant as soon as he passed through the doors. Getting to his feet he waved his hands in excitement and relief at the sight of Darby. But, Fergal's excitement diminished, at once when he noticed that Darby was empty handed.

"Where is the evidence?" Fergal asked in a raised whisper when Darby took his seat.

"The guards would not allow me to bring it into the inner court yards of the castle," Darby answered. "I had to give it to the master-at-arms." Hearing this Fergal stood up and waved to get Seamus' attention.

"Seamus, Seamus! Pray come here I need to talk to you." Fergal said in a slightly loud voice to get Seamus' attention without causing a disturbance.

"Yes, my Lord. How may I be of assistance?" Seamus asked in his thickly Scotia-accented voice.

"Darby left a large arrow with the master-at-arms when he came in. We now need that arrow here. Can you have someone bring it to us as soon as possible?" Fergal asked with an anxious voice hands clenched to the point of turning his knuckles white.

"I will see to it at once my Lord," Seamus answered. "As soon as King Fios has been piped in and the court is called to order." Seamus bowed slightly and turned away.

The court started to quiet down when Seamus banged his long jeweled scepter on the flagstone floor. "Hear ye! Hear ye! Come to order in the Court of the Honorable King Fios Crann O'Darach." The pipers stood beside the door where the King would enter and began to play the traditional 'Long Live the King' anthem. Everyone in the court stood up and the king's entry doors swung wide.

King Fios strode into the court with all of the pomp and pageantry due a royal personage. His long orange-red head of hair topped with a jeweled crown of gold, flowed over his shoulders. A short curly beard matched the color of his hair. His thick yellow cloak trimmed in red with a large rampant dragon embroidered on the back hung heavily on his shoulders.

The cloak he wore had been passed down from father to son for over three hundred years. The fur was that of the Allta Bui Madra, a species of yellow-furred dragons that became extinct less than seventy years ago.

The loss of this spectacular creature was the final step in passing the Endangered Dragon Species act of 1754. With this law passed the hunting of dragons in the Celtic Islands Kingdom became prohibited. It also required every dragon-bearing island to designate fifty-acres for each living dragon in the form of a sanctuary. These sanctuaries were to include all nesting, feeding and breeding areas known to be current and past dragon refuges.

King Fios climbed the steps to his throne platform and seated himself in his chair. The court attendees sat down and the court became quiet.

"At this time, on this day, in this year of 1814, of the 25th year of our great King Fios Crann O'Darach's reign, I declare this special meeting of the Dragon Council in the O'Darach throne room of the Kings Court now in session," Seamus bellowed in a loud, clear voice without taking a single breath.

Seamus struck his scepter on the stone floor three times and yelled, "Who comes now to address His Majesty King Fios Crann O'Darach?"

Fergal stood up and shouted, "I Fergal O'Shannessey Gruaige, Dragon Councilor for Whidley Island, Your Majesty."

"Come forward Councilor Gruaige." King Fios beckoned, his hand raised in acknowledgement.

Fergal made his way past the other seated attendees and out into the open area in front of the throne platform. He caught Seamus' eye, who nodded and signaled the Master at Arms forward.

"Your Majesty, as you are aware the Dragon Council has been investigating the slaying of five dragons in the Celtic Islands. Some of the dragons were found disemboweled and drained of blood. It was thought that all of the dragons slain so far have been older ones, none under one-hundred years of age and all bulls. The islands that have reported dragon deaths are Failte, Skellig, Anglesey, Ynys Dysilio, and Islay " Fergal said, reading from his now unrolled scroll which Darby held up for him to read. "And now Whidley," he added.

"My son, Risteard Gruaige of Whidley Island witnessed a dragon dying with an arrow in its chest. He pulled it from the dragon Volcae and took it to the sheriff of Paraic, the seat of Whidley. The sheriff brought it here to Scotia but not before he was attacked by someone trying to get the arrow back or so it seemed to him." Fergal continued, "The only thing more horrific than the slaughter of these creatures is the hallmark found on the arrow's brass tip."

The Master at Arms presented the large cloth draped arrow to Fergal and then retreated from the court room. Fergal carefully uncovered the long arrow. Council members strained to see it from where they sat. Fergal handed it to Darby who in turn gave it to Seamus. Seamus climbed the steps to the king's throne, bowed and placed it in the outstretched gloved hands of King Fios.

The King turned the large arrow over and gestured for Seamus to bring a large candelabrum closer for his inspection.

"I know this mark," King Fios said, visibly stunned by what he saw. "It is the hallmark of King Victor Van Slauthe's armory." Crimson flashed across the Kings' face.

A loud throng of angry voices echoed to the top of the cathedral ceiling. Disbelief, arguments for and against the news filled the room.

Someone yelled, "Bloody bucket-heads!" another shouted, "Crown King of Fartdom!" Others yelled more insults about the King of Saxony and his country; while there were also many who argued that it was untrue, a lie, or a horrible mistake. Sometimes the believers and the disbelievers were only feet, if not inches apart shouting at each other at the top of their voices.

"Order, my Lords! Order now, I say!" Seamus' voice raised above all others. "I will have order in this, the King's Throne-room!" He pounded his scepter hard on the floor his face stone without emotion or temper.

Seamus' ever calming presence had kept the court from upheaval on more than one occasion in is thirty plus years of service to this king and the kings' father before him. He was well respected by all and the council members began to quiet and retake their seats.

"King Van Slauthe thinks he can do as he pleases with our dragons," Finbar O'Shea Bresnahan of Failte Island grunted just loud enough for some members to hear.

"And our laws, too!" another added.

"This is nonsense!" cried Councilor Sciltin (Scilty) O'Shannessy McMillan, a supporter of King Von Slauthe.

"It makes perfect sense!" yelled Councilor Grufton (Gruf) Y Llanrwst Cyrff of Foite Island, who stood with one fist raised, tightly clenched and the other grasping the rail in front of his seat. "His family hunted trophy dragons on Foite Island for generations!"

"Trophy dragons were always taken whole! With the blessings of the islands where they were hunted on before they became a protected species. I might add that a few island politicos became very rich off of those paid dragon hunts!" retorted Scilty McMillan.

"What are you getting at, McMillan?" Gruf Cyrff roared back.

"We never allowed trophy hunting on our island and never had any trouble with dragon poaching in our history!" Scilty McMillan shot back. "Foite Island Dragon Keepers tried to claim dragon over-population twenty years ago as a good reason to hold a 'special' dragon hunt permit."

"Gentlemen, gentlemen!" King Fios said in a raised and agitated voice. "Let Councilor Gruaige continue with the result of his investigation." King Fios raised both of his hands gesturing the council members to sit down. Then he turned his attention back to Fergal.

"Did anyone see who loosed the arrow, Councilor

Gruaige?" he asked, his tone cool.

"Not that I could find, Your Majesty." Fergal answered.

"Is your son here today?"

"Yes, he is on Scotia, but not in the castle. He and his family are here for the Faire," Fergal said. "Would you like me to send for him?"

"Councilors as guardians of our dragons and leaders in your own communities you must use great caution and let calmer heads prevail before leaving this room." The King's voice rang out steady and strong in resolve.

"I do not want my subjects panicked by wild allegations or accusations towards King Van Slauthe and Saxony. More investigation is required in this matter. I command you to use restraint and not discuss this matter with anyone outside of this body of attendees."

Grumbling and murmurs of objection rose from the audience, but were squelched with two hard pounds of Seamus' staff on the floor.

"Holiday makers have come from all over the Celtic Islands and the continent to enjoy the Faire and archery competition. I will not have them frightened out of their merriment," King Fios said. "I believe we could all use a break and I must make ready for the trophy ceremony. We will pick this up early tomorrow morning," King Fios added standing up to make his departure.

Seamus MacDougal banged his scepter three times announcing, "Everyone rise this session has now concluded for the day." He pointed his scepter at the waiting pipers who had been standing at attention the entire time.

"Pipers! Pipe out your King," Seamus said in a loud voice and stamped his scepter three more times. The pipers thrust their pipes' under their arm pits and blew into the chanters. The loud shrill of highland pipes came to life. In unison they marched to the Kings' chamber door and stood on both sides. The King waved his good-byes and walked through the doorway followed by the pipers.

"We accomplished nothing, today!" bellowed Council member Kauri Patrish MacCloud of Islay Island as the mutterings of discontentment started to resume.

The assembly slowly started to make their way out of the throne room. There was much discussion and disbelief regarding the hallmark on the spear. King Van Slauthe had many advocates in the council and two distant relations through marriage as well.

Fergal was in deep discussion with Scilty McMillan when Seamus MacDougal caught his attention with a wave. Next to Seamus stood the master at arms who held the draped spear. Fergal patted Scilty on the shoulder, promised to talk with him more before he left the castle and walked toward Seamus.

"The arrow will be locked in the armory until King Fios instructs otherwise," Seamus said.

"It may be wise to have an expert look at it to authenticate the hallmark on the brass tip," Fergal suggested. "The whole arrow should be examined as it appears to be hollow. Plus, that tip could have been placed on the spear at a later time. We can leave no stone unturned before any dialogue starts with King Van Slauthe."

"I will be speaking with King Fios before the trophy ceremonies and bring your concerns to his attention. We will have the arrow thoroughly inspected before the council meets tomorrow," Seamus assured.

# CHAPTER #11

## *THE TUNNELS*

Tharill and Rory walked to the open gate and stood for a moment considering tunnel or passage way beyond. "This was locked this morning. Wasn't it?" Tharill asked setting his bow and quiver down.

"I do believe you are right!" Rory piped over his shoulder as he walked past Tharill and into the darkness of the tunnel.

"Wait!" Tharill yelled and glanced around to see if anyone was nearby or looking in their direction. "We can't go in there," he continued in a whisper.

"Why not, it **is** unlocked," Rory said.

"Unlocked because the lock is broken," Tharill barked. "Look." He picked up a broken lock from the ground and tossed it to Rory, who glanced at it and threw it back. At this point Tharill knew his brother would not stop so he picked up his bow and quiver and slung them over his shoulder. "Wait I'm coming with you." Tharill knew there was no turning Rory back once he had his mind set.

"I wonder who broke the lock." Rory said.

"I wonder why it was broken." Tharill replied with a sidelong glance. "I think this might be part of the old underground escape tunnels from the castle."

"Hey! What are you lads doing in there?" Shouted a loud voice from behind them, startling both.

"Do you want to come with us?" Rory yelled back without turning as he recognized the voice of Miss Reesa Burlong.

"Of course not you fool!" She retorted, feigning shock, at an impertinent question and added, "Get out of there before you get caught!" But then she leaned through the open gate as if considering to enter as well. Her curly black hair tied back with a yellow ribbon that matched her dress. Reesa blinked as a torch burst into a bright flame and filled the tunnel with a quivering iridescent glow. Tharill's muscular frame was outlined against the darkness where he stood with one arm out stretched in her direction. She felt his eyes gazing at her and she noticed her breath caught in her chest for an instant.

"Come on, it will be fun." Rory said in a cool, confident tone grabbing the torch from Tharill. "We'll be back in plenty of time for the awards ceremony."

"No, I shouldn't, you shouldn't!" Reesa pursed her lips and added, "Get out of there before a castle guard catches you or worse, replaces the broken lock and locks you in!"

"We won't go too far. I am guessing these turn into catacombs at some point. We'll turn back there." Tharill said watching Rory as he proceeded forward into the tunnel, the thick black smoke of the torch rising to the top of the tunnel.

"Tharill! Please, come out of there!" Reesa pleaded, turning back to look in the direction of the archery field. The competition was over but several people were milling around the ale tent.

"This coming from the same girl we found hanging off a cliff less than two weeks ago," Tharill said in a slightly raised voice to make sure she heard him.

"That was different!" Reesa yelled back into the tunnel.

"I need to go with my brother and keep him out of trouble," Tharill said. "There is no telling what he might find down there. Are you coming or not?"

"No," she said, a ting of regret edging her voice.

Tharill hurried to catch up with his brother and as the light of the torch grew dimmer between them. He could hear water trickling somewhere in the distance. *Part of the underground water system?* He wondered if the designers of the five-hundred year old O'Darach castle had included all the normal precautions for drought, siege, natural catastrophes and invasion. He had read that most underground tunnel systems like this one connected parts of the castle with access to secret passages and escape routes to hidden openings a safe distance from the castle walls. The best ones also had access to an endless supply of fresh water from underground springs.

Rory and Tharill continued their descent into the depths of the dark tunnels. As they walked Tharill looked for another torch to light. "I should have grabbed the other torch from where we started. I haven't seen anymore. You know that we will be hip-deep in dragon dung if this torch goes out for any reason."

"It won't," Rory said without breaking his stride.

The words, "Hi, what are you doing?" startled Reesa to the point that her heart felt as though it had leapt from her chest. She spun around to find Prince Rutgar Van Slauthe standing behind her, smiling.

"I am so sorry, Miss Burlong!" he cried! "I did not mean to startle you so, truly. I saw you standing here alone and thought I would make sure you are alright. Oh, look someone has broken the lock on this gate." Prince Rutgar picked up the lock and turned it over in his hand, examining it.

"What do you make of that?" He said handing it to Reesa.

She looked at him feigning a smile and said nothing at first.

"Are you well?" he looked genuinely concerned.

"I am fine." She managed to answer.

"I am truly sorry to have disturbed you, Miss Burlong." He bowed and turned to leave.

"No, wait." Reesa said, touching his arm with her hand. "I'm sorry. How rude of me. I was simply lost in thoughts of how my day has gone." She smiled adding, "Please stay, Prince Rutgar."

"Your day appeared to go very well according to the score board," he said.

"Thank you,"

He looked at the lock she still held in her hand. "What do you make of that?" he asked again, pointing at the lock.

"I don't know. It was not broken earlier in the day. I sat under that tree," she turned and pointed at a bench under a large oak tree, "and ate some fruit with friends not more than two hours past. The gate was securely locked then."

"We have tunnels like this at home," he noted, "there should be a torch or two just within. Shall we check it out?"

His bright blue eyes gleamed with curiosity or mischief. Reesa was unsure to which.

"No we mustn't," she said.

"Why not?" Prince Rutgar asked, his hair, the color of freshly fallen snow braided in rows to the back of his head where beads of ceramic, wood and bone tinkled in the light breeze.

"It was locked for a reason," She answered, matter-of-factly.

Rutgar chuckled and proceeded to walk into the passage way.

*What is it with these lads and exploring passage ways?* Reesa thought and then stepped across the open gate's threshold.

"Okay, I will come with you." Reesa said, wishing she had some trousers to change into. Her mother would kill her if she ruined her new archery costume.

The walls of the tunnel were a mixture of brick and stone. Reesa pulled off one of her gloves and slid her fingers across the stones. They were cool and slightly moist. She noticed the floor was lined with large slabs of gray and blue flagstone. The first

125

sconce they came to was empty. This is where Tharill had taken the torch from.

"It seems there should be a torch here." Rutgar said before spotting another one across the way.

*Should I tell him that Tharill and Rory took it? Why shouldn't I tell him?* She felt very uncomfortable about the confrontation Rory and the Prince had earlier.

Rutgar struck a match and put it to the torch flashing it into a blaze of light. "This torch has been recently wrapped and oiled," Rutgar said, noting how quick and brightly it fired up.

He held out an open hand, "Here my lady, may I take your hand?" he offered.

Reesa caught herself blushing. "Thank you, I can manage." She replied and waved him forward. *Why blush, now? I've always been treated like a lady, well, except when mistaken for a boy hanging by a rope off the side of a cliff, anyway. Maybe it was that Tharill more than likely would have handed me the torch and then pushed me ahead, there you go Explorer Girl! You lead the way!* The thought caused her to laugh out loud.

Rutgar puzzled by Reesa's sudden laughter, asked, "Something I said?"

"No, it's just funny that I am going with you to explore this passage. That's all." Reesa answered and what she said was true. She just left out the part about Tharill and Rory.

They could hear the sound of water trickling in the near distance and saw two open doors leading to rooms on the side of the passage. Rutgar reached his arm out with the torch and lit up the interior of one of the rooms. "It looks like a livestock room." Rutgar said pointing to feed and water troughs. "In case of a siege livestock would be brought here and housed if it was unsafe to keep them in the inner courtyard."

Reesa moved close beside him to get a better look, locks of her curly hair brushing his shoulder as she did. A sweet scent of vanilla wafted into his nose. He inhaled deeply, almost instinctively. Reesa appeared not to notice or if she did she gave no indication.

Stepping back out of the room and holding the torch toward the other side of the passage they saw a closed door. With Reesa close at his side, Rutgar opened the door. "Fodder and grain storage for the animals." He explained. "Although, it is empty now. We always keep our siege stores full and regularly rotated to prevent spoilage."

"I see."

"That is one of my duties at home." Rutgar proudly added. "I inspect all siege stores monthly and keep the stock rotated."

"Have you ever been under siege?" she asked. "I mean you personally?"

"Yes, once but I was only five years of age and do not remember much. I do remember being very frightened and my mother and I became extremely ill. My mother died during the siege. The attack on our castle lasted for almost six months, or so I am told."

Reesa stopped and put her hand on his arm, "I am sorry about your mother."

"Thank you."

"Do you remember much about her?" Reesa asked as they continued to walk into the darkness beyond the torch.

"I remember she used to sing or hum when she was sewing or embroidering. There is a portrait of her over the fireplace in our great hall. From that single portrait, my father has had many smaller paintings done. There is some type of painting of her in every chamber in the castle," he said, smiling at the thought.

Reesa stopped. "I think that is a stairway," she said pointing ahead.

Walking closer to a curve in the passage they did indeed find a wooden stair case. Rutgar tested the first step with the weight of his left foot. The stair creaked but held. He then tested the next one, it held.

"We should be okay going up." He said over his shoulder.

"It does not appear that anyone has been up this stair case in a very long time." Reesa said eyeing Rutgar's boot print in the dust.

The two slowly climbed the stairs towards a beam of light where voices could be heard. They reached the top of the stairs which turned into a corridor similar to that of a servant's bypass. Light streamed in under the closed door and through the door's keyhole.

Rutgar placed the torch in an empty scone on the wall. Reesa peered into the keyhole.

"Oh, my!" She said, covering her mouth with her hand.

"What?" Rutgar asked and leaned over close to her to look through the keyhole, too. What he saw made him stand up straight and then slowly back away. Reesa joined him, pressing herself against the wall opposite from the door.

"It is King Fios' throne room," Rutgar said.

"Yes and there is a meeting going on. We should not listen. We should leave immediately," She said, her voice cracked in panic.

Rutgar cocked his head grinning and said, "No, let's listen. How often do you get to observe the inner working of the law makers?"

Reesa note the twinkle of mischief was back in his eyes. "Oh, my," she said, as he grabbed her hand and pulled her closer to the large keyhole he was again peering into. She noticed that the voices from the other side of the door were loud and combative.

"Rutgar," she started to protest.

"Shhhh, I think I heard Saxony mentioned."

"He is planning to invade and this arrow is the proof! My Lord, what other evidence do you need?" The voice of Councilor Sciltin O'Shannessy McMillan was loud enough to be clearly heard on the other side of the locked door where Reesa & Rutgar stood.

"Here is Van Slauthe's coat of arms stamped right into the bronze of the arrow tip!" The sound of feet stomping and voices agreeing and disagreeing spilled through the keyhole.

Reesa turned abruptly, staring at the confused expression on Rutgar's face.

"What are they talking about?" Reesa asked in a soft voice.

"I don't know," Rutgar said, shaking his head.

"Sure you don't!" Rory's voice barked from the stairway he had just come up.

Reesa and Rutgar spun to see Tharill and Rory walking out of the shadows into the light cast by Rutgar's torch.

"What do you mean?" Rutgar demanded.

"Be quiet! They will hear us," Reesa hissed, shooing them down the hall and away from the door.

"Don't play the innocent, Prince Van Slauthe. The arrow was pulled directly from a Whidley Island dragon, Volcae by my uncle less than three weeks ago," Rory retorted.

"Take it easy, Rory," Tharill cautioned putting a hand on his brother's shoulder which was immediately shrugged off.

"Rutgar, what is he talking about?" Reesa asked, stepping forward.

"Rutgar? Rutgar is it now?" Tharill said slight tremor of shock in his voice.

"Well, you two got pretty close in less than a day. I should have guessed," Rory threw back at the girl.

"And what do you mean by that?" Reesa snapped.

"Let's all just take a step back for a moment," Tharill said, trying to sound the voice of reason.

"I don't know what they are talking about!" Rutgar objected. "Or what arrow you are talking about?"

"Liar!" Rory yelled and lunged at the prince. He slung Rutgar against the wall. Rutgar pushed back and slammed a left hook into Rory's cheek splitting it open. Rory responded with two quick jabs to Rutgar's jaw and eye, stunning him.

"Stop! Stop!" Reesa screamed.

Tharill rushed forward and grabbed Rory by the shoulders from behind. Rory drew back his fist to hit Rutgar and struck Tharill square in the face with his elbow. Blood burst from his nose. "Ohh, ohh!" Tharill cried out in pain as he lost his balance and fell back against Reesa sending her into the wall.

Rutgar threw up his right arm sending Rory's blow wild but his other fist connected with Rutgar's jaw again. Rutgar lashed out with both fist's one pounded hard into Rory's chest the other into his stomach. He fell to the floor gasping for breath. But, Rory was quick to recover and tripped Rutgar by hooking his foot on Rutgar's ankle and yanking it back. Rutgar smacked the back of his head on the wall and he slid down in a daze. Rory clambered to get on top of the Prince and preparing to strike him again, drew back his fist.

Reesa shrieked at the sight a large man rushing into the room brandishing what appeared to be a long curved dagger. In an instant the man had the dagger at Rory's throat.

Tharill started to move forward to defend his brother but stopped as the turban clad man swiftly pointed another dagger in Tharill's direction.

Reesa grabbed Tharill's shoulder and he protectively shoved her behind him with the bloody hand he had been holding his wounded nose with.

"Be so kind as to step away from my Prince," said Rastom Razmadze, in his calm, middle-eastern accent as he held a scimitar at Rory's neck.

"I am okay, Rastom, let him go," Rutgar said, shaking the fog from his mind.

"As you wish Your Highness," Rastom said removing the knife from Rory's throat and pushing both blades back into their jeweled scabbards. "May I ask what is going on here?" Rastom looked from Rutgar to the Gruaige brothers and then at Reesa. Seeing the blood on her dress he asked, "Are you hurt, Miss Burlong?"

"What?" She looked puzzled. "Hurt?"

"The blood on your dress," Rastom pointed.

She looked down and saw dark red streaks on the front and side of her once sunny yellow and crème colored archery frock. "Oh, no!" she blurted out. "Mother is going to kill me."

"Are you injured?" Rastom asked again.

"No, this is Tharill's blood."

Rastom's right eyebrow rose slightly as if considering the situation and then returned his attention to Rutgar.

"Rory and I had a misunderstanding," Rutgar said.

Rastom extended his hand to help the Prince stand then Rutgar handed Reesa a handkerchief to wipe at the blood on her dress. "Yes, I can see several points of the discussion starting to swell on Your Majesty's lips and right eye," Rastom said and turned to look at Rory and Tharill. "Two against one?" He asked pointing to Tharill's face.

"No, my brother did this to me," Tharill said through cupped hands covering his bleeding nose.

"Not on purpose!" Rory defended, frowning at Tharill.

Rastom pulled a cloth from one of his billowing shirt sleeves and handed it to Tharill. "I would say your nose may be broken, Master Gruaige."

Looking closely at Rory's bleeding cheek Rastom added, "You may need stitches for that cut on your cheek," which had a steady stream of blood flowing down from it.

The shouting from beyond the door down the hall grew louder and more violent.

"I do not believe guests are permitted in this area," Rastom said. He then plucked the brightly burning torch from its sconce and said, "Shall we go, Your Majesty?"

"Do you know what is behind that door, Rastom?" Rutgar said pointing down the hall beyond where the group stood.

"No and it is none of my business your highness as you may also consider it may be none of yours," Rastom replied holding the torch toward the staircase to light the way.

"It is my business when they accuse my father and your King of ruthlessly having dragons killed on the Celtic Islands," Rutgar's voice was loud and echoed down the hall, apparently not caring if he were heard by those on the other side of the door.

Rastom started to lead the way back out, but stopped and ushered the young people to go first. Something did not feel right. He stopped and looked back from where they had just come. Nothing caught his eye but there was something or someone back there in the dark he was sure.

131

Curro Delagarza stood silent in the shadows and watched the group proceed slowly back toward the tunnel entrance. His plan was starting to come together.

# CHAPTER #12

## *DIARMAID'S BOAT YARD*

Prince Rutgar paced between his chamber windows like an expectant father. His brow furrowed and hands clasped so tightly his knuckles had turned white. Rastom Razmadze stood in silence by the front door watching his charge nervously pacing back and forth. When a knock sounded on the door, Rutgar stopped and looked at Razmadze. The calm expression on his body-guard's face gave him a sense of security, if only in a small way.

The knock came again and Rutgar nodded his head, ready to accept visitors. Rastom acknowledged with a slight bow and with only a slight detectable movement put one hand on his scimitar as he turned the door handle with the other. He opened the door and stood aside. "Please enter, my lord," he said, with a respectful bow.

"Thank you Rastom Razmadze," replied, Madog ap Gruffydd making his way over to the window where Prince Rutgar stood a smile of relief spreading across his face.

"Prince, I have some disturbing and regrettable news to share with you." Madog said in a thoughtful tone.

"A large arrow with the Van Slauthe hallmark was recovered from the carcass of a slain dragon on Whidley Island."

"I know," said, Rutgar. "I was exploring the siege tunnels and came upon a door that led to the king's court."

Madog's eyes widen in surprise and he said, "What?" Turning his attention to Rastom he scorned, "and you let him go into another castle's siege tunnels? Are you out of your mind?"

Rastom started to speak but Rutgar stopped him with the wave of his hand. "It was my doing. I asked Rastom to get something for me and then I left the archery field. Childish, I know." Rutgar said a sheepish expression on his face. "Anyway, I heard what they were saying. It is not true and you know it, too. My father would never allow such sport." Rutgar turned and looked out the window.

Madog stepped closer to the young man and put his hand on Rutgar's shoulder. "Of course it is not true. That tip could have been plucked off any lost or discarded arrow. It was also peculiarly long and hollow. I've not seen any tip like it before," Madog said. "The council meets again in the morning for further discussion."

"Hollow?" Rutgar asked.

"And filled with poison," Madog continued.

"I wondered how a single arrow could take down a fully grown Whidley bull dragon," he pondered. Then added through questioning eyes, "Why would anyone want to kill a dragon and then make it look as if someone from our kingdom had done it?"

Another knock sounded at the door directing attention away from the conversation between Rutgar and Madog. "That should be my cousin Feylan." Madog said.

Rastom waited for Rutgar's approval before opening the door. Rutgar nodded and Rastom opened the door cautiously as he had before.

"I am Feylan O'Shea ap Gruffydd," announced a deep voice from the hallway. "I believe I am expected?" he asked more than stated.

Rastom stepped aside and invited the new comer in with a bow. Glancing down the hall he noticed two men leaning against the wall talking. He closed the door and relocked it. Rutgar approached the large, thickly-bearded man and held out his hand. Feylan grasped the young prince's hand with such strength and affection Rutgar tried not to cringe in pain.

"I am so glad to meet you Prince Rutgar!" Feylan's deep voice spoke with a youthful glee and an infectious smile blossomed from his cheeks. "Your aunt Helga and my dear Rosheen are the closest of friends. Helga speaks very fondly of you."

Feylan then turned his attention to Madog. "My ship *Mor Telyn* is in ready should you need it."

"A ship?" Prince Rutgar questioned. He looked from Feylan to Madog and then over to Rastom. "What do you propose? That I flee and hide like a common criminal?"

Madog held up his hand to reassure, "We are concerned for your safety once the hallmark on the arrow is made public," Madog replied. "What you decide to do is totally up to you Prince."

"My father must be notified at once." Rutgar said.

"I am preparing a dispatch to send with my fastest long range balloon this evening," Madog said. "I will include any message you choose to send as well."

"Why can the prince not go in the balloon and deliver the message in person?" Feylan asked.

"It is a correspondence transport with just enough room for the pilot and a twenty-pound mail bag. It will take only two days to get to Saxony," Madog answered.

"I will send a message asking my father what he wants me to do. I can speak for him in his stead, if need be." Rutgar said and seated himself at a writing desk where pen and paper were at hand.

"I will include it with my correspondence to him," Madog said, adding, "I would advise you to leave this evening on Feylan's ship for a visit to Dunsey. Your Aunt Helga would very much want you there until this is resolved, I am sure."

"I will not run and hide!" Rutgar exclaimed firmly and handed Madog his sealed message. "The Van Slauthe's have done nothing wrong and I will not lend truth to any speculation that we have done so by running away."

"I agree whole heartedly with the young prince," Said Feylan. "But we should make ready in case things turn to gnart dung. I will send messengers to all Gruffydd councilors, Sciltin McMillan, and Hugh McRae who I know are supporters of the Van Slauthe family to meet this evening and discuss the matter."

"You are right Feylan," Madog conceded. "I believe the best place to meet without drawing attention is Diarmaid's Boat Yard."

"Isn't it outside the castle walls? Won't that many Gruffydds leaving the castle and heading in the same direction draw attention?" asked Rutgar.

"Not at all. Tonight is stone-throw night and we Gruffydds are great for the gambling!" Feylan said, a resounding chuckle in his voice.

"Have you not been to Diarmaid's yet?" Feylan asked the prince who shook his head. "Well, then we shall mix business with please, tonight!"

"Come to my chambers and let us sup together before leaving for Diarmaid's," Madog invited. "Would half seven suit?"

"Excellent," Rutgar agreed.

Madog shook the young prince's hand and patted Feylan on the back. "Let us be on our way, Feylan."

"We shall see you then," he said as they parted. Rastom held the door open for the two and locked it behind them.

"What do you say to this plan?" Rutgar asked Rastom.

"I think we shall see where it takes us," Rastom replied, and left the room to fix the Prince a snack of fruit, nuts, and a glass of wine.

Rastom would eat a meal and rest before escorting the Prince to dinner and then on to Diarmaid's for the meeting. He would be on full alert tonight.

The large wooden structure was not only run down but dark with tobacco smoke and smelled of sour mash. The sound of cheering was almost deafening. The men looked like they were convicts, ruffians, and scoundrels in general. They were crowded into small groups watching Faire of colored stones being tossed.

The little group of well-dressed men, looking so out of place, walked in. But, it was apparent to Prince Rutgar that both Madog and Feylan felt quite at ease in such a place. Rutgar, himself, was very much on edge even though he knew Rastom was close on his heels.

Feylan pointed to a door toward the rear of the building and they started making their way in that direction. As they proceeded through the crowd, Rutgar noticed that almost everyone knew both Madog and Feylan. Handshake after handshake and pats on the back came with "hello and join us!" yelled across the room. Rutgar glanced at Rastom who was watchful but did not show any concern. Feylan and Madog were friendly to the greetings with head nods and hand waves, but they did not stray from their path to the door at the back of the great room. A large surly looking man opened the door for them without saying a word.

The room inside was well lit and much quieter than the large boat warehouse type room they just left. All were greeted by other well dressed individuals as soon as they entered the room.

"Madog! Prince Van Slauthe," A deep voice rang out from a thin man seated at a table.

Rutgar at once recognized the thick Llanddwyn accent of Broslin ap Meryk. Standing up, Broslin beckoned them to the table. He bowed to the young prince and greeted the others. He banged his empty ale mug on the table to get everyone's attention. "We should get this meeting started," Broslin said. "Now that the prince, Madog, and Feylan are here."

Of the twenty-seven dragon council members, fourteen were in attendance at this meeting to show support for the Saxony and King Victor Van Slauthe. The prince knew several of the councilors and was introduced to those he did not know. Rutgar thanked each one and then was courteously directed to sit at the head of the long table.

Unlike the unruly meeting of the dragon council there was no shouting or pounding of fists. Broslin opened the meeting by stating the facts about the dragon kills as known. He asked Rhodri Mauer ap Rishton of Dunsey Island to write down everything said. Rhodri must have expected this request of him for he pulled parchment, ink and pen from his satchel and arranged them in front of him on the table.

Rastom Razmadze was the first to react to the commotion outside the door. His scimitar instantly twirled into a defensive position. He stepped closer to his charge, Prince Rutgar Van Slauthe. Several around the table rose to their feet, pulled hidden pistols from trousers or jackets while others just sat dumbfounded.

The doors crashed open and several well-armed men wearing King's Guard uniforms entered the room. "Prince Rutgar", yelled a man who appeared to be in charge of the group. "We have a warrant for-" his words cut short by the sound of shots being fired.

"Run, my prince!" Razmadze shouted over his shoulder as he stepped into the frenzy of fighting men. The prince pulled his own dagger and started to approach the melee of fists, knives, and pistol fire. But, Razmadze turned back just in time to deflect a blow from an axe, directed at the prince, with a single thrust of his blade into the man's chest. "Now! Go now!" His angry words were aimed directly into the startled ice-blue eyes of the prince. Without another word he fended off a charging man with a single swipe of his scimitar.

"Come! This way Rutgar!" yelled Madog from across the room. Rutgar felt himself being propelled forward with a push from behind. He glanced back and realized it was Feylan's hand on his shoulder so he did not resist. Rutgar found himself with three or four other men heading through a panel in the wall that opened into a hidden passage. The panel closed behind Feylan with the pull of a rope. Silently the fleeing men rushed through the narrow passage followed by sounds of fighting and men crying out in pain. The passage appeared to be between fake walls in the rooms of the boat construction building.

Rutgar thought of Razmadze and regretted leaving the man who had always been at his side. Rastom was more than a body guard. He was a friend, a confidant and a constant companion for as long as he could remember and he was not getting any younger. Would he be okay? Rutgar shuddered at the thought of losing him.

Madog stopped suddenly directly in front of Rutgar. "Do you smell smoke?" Madog asked sniffing the air.

"Yes," Feylan answered.

"I smell it, too," Rutgar said, looking around in the barely lit passage.

A panel in the wall crashed to the floor out of sight behind them. Next the sound of yelling came from the same direction.

"A secret passage, my lord!" yelled a man in the distance.

"Go, go!" Feylan hissed just above a whisper to Madog and Rutgar. The three started to run again. They could hear their pursuers were getting closer. At the end of the passageway a door lay off its hinges on the ground. They ran out into the moonless dark night, Madog leading the way.

"There they are!" a voice yelled from inside the passageway the three had just left.

"I'll hold them off, you two head for the docks!" Feylan said in a low but commanding voice, pulling two concealed pistols from his belt under a long thin lined coat.

"This way, Rutgar," Madog said, pulling a pair of ivory-handled flintlocks from his belt as well. Rutgar followed without question. He had never seen this side of his uncle, whom he had always thought of as meek and a bit elderly.

They ran in the shadows of buildings and dry-docked boats. They stopped only once at the sound of pistol-fire coming from the direction they had just left. "That's Feylan." Madog said, "I would know the sound of those Saxon pistols anywhere. I had them specially made for his fiftieth birthday." Rutgar saw his uncle's face fraught with worry.

"I can find my way from here, Uncle Madog. Go back and make sure Feylan is okay," Rutgar said resting his hand on Madog's shoulder.

Madog gave him a thoughtful glance and said, "No, let's keep going." Rutgar did not move but instead tightened his grip on his uncle's shoulder.

"Really, I know the way from here. Go, go back."

Madog placed his own hand over Rutgar's and said, "Feylan and I are getting a little too long in the tooth for this sort of thing." Then smiled and ran back the way they had come.

Rutgar continued his stealth like maneuvering between boats and the shadows of warehouses along the shipyards. In the light of an oil lamp on a pole he saw the words, 'pier 57' and an arrow pointing down a lane. From what he remembered, the lane was lined with shipping businesses, mariner supply shops, and a few rowdy seafaring pubs. It was also well-lit with oil-lamp posts. This was the only lane to the pier and there was no way around it with enclosed shipyards on both sides.

He stepped around the corner into the dimly lit lane. There were four obviously drunk men stumbling and laughing as they sang 'Paddy Doyle's Boots'.

*"Yes, aye, and we'll haul, aye,*
*To pay Paddy Doyle for his boots;*
*We'll tauten the bunt, and we'll furl, aye,*
*And pay Paddy Doyle for his boots."*

Rutgar thought he would blend in better if he were also to appear drunk. So, he lowered his head and staggered slightly as he approached the men.

*"Yeo, aye, and we'll sing, aye,*
*To pay Paddy Doyle for his boots;*
*We'll bunt up the sail with a fling, aye,*
*And pay Paddy Doyle for his boots!"*

They passed each other with nothing more than a nod of the head and Rutgar heard them continue to sing as they turned the corner out of sight.

*Yeo, aye an we'll haul, aye,*
*To pay Paddy Doyle for his boots;*
*We'll skin the ol' rabbit an' haul, aye,*
*To pay Paddy Doyle for his boots!*

Rutgar looked cautiously about and continued to emulate a drunken stagger. Most of the shops were closed at this late hour and the pubs appeared to be thinning out as there were only four or five people meandering about. The hair rose on the back of his neck as he hurried past a dark alley when from the alley a thickly accented voice said, "Prince Van Slauthe."

Recognizing the Spanian accent, the accent of a country Saxony had been embroiled in bitter border dispute for decades, he immediately ran.

He could hear at least two men chasing him. Rutgar was sure he could out-run them, but to where? Would others be waiting by his uncle's ship, the Mor Telyn? They must have figured he would head to the ship.

Rutgar flung a pub door open and ran inside. It was dark, smoky and crowded with celebrating archery contestants. Finding a hat and coat hanging on the back of an unattended chair, he put them on and slung his own under a table.

"Hey, looook whoooo's heeere," Came the slurred words of a familiar voice. Rutgar hurried in the direction of the voice. Rory staggered to his feet and pulled a chair out for Rutgar. "Pleeease have a sit-down, Your Holiness," Rory said with a mock bow that almost caused him to fall into Rutgar.

Rutgar immediately sat down and pulled the chair close to the table with his back to the door. He jolted at the feel of a slap on his back. "Slumming, your most on high excellent one?" Tharill laughed his speech more clear than Rory's slurred greeting.

"Or have you come to admire my shinnnny new trophy? Thank you, by the way for losing sooooo gracefully your worshipfullllness." Rory said holding up a silver trophy topped with the figure of an archer, bow drawn and then kissed it.

Rutgar kept his head low as he looked toward the front door which had just opened. From the corner of his eye, he caught the outline of two men entering the pub.

"You look different your holiness," Tharill chided leaning forward. At once Tharill noticed the subdued panic in Rutgar's eyes.

"What?" Tharill said and looked toward the closing front door.

Rutgar sat quiet looking down at the table. *Should he ask these idiots for help?* His pride said, *No way!* But he truly needed help, if he were to get through this night with his life.

Tharill pushed a half full beer glass in front of Rutgar.

"No," Rutgar whispered, an anxious look on his face.

"Pick it up and look like you are drinking you fool!" Tharill hissed, leaning forward with his elbows on the table cupping his own drink with his hands.

Rutgar nodded his head in understanding and picked the glass up. Tharill pushed his chair closer to Rutgar and put Rory's trophy in front of him.

Rory began to object, his dislike of the prince apparent, but the look on his brother's face checked him. Even with his brain thick in a drunken fog, he knew in an instant something was amiss.

Tharill removed his new red and black scarf, a traditional piece of attire worn by competitive archers showing their rank of skill, and slipped it around Rutgar's neck. Pulling his old scarf from his pocket and put it around his own neck.

Tharill signaled for the barmaid and ordered three stout mugs of coffee for the table. When she left, Rory leaned back on his chair and whispered something to a fellow archer at the next table. Tharill could see two tall dark-haired men wearing black shirts and trousers making their way through the pub. They appeared to be looking for someone and Tharill was pretty sure he knew who they wanted.

The man Rory had whispered to got up and walked over to the bar where the two strangers stopped to talk. The archer ordered more beer and waited for the strangers to move away before returning.

The strangers left the pub in a hurry without anymore conversation or investigation. It was evident their prey had eluded them, for now.

Returning to his seat with two pints of stout, the archer leaned over and spoke with Rory, then nodded his head at Rutgar and Tharill and then turned his attention back to his own table.

Tharill thanked the barmaid and paid her for the coffee after she sat them on the table. He pushed one in front of Rory, who took a quick draw. "Sweet dragon's breath, this is hot!" he cried. Slightly embarrassed by his outburst, he looked around to see if anyone was paying attention. No one was, the hour was late, the spirits had been flowing for hours and no one cared. Fanning his mouth with one hand in hopes that air would ease the pain, Rory whispered, "Those men were Spanian, Rutgar. What the dung heap is going on?"

Rutgar picked up his mug and blew on the coffee, "I don't know."

"This has something to do with our dragons," Tharill said. "I bet my life on it."

"I think it is my life you are betting," Rutgar gloomed.

# CHAPTER #13

## *BOAT YARD AFTERMATH*

The marble pillars in the Kings throne-room stood cold and silent in contrast to the loud, fuming voices that rose in volume like a newly lit flame grabs hold and begins to thrive. Tension and discourse thickened the air like smoke.

"We were attacked by the king's own guards and sheriff !" Broslin ap Meryk yelled, repeatedly slamming his fist on the banister in front of his chair. The king's court roared with men shouting at each other and no one in particular.

"Come to order!" Seamus MacDougal, the king's court valet, shouted into the crowd striking his scepter onto the floor with loud reverberating clanks. "We will come to order, gentlemen. Come to order I say and all will be heard."

King Fios sat on his throne, his face wrought with concern and worry. The charges the dragon council members were flinging about were preposterous in his opinion, but the members believed them to be true, which for King Fios was even more troubling.

"I have sent for my Sheriff. He will answer for this or I will know the reason why," King Fios said.

"I ordered no raid on Diarmaid's Boatyard. I have been aware of the stone throw gambling there for years. I could care less how men choose to squander their hard earned monies." King Fios waved his hand in an annoyed manner at such a ludicrous accusation.

Sheriff Vallyn Tearjoy entered the court to a booing and hissing crowd. He looked about with a defensive glare in the direction of familiar faces.

"Your Majesty," He said with a respectful bow. "How may I be of service?"

"It has come to my attention that a raid was led on Diarmaid's Boatyard last night. Please explain," the King said, leaning forward with elbows on his knees.

The crowd started to become noisy again and Seamus struck his scepter, casting accusatory glances at the individuals causing the ruckus. The court room settled once more.

"My deputies and I went to Diarmaid's last night. This is correct, but it was not to raid the place, Your Majesty. We were in search of a murderer that was reported to be there," Sheriff Vallyn explained.

"Your men attacked me! I barely escaped with my life!" Shouted Broslin ap Meryk in defiance of Seamus' rebuking glare.

"I can assure you councilor ap Meryk, my men only acted in self-defense while trying to arrest a murder suspect," the sheriff said in a respectful, albeit slightly defensive tone.

The court room again had to be quieted by the repeated striking of Seamus' staff upon the flagstone floor. The King raised and lowered his hands to convey his desire for everyone to retake their seats.

Returning his attention to Sheriff Tearjoy, he said, "tell me about the murder suspect."

"We went to arrest Rastom Razmadze for the murder of Christian Wallace. He resisted, killing two of my men and wounding four others before being over powered, My Lord."

"Do you refer to Prince Rutgar Van Slauthe's Mameluk body guard?" the King asked, shock flashing across his face.

145

"The same, My Lord," The Sheriff said adding, "We had a valid warrant naming him and signed by yourself." He pulled a folded paper from his vest pocket and handed it to Seamus. Seamus unfolded it and presented it to the king.

King Fios looked the document over carefully and asked, "who gave you this warrant and when?"

"It came by messenger early last evening," the sheriff answered.

"I signed no such document," the King snarled. "This is a fake!" He slapped the paper on his knee and tossed it back to Seamus.

The room broke into a roar of shouts, pounding fists and the stomping of booted feet. The sound of Seamus' staff pounding on the floor could not be heard over the pandemonium in the court room.

King Fios stood, shouting, "Quiet, quiet!" and returning his attention back to Tearjoy, he growled, "Where is Rastom Razmadze at this time?"

Startled by the question, Tearjoy said, "castle guards came for him shortly after we arrested him last night, Your Highness."

"What the dragon's breath is going on here?" King Fios' disbelief resounded through the court room. "I know not of any such happening!" he shouted in growing anger. "But, I will get to the root of it all!" The King glared at Tearjoy. Verbal instructions were not needed, as the expression on the King's face told all.

"Yes, Your Majesty. I will conduct this investigation myself," Tearjoy said, determination showing in his hardened jaw line.

"If your men were not chasing and shooting at us," Feylan shouted from his chair, unable to stand, "then who was? I am not imagining this bullet wound here in my leg!"

"I assure you, they were not my men, councilor ap Gruffydd," Tearjoy vehemently denied.

"I killed one of them; did you not recover the body?" Feylan retorted.

"We recovered only the bodies of the two deputies that

Razmadze killed during his arrest. We had several injuries but no other deaths, and all of my men were accounted for after the arrest," Tearjoy said. "Where did you kill this man, counselor ap Gruffydd? I will send my sergeant to retrieve the body."

Feylan relayed the location to the court and Tearjoy charged his sergeant with the task of discovering the identity of the dead imposter.

"Where is Prince Rutgar Van Slauthe, at this time?" the King demanded. No one offered an answer and all eyes turned to Feylan and Madog who sat next to each other.

"My nephew, the Prince, was to meet us at my ship the Mor Telyn last night after our escape from Diarmaid's," Madog said. "But he did not arrive there."

"Escape? Prince Van Slauthe should not have needed to escape from anywhere or anything!" King Fios bellowed.

"I want the Prince found!

I want his body guard found!

I want the man who forged my signature on that damnú warrant found!

I want the fake guards found and I want them found now!" the King howled pounding the arm of his throne-chair with each demand.

The room grew very quiet as pale and astonished faces stared at their King, who was renowned for his even tempered nature. This outburst of un-vetted anger had shocked all those in the room.

Turning to his Court's Valet he said, "Seamus, we must get word to King Victor at once! It would not bode well for him to hear of this extraordinary situation through the fast-moving gossip mongers on Scotia. Have our fastest message balloon readied for launch."

"Yes, your majesty."

King Fios said, "I must write this letter at once in private," and stomped off the throne platform.

"All rise for the King's departure!" Seamus bellowed and struck his staff to the floor three times. "Councilors I will have food and refreshments brought to you in the guest-hall. Please make your way there at this time."

The kilted pipers thrust their bags under their arms and the sound of the highland pipes drowned out all other noise in the throne-room as they followed King Fios through the open doorway.

Sheriff Vallyn Tearjoy stood before the great door leading to the King's chambers. *How can I report on what I cannot find?* he thought, looking down at his shoes. He and his men had searched the whole day for the messenger and the guards that removed Razmadze from their custody. Plus, the body of the man councilor ap Gruffydd claimed to have shot had not been located, either. There was also no record of a warrant being issued or any messenger sent from the King's court.

King Fios Crann O'Darach was not a vindictive man, but he did expect results from his subordinates. At this time Sheriff Vallyn Tearjoy had only uncovered more questions during his searching. There was one thing he knew for sure, whoever had organized the events of last night had gone to a lot of effort to implicate King Fios in the arrest of Rastom Razmadze and the attack on Prince Rutgar.

*Well here I go.* Tearjoy thought and sternly knocked on the door.

"Come in," a voice came from behind the door. *Seamus MacDougal* he assumed. Tearjoy opened the door and stepped through.

"Is the messenger dead?" Curro Delagarza asked his sergeant.

"Si, mi Comandante," Felipe Quesada answered and handed Delagarza a parchment bearing the Crann O'Darach royal seal, still intact.

Delagarza picked up a candle from the table and set the parchment a light and then threw the burning paper into the unlit fire hearth where it blazed for a moment and then smoldered into ash. He stood for a minute staring down at it.

A tall man standing over six-feet tall, Delagarza presented an imposing figure of a man. Dressed in black pants and beige tunic drawn tight at the waist by a double-wrapped red sash he stood silent nudging the last remnants of the parchment into the hearth with the tip of his boot.

"Where is Razmadze, now?" Delagarza asked, not looking away from the hearth.

"Él está en el buque," sergeant Quesada said pointing out the window to Delagarza's fourteen gun ship, Hav Fuglen.

The Hav Fuglen flew the Noreg national flag, a neutral country located on the continent sharing its southern border with Spana and Saxony. As Delagarza's mother was Noregn he claimed citizenship in both Noreg and Spana, speaking each language fluently, as well.

"Have the fire-proof cages been assembled in the hold of the Hav Fuglen?"

"Si, las jaulas están listas," sergeant Quesada answered.

"As soon as you have captured the prince and Professor Burlong we will make sail." Delagarza said, strolling over to the window to view the docks and harbor. From this window he could see most of the ships in the harbor and more importantly he had a clear view of the ship moored across from his, Madog ap Gruffydd's schooner, the Mor Telyn.

"¿Qué hacemos con su esposa y su hija,"

"Oh, that's right," Delagarza answered with a sigh of annoyance. "He travels with his wife and daughter." He stood for a few moments gazing out the window at the gently rocking motion of the ships anchored in the harbor. "Kill them."

"¿Estás seguro, Comandante," Sergeant Quesada blinked in surprised at Delagarza's answer.

"Make it look like an accident," Delagarza said. "And do it tonight. I want to be away from this island within the next two days."

"Si, mi Comandante," Sergeant Quesada saluted and left the room.

# CHAPTER #14

## *SMUGGLING A PRINCE*

Tharill woke to a painful throbbing headache. It hurt to even open his eyes, the after effect from a night celebrating with Rory and other fellow archers at the Anchor Inn Tavern on Quay Way Lane.

Tharill looked up at the ceiling rafters. He blinked several times before he realized he was lying on the floor, and not on a bed. Although, he could feel the pillow under his head and a blanket about him he wondered how he ended up on the floor. He laid quiet for a bit thinking about the night before.

He turned his head to the left and squinted at the sight of what appeared to be a pair of brown boots with the Van Slauthe crest on the buckles. *Rutgar*. Tharill slowly sat up, but his head began to spin so he dropped back down. Rolling over onto his side, Tharill felt queasy but managed to prop himself up into a half-sitting, position. He saw Rutgar sleeping in the bed across from Rory. He was still fully clothed, except for boots and hat, with one hand on the hilt of a dagger protruding from under his vest.

*The royal gnart's ass is sleeping in my bed!* Tharill rubbed at the stubble on his chin. *We must have tossed stones for it.* He surmised.

Tharill staggered to his feet and made his way to the open window. He took in a deep breath and unexpectedly spewed chunks of last night's dinner and ale out onto the guesthouse courtyard below. He looked at the other second story windows and thankfully saw no one else. The early morning fog was as thick as his aunt's gnart-bean soup. The cold, dark grey mist extended from ground level to about 12 feet high. He saw no movement other than a flock of pigeons, fluttering this way and that, above a water fountain.

"My thanks to you Tharill," came the quiet, gravelly voice of Rutgar Van Slauthe, who was now sitting up in the bed, his stockinged feet on the floor. Tharill turned at the sound, wiping tidbits of slime from his chin, and gave Rutgar a sheepish grin.

"Well, we couldn't let our only royal acquaintance get murdered right in front of us, now could we?" Tharill asked. Then he looked over at Rory to see if he was awake yet.

"Tharill, I want you to know that I have always respected your family's long history as Dragon Keepers. I also admire your ability as an archer. Even though we've long had a competitive rivalry in archery, I always enjoy my encounters with you at the matches. But, I never imagined you would help me in the manner that you have." Rutgar said rubbing the sleep from his eyes with the palms of his hands. "I just want to say ..." he stopped as if the words came hard to say.

"It's okay, Rutgar, forget it, really," Tharill replied a little embarrassed by the unusually personal nature of the Prince's words.

"Who the dragon's breath were those guys after you last night?" Tharill asked and turned from the window to slump in a chair next to it. "Where is your Mameluk, Razmadze?"

"I don't know where Rastom is or if he is even alive." Rutgar said the pain of not knowing showing on his face and in his voice.

"Alive?" Tharill echoed. A wrinkle furrowed his brow.

Tharill slowly reached for his shoes, put them on and began lacing them up. "What was all that about? Who in their right mind would chase after the crown prince of Saxony and why?"

"They had Spanian accents," Rutgar said.

"What would Spanians be doing on Scotia? Their ship would have been noticed the minute it came within sight of the island lookout towers." Tharill muttered, and then answered his own question. "They must have landed in a smaller boat. So, where is their ship?"

"Maybe they came by transport balloon." Rory, now awake, suggested.

"No, there are very few places to land a balloon on Scotia and none where a landing would go unnoticed. They must have a ship anchored out to sea but close enough to reach by a rowboat." Tharill said.

The three teens were startled by a loud knock at the door. Looking from one to the other, Tharill asked, "who is it?"

"It's me." The cheerful voice of Reesa Burlong rang out.

"I'll be right there." Rory replied. "Are you alone?" Rory asked his hand on the door handle.

"No, I have the entire St. Brigid's All Girl Choir with me to sing you a wake-up song," Reesa said in a matter-of-fact tone.

Tharill nodded his head at Rory, who rolled his eyes and frowned. Rory opened the door, pulled Reesa quickly inside, and glanced down the hall before shutting the door.

"Hey!" Reesa protested yanking her arm free from Rory's hand. Instant fury glinted in her eyes for being man-handled in such a way. She snapped, "watch your hands!" but stopped cold at the sight of Prince Rutgar Van Slauthe sitting on the edge of one of the beds.

"Hi," Rutgar said, leaning forward to pull on his boots.

"Rutgar! The king's guards are looking everywhere for you!" Reesa yelped. "What are you doing here?"

"Rutgar was chased by two Spanians last night," Tharill answered. "They chased him into the Broken Bow where we were celebrating."

"Spanians, on Scotia? Really?" Reesa frowned, obviously skeptical. Moving from the door to sit in the chair vacated by Tharill, Reesa crinkled her nose. "What is that horrible smell?"

Rory shoved his sockless feet into his shoes, averting Reesa's sidelong glance.

"I can assure you they were most definitely from Spana," Rutgar said, annoyed at Reesa's comments.

"You must go to the sheriff and let them know you are all right," Reesa urged.

"No! I will not!" Rutgar exclaimed.

"But, why?" Reesa asked, and caught the puzzled look on the faces of both Rory and Tharill who were silently watching the confrontation.

"How do I know it is not the sheriff, the king's guards or even King Fios Crann O'Darach himself who has set these Spanians after me?" Rutgar snapped back.

"You can't be serious," Reesa said, obviously astonished at such a thought.

"He has a point," Rory said.

Her eyes blazed at such a horrible accusation and she began to object, "Here now! I-"

Tharill held up a hand interrupting her, "wait a minute Rutgar may really have something here. I'm not saying it is the King himself, but perhaps a council member or some King's Court underling may be behind this."

"You heard members of the council just yesterday in the King's Court accusing my father of involvement in the dragon slayings," Rutgar reminded her.

"Yes, but we know that it's not true. You said as much," Reesa protested. "You and Rory came to blows over it."

"Well, as far as that goes..." Rory's expression was apologetic and Rutgar just smiled in acceptance, waving any further discussion of the fight off.

154

"I am honored that you take me at my word, my lady." Rutgar bowed.

"I believe that you *are* a man of your word," Reesa replied, a twinkle of undisguised affection in her eyes.

"Can we move on?" Tharill barked. "You two can plan your wedding later."

"Tharill!" Reesa objected. A blush of crimson flashed across her cheeks, highlighting her bright blue eyes. Amused by the exchange, Rory tried to stifle a laugh but it came out as a loud 'snorting 'sound which drew harsh looks from both Tharill and Reesa.

"We need to keep Rutgar safe as well as get word to his family," Tharill said to Rory.

"But we return to Whidley today on the afternoon balloon," Rory reminded Tharill.

"And we leave for Dara by ship on this morning's tide," Reesa added.

"I am far too well known to go unnoticed on balloon or ship," Rutgar stated.

"That white hair of yours might as well be a lighthouse beacon," Rory laughed.

Rutgar frowned, "he is right. My accent is a give-away, too. So what can we do?"

The silence of quiet thought and ideas filled the room. Minutes passed, sitting positions changed. Song birds chirped outside the window.

Tharill slapped his knee, startling them all. "I've got it!" he raved.

"My head itches!" Rutgar complained.

"Stop whining Your Worshipfulness and keep walking," Tharill ordered. "We are almost there."

"If my hair falls out because of this dye, I am going to beat the gnart snot out of you!" Rutgar shot back.

"And stop talking!" Tharill halted mid-stride, "you are going to blow this whole thing if you don't keep your head down and royal gab shut."

"I am Denis O'Shea your cousin from West Faelog Island and I have 'Cat's Tongue' and am unable to speak until it heals." Rutgar recited, putting on his best obedient-school-boy face.

"We'll make a king out of you yet, carrot head," Tharill chortled with a slap to Rutgar's back.

"I look like my hair is on fire!" Rutgar protested.

"Then you will fit right in as an O'Shea," Tharill laughed.

The boarding line at the balloon dock was long but moving swiftly.

"*Keltic Queen*," Tharill read on the passenger ship's side. "This is the newest addition to the Celtic Island Transport Company's fleet and the largest." Tharill leaned back on the dock rail and peered up at the expansive oblong balloon above the passenger ship. "She's not only airborne but seaworthy as well."

"What a wonder!" Rutgar whispered his agreement.

"She is a clipper class ship 114 feet in length with her balloon being close to twice that," Tharill clapped his hands together, "We are traveling in style!" he exclaimed in delight.

"I feel bad, using Rory's ticket like this." Rutgar said quietly. "I know how excited he was about taking this transport home for the first time."

"He understands," Tharill answered thoughtfully, "besides, someone has to contact your uncle. I would trust that important task to no one other than my brother."

"Ticket, please," a tall man with a long nose in a Celtic Island Transport uniform thrust his hand out toward Tharill.

Tharill handed the man his ticket who stamped it and handed it back. Rutgar handed his ticket next and the man gave the prince a questioning look. Rutgar smiled back but said nothing.

"Thank you, enjoy your trip and watch your step on the gangway," the man said, still looking at Rutgar.

"Keep walking," Tharill whispered, "and don't turn around."

Tharill turned as if to wave good-bye to someone and caught sight of the man still watching Rutgar. The man noticed Tharill looking in his direction and returned his attention to stamping tickets.

"Well?" Rutgar asked softly.

"I don't know. Let's find our seats for now."

"I don't think I can just sit. Is there anywhere else we can go?"

"There might be an observation deck." Tharill said, "Wait here, I'll go ask," he instructed and walked away.

Rutgar pretended to admire the drawings of other Celtic Island Transport Balloon-ships hanging on the corridor wall. He did not hear the sound of booted footsteps behind him. He only felt a gloved hand grab his shoulder from behind.

He whirled around to find the long-nosed ticket agent standing next to a transport constable. "This be him, constable."

Rutgar stepped back, his hand on the hilt of his dagger, feet spread ready to defend himself.

"Hand over your dagger. There's a good lad," the constable said, his hand out.

"You must check all weapons before boarding," the ticket agent snapped, "don't you read the signs posted everywhere?" The agent waved his hand about, pointing here and there at the very signs referred to.

Rutgar frowned, cocked his head and easily slid the dagger from its sheath. He flipped it over and handed it butt first to the constable.

"You can pick it up when we land. What name do I list it under?" He asked.

Rutgar said nothing merely grimaced at the question.

"Here now, what is this?" the ticket agent's tone was impatient.

"His name is Denis O'Shea." Tharill's voice sounded loud and clear from the stairwell he had just descended. "He's my cousin visiting from West Faelog Island and he's got cat's tongue."

"Well, well," the constable laughed. "My wife had cat's tongue from yelling at me one time and it lasted two weeks! Best two weeks of our marriage, come to think of it."

Rutgar swiped a few drops of sweat from his forehead, and crocked out a raspy, "Uha, uha," in agreement.

"How did you get it?" the ticket agent questioned.

"Too much cheering at the archery tournament. I've just started to teach him how to handle a bow." Tharill quickly answered. "We are hoping that one day he might be good enough to compete." Tharill gave Rutgar a pat on the shoulder.

Rutgar bit his lip, "Uha-uha-uha," he growled.

"Come on, coz, it is off to the observation deck. We are going to be on this tub for the next two days, we might as well check her and the other passengers out."

Rory walked down the pier, looking for a ship listings board. Out of the corner of his eye he could see a massive transport balloon ship rising into the sky. He stopped and watched as the tethers were cast free and the studding sails blossomed into life on both sides of the enormous balloon.

"How do they steer that thing?" he wondered aloud. He sighed at the thought of missing his chance to take the transport home. "Well, I'll be riding back with Bull and the other horses, instead," he sighed. "Bull will be glad."

Returning his attention to the numerous post boards on the pier he spotted what he was looking for, the in-port ship roster and locations. Rory dug through his pockets to find the paper on which Rutgar had written the name of his uncle's boat, but it was not there.

"Dung nuggets!" he swore softly, "where is that piece of paper?"

"Looking for this?" asked a thickly accented voice. Rory jerked his head to see who had joined him on the pier, and saw two tall dark-haired men dressed in black shirts, pants and wide-brimmed straw hats. One held up a piece of paper. Rory's piece of paper. He looked around for an escape route and saw a group of sailors walking up the pier in his direction.

"Hey there, mates!" he shouted, "what is the name of your boat?"

"*Rose of Tralee*" a snaggle-toothed sailor yelled back. "Why do you ask, young lad?"

"I thought so," Rory answered back with a frown. "Those two guys in the black shirts are looking for the *Rose of Tralee* to condemn it as rotten to the beam and turn it into a garbage scow."

"What?" a burly sailor growled tossing down his duffle bag. Another started to roll up his sleeves and walk towards the two men who were now beginning to look rather anxious about the situation.

The two men turned and bolted, but the sailors were already on them before they were off the pier.

Rory stooped to pick up the piece of paper the man had dropped in his haste.

It read:

## *Mor Telyn pier 12*

"Got it!" Rory chirped and tossed the paper into the water as he ran to the next pier. He slid to a stop and read the pier number '12' before sprinting toward the only ship docked there.

"Ahoy the ship," he yelled and waited a moment expecting a reply. He yelled again, still no reply. His neck tingled, the nape hair bristling in apprehension.

"They are all dead and cannot help you lad," responded a man from the deck of the ship. "Where is the prince?"

Rory spun around to flee when a shot from a gun rang out. The bullet hit him with such force he was flung from the pier into the cold sea water below. He splashed heavily and felt himself sink into the dark water.

"Did I tell you to shoot him?" An angry Curro Delagarza shouted at his sergeant.

"No, sir, but.." Felipe Quesada was stopped mid sentence with a backhand from Delagarza.

"He is no good to us dead and firing that gun will attract unwanted attention," Delagarza snapped. "Over the side now, everyone! Back to our launch before a constable shows up!" Sergeant Quesada waived his hand at the six other men on the *Mor Telyn* and yelled, "Hágalo ahora".

# CHAPTER #15

## *SANDY BLU GRAUIGE*

Tharill closed his eyes and took in a deep breath of the cool and fresh ocean air. Three hours into the flight with only the ocean in sight Tharill felt relaxed for the first time in two days. He and Rutgar leaned lazily on the railing of the transport balloon's observation deck.

"Look, Tharill a pod of red whales!" Rutgar yelled, shaking Tharill from his daydream.

"Where away?" Tharill yelped, the meaning of Rutgar's words sinking in.

Rutgar stretched out his arm, his index finger pointing in the direction of the whales below, breaching the surface and then slamming back down into the water.

"Six, seven..." Rutgar counted.

"Eight, nine, ten!" Tharill howled.

"Look!" Rutgar pointed in another direction. "There are two more just below the surface."

Tharill strained to look through the deep water at the outlines of two whales. "A mother and her calf?"

"I think so," Rutgar replied with glee.

A man and young boy approached the railing.

"Keep your voice down. Someone might pick-up on your accent," Tharill prompted. Rutgar nodded."

"Good day," the man said, smiling at Tharill and Rutgar. He then turned to the boy, "The red whale like the dragons of the Celtic Isles were hunted to near extinction less than 18 years ago. To date, less than forty whales survive. They are long lived creatures and the cow will carry the unborn calf for a matter of years, not months. Regeneration for them will take decades..." The man's voice trailed off as he and the boy walked past.

Voices rang out from all around the deck as more passengers saw the splendor of the whales breaching and crashing down into the water.

"'Tis a handsome sight to behold, indeed," roared a deep raspy voice from down the rail. Tharill pulled back from the railing to look over Rutgar's shoulder. The voice sounded familiar. He saw a tall, thick-framed man in a dark brown sealskin boat cloak and tall, loose fitting boots rolled down at the tops. The man was tapping a long whale bone pipe on the rail.

"I don't believe it," Tharill muttered with a grin.

"Don't believe what? Who are you looking at?" Rutgar whispered, peering in the direction Tharill was gazing.

Tharill walked away from Rutgar, "come on. I want you to meet someone."

"Is that wise?" Rutgar questioned, his eyes scanning the area to make sure no one was within earshot.

"Probably not, but come on anyway."

The burly man backed away from the rail as Tharill and Rutgar approached. His face came alight, his gaping smile revealed a set of ill-fitting gold and bleach-white whalebone teeth, yet jolly personality. "Haul me close to the wind," he shouted, shoving his pipe into a little pouch and ambling toward Tharill.

Holding out his hand he said, "Tharill, my lad. It is so good to see you."

Tharill grasped the man's hand and was instantly pulled close into a near bone-crushing bear hug. Rutgar stood back his eyes wide, head cocked, curious at the exchange. The embrace lasted just long enough for Tharill to gasp out, "I...I can't breathe."

"If you had more meat on your bones, your hull would not cave so easily. Where is your hot tempered shadow?" the man asked in a surprisingly jovial tone for such a gruff-looking character.

Tharill's facial expression grew quizzical.

"Your little brother, Rory," the man chuckled. "And who is this?" he added, indicating Rutgar.

"Rutgar, this is my uncle, Captain Shandy Blue Gruaige," Tharill whispered, leaning close to Rutgar. "Of the privateer ship, Sea Pucca," he continued. Also in a soft voice he said, "Uncle Shandy, I'd like you to meet my good friend, Prince Rutgar Van Slauthe of Saxony."

"Glad to meet you, Your Highness," Shandy said with a deep bow. Rutgar's eyes widened and darted from left to right.

"No, Uncle," Tharill hissed, the color draining from his face.

Shandy straightened, puzzled by the lads' reactions to what he thought merely proper etiquette for royalty. "Why are we whispering and what happened to the prince's hair? It is the color of a carrot," Shandy quipped staring at Rutgar's bright orange/red hair.

"We could really use your help, Uncle. We need to talk somewhere private though," Tharill said, glancing around to see if anyone was watching. The other passengers appeared to be focused on the red whales as they swam from sight.

"Let us go to my cabin," Shandy responded, a note of concern edging his voice. They walked down the stairs of the observation deck into the main cabin and then descended another set of stairs to the cabin and berthing areas.

The Keltic Queen could accommodate all class levels and purse sizes, from a single seat ticket to a luxurious cabin. Tharill knew his uncle was not a wealthy man and wondered how he was able to afford a cabin on such a fine ship. *Perhaps he captured a large prize ship this year,* he surmised.

They walked through a brightly lit corridor, passing fancy gilded cabin doors with large engraved numbers on each. Tharill could hear music and smelled perfume. Shandy turned a corner and another stairwell appeared. Down they went, deeper into the belly of the huge ship.

Tharill's chest tightened. He grimaced at not being able to see outside. With each step the stairs seemed narrower, the walls closer and the air thicker. Tharill stumbled and Rutgar grabbed at his shoulder to steady him. "You alright?" he asked. Tharill nodded, took a deep breath and continued down the stairs.

Shandy stopped, looked back and said, "Not much further, lads." Without breaking stride, he pulled a large key from his pocket and scratched at his bushy beard with it as he reached the last of the steps. "The captain is a friend of mine and he put me up in this here cabin," he said. The stairs ended in front of a plain set of double doors. Shandy turned the key and swung the doors open to reveal a large, bright room with four windows. He strode over to the windows unlatching each and throwing them open wide.

Tharill's face was brushed by a blast of fresh air. He instantly felt revitalized and steady on his feet. He breathed in not only the air but the warmth of sunlight as well. The cabin appeared to be a quarter the width of the stern of the ship, port side. It was spacious and furnished with two arm chairs, a settee, writing desk, table with two chairs, sideboard with cabinets, a bed, and two storage lockers.

"Sit down lads and tell me what the matter can be," Shandy said, his large frame settling into a rather tall arm chair next to the desk. Tharill sat on a rose-colored settee across from Shandy and Rutgar in the other arm chair.

"Where do we start?" Tharill sighed, "the last two days have been one paddy-jack after another, to say the least."

Rutgar nodded and looked back at Tharill through weary, bewildered eyes, and said, "it all started with Rastom getting arrested for a murder he could not have committed."

"Who is Rastom?" Shandy questioned.

"Wait, it really started with the Van Slauthe hallmark on the arrow head," Tharill objected.

"What arrow?" Shandy asked a confused looked crossed his face.

Tharill looked past the open windows and said, "it was the killings of-"

"It was the dragons," Rutgar interrupted. Tharill turned to Rutgar, their eyes meeting.

"It was the dragons," he agreed with a nod of his head.

"You dodgy land-lubbers flush-out your scuppers and spill your tale!" Shandy roared with a slap to his knee and chuckle in his voice. His tone was impatient yet also mildly amused.

Tharill leaned forward, his elbows resting on his knees looking perplexed.

"How about some snowberry wine to settle your nerves," Shandy offered standing up and walking to the nearby sideboard. He removed three glasses and a large bottle of wine from within the cabinet.

Shandy handed each lad a glass and poured a good measure into the glasses, setting the bottle down on the floor next to his chair. Settling back down in the chair he raised his glass and said, "Cheers." Shandy took in a long draw of the milky white liquid.

"Slainte." Tharill raised his glass in a return toast to his uncle and Rutgar.

"Prost!" Rutgar cheered and gulped the wine down.

Shandy refilled their glasses and re-corked the bottle dropping it on the floor next to him again. "Alright lads, now that we have completed the proper international toasts to all," a bright smile lit up his scruffy face. "Tell me about your troubles before too much wine spills the wind from yer sails."

Tharill took the lead, "You are aware of the dragon killings." It was a statement more than a question and Shandy listening intently, nodded his head in agreement.

"On the way to market two weeks ago, Uncle Rist and I found the old bull dragon Volcae dying from a wound. The large arrow had the Van Slauthe hallmark on the tip."

"Are you sure it was the Van Slauthe hallmark?" Shandy questioned, visibly shocked he straightened in his seat.

"Oh, yes. Uncle Rist pulled the arrow from the dragon's body and sent it to Grandfather Fergal. Grandfather took it to the dragon council meeting and showed it to the King."

"There is no way my father would have sanctioned such a profound act," Rutgar barked rising to his feet.

"Calm down, my lad," Shandy reassured, "I agree with you. But, how did an arrow with the Van Slauthe hallmark come to take down such a mighty and well-known bull dragon?"

"I do not know. But, I will find out," Rutgar said, his anger swelling through his voice.

"Maybe the question we should be asking is *why* at this point. If we find out the *why,* the *who* may answer itself." Shandy continued, "What happened next?"

"We were exploring the tunnels under King Fios' castle when we ventured into a passage that took us next to the King's throne room. We heard the whole tale of how the arrow was found then presented to the king and the Dragon Council," Rutgar wiped a bead of sweat from his brow.

Tharill leaned forward and said, "the Dragon Council members were yelling and screaming at each other as to who believed King Van Slauthe would break the dragon treaty and several who did not believe it at all," Tharill said, excitement showing in his voice as he recalled the incident.

"My uncle, Madog ap Gruffydd came to my room later that afternoon," Rutgar said, holding out his glass for more wine. "He said a meeting had been planned by Van Slauthe relatives and supporters to discuss the matter and I should attend. He also said he thought it would be best for my body-guard, Rastom Razmadze, and I to leave that night on council member Feylan O'Shea's ship."

"They were holding the meeting in a building at Diarmaid's Boatyard," Tharill added.

"Aye, I know that bilge-smelling dump of a boat yard well. I have won and lost more than one treasure chest of coins there," Shandy said with a shake of his head and wink of an eye, in recollection.

"Rastom and I went with my uncle and Feylan to the boatyard. The building was very large with partially built boats and crowded with groups of men engaged in stone-throw gambling." Rutgar took in a deep breath and continued, "we went into a back room and had just sat down when the door burst open and armed men stormed in." Rutgar gulped down his wine and held his glass out to Shandy to be refilled.

Shandy poured more wine. "Go on lad," he said and waived the bottle toward Tharill who held out his glass as well.

"Rastom stepped in front of me, brandishing his scimitar," Rutgar said, his brow knitted in thought, "Uncle Madog told me to follow Feylan out of the building. I did not want to flee like a coward, but Rastom insisted he would catch up with us at the boat."

"What is the name of the ship?" Shandy asked.

"The Marc Teller, I think," Rutgar said an eyebrow raised in thought.

"Marc Teller? I know of no such vessel. Are ye sure?" Shandy asked, a puzzled look crossing his face. "Could you mean the Mor Telyn?"

"Yes, that's it," Rutgar snapped his fingers.

"Aye, fine little brig based out of Ynys Catrian Island. Know her well. Captained by Sean O'Casey, good man that O'Casey," Shandy said nodding his head. "Low crew turn-over, fast cargo delivery turn-a-rounds."

"I don't know who the captain is," Rutgar responded.

Shandy gave a slight wave of his hand in dismissal. "Continue, my lad."

"Once clear of the building Uncle Madog and Feylan said we should split up and meet at the ship. I was instructed to head directly for the docks."

Tharill sat forward and picked it up from there, "that's when Rutgar ran into Rory and me at The Anchor Pub," Tharill added.

"I was being chased by two Spanians-".

"Spanians?" Shandy interrupted. "Are you quite sure they were Spanians, lad?"

"Yes, I would know a Spanian accent anywhere. We've had an ongoing border dispute with their nation for as long as I can remember," Rutgar said through narrowed eyes.

"That is—"Shandy began to say when he was jolted out of his chair. The whole room shook violently. Both Tharill and Rutgar toppled over backwards in their chairs. Loud bells rang out. Crew members and frightened passengers could be heard shouting from the decks above.

Shandy lumbered to his feet. "We've lost way, I do believe," he said and walked to the windows. "Yes, we have and dropping closer to the water, to boot," he added in a calm matter-of-fact tone.

"What is happening?" Tharill asked, putting his chair up-right again.

"You lads stay here; I'll go topside to see what is amiss," Shandy shut the door behind him, and then opened it again. "Don't let anyone but me in. You hear me lads? No one." He pulled the door shut and Tharill could hear the thud of Shandy's heavy boots bounding up the stairs.

Rutgar leaned out the window trying to see around the massive stern of the ship. "I don't see anything but water and it is getting closer," he said.

Tharill pulled a chair over to the window and stood on it to get a better look. "Good idea," Rutgar nodded and pushed a footlocker over to the window he had been looking out.

"Careful there Your Worshipfulness," Tharill chided, "we don't want to have to go prince-fishing."

"Suck gnart-snot," Rutgar retorted.

They stood silent side-by-side for several moments, like birds of prey scanning a meadow for any movement.

"See that?" Tharill asked. He pointed at a small plank of wood as it floated into view, followed shortly by a very large smoldering hulk of wreckage.

"Yes, but what is it?" Rutgar peered down at the remains of a blackened ship burnt to the waterline. *A vessel of some-sort?*

The Keltic Queen shuddered, shaking the room and Rutgar grabbed Tharill who teetered at the open window.

"Fishing for who?" Rutgar grinned.

"We've come to a complete stop," Tharill said without acknowledging the comment and shrugged off Rutgar's cautious grasp of his shoulder.

Rutgar removed his hand, puzzled at Tharill's reaction, but said nothing.

Jolly boats lowered from the Keltic Queen were now in sight, manned with stout sailors rowing briskly towards various floating debris where men could be seen waving their arms as they clung on for their very lives.

Tharill and Rutgar watched as survivors and then later the dead were pulled from the water. They could not see where the boats were being hoisted back up to the ship, but could hear as commands and responses were yelled between those in the water and crew members.

It grew dark and the air chilled as the last of the jolly boats disappeared, *back up to the ship*, Tharill assumed. It had been a long day and both lads were starting to feel tired and hungry.

"It's getting cold," Rutgar said, rubbing his arms, "I guess we should close the windows."

"Leave this one open," Tharill said, pointing to the one behind him. "I'll close it shortly."

The ship shuddered and then jerked in a fore and aft motion. Tharill felt himself being slightly pushed back and down. His weight felt heavy in his boots.

"We must be underway again," Rutgar said, "Do you feel the pressure?"

"Yes. I don't remember it being this strong when we left the port though," Tharill said.

"That is because it was a slow ascension," chimed Shandy from the doorway. "The captain must make up lost time, so he is now preparing to bend on every sail."

Shandy closed the door with a kick of his boot and strode over to the sideboard where he laid out six large gnart-bacon sandwiches, a few boiled eggs, and a fair sized hunk of cheese. "I thought you'd be hungry so I stopped off at the galley," he smiled wiping crumbs off his beard. "Of course, I sampled a few things while I was there."

"I'm sure you did Uncle Shandy, I'm sure you did," Tharill laughed.

"We'll sleep sound tonight and be in port by the noon," Shandy said as he offered the lads wine. They each grabbed a sandwich, a couple of eggs and carved pieces of cheese which all went on to plates to be consumed between gulps of wine and questions about the wreckage.

"Well, hoist-my-anchor," Shandy said with a slap to his knee, "I almost forgot." He shoved another piece of sandwich in his mouth and walked to the door. With a quick jerk the door was open and he pulled a two foot long piece of wood inside. "Had to set this aside so I could open the door when my hands were full of what you're stuffing your gobs with."

He handed it to Tharill pointed to the scorched area, and said, "now, what do you make of that my lad?"

Tharill wiped his hands on his pants picked up a knife and scratched at the scorch mark with it. Startled by what the knife revealed, he jerked his head up, "no, it can't be..."

"What?" Rutgar took the wood and turned it over in his hands, "what are these deep white marks? I've never seen scorch marks like these before."

Tharill tapped the edge of the wood with the knife, "that is caused from the heat of a dragon-blow."

"Dragon-blow? You mean flame? Are we now to be attacked by dragons?" Rutgar's eyes were wide, the muscles in his neck tense and back rigid.

"No, no of course not lad," Shandy laid a hand on Rutgar's shoulder. "Dragons blow in self-defense only, like a skunk sprays its stink."

"Well, I've never heard of a skunk's spray burning a boat to the waterline before!" Rutgar objected.

"Uncle Shandy, dragons will blow to protect their draglings," Tharill offered, "but who would be eejit enough and mess with a dragling to the point of pushing its mum into a protective attack?"

Shandy sat back down in his chair and lit his pipe, "yes, that is the question or is it again the *why* not the *who*, we should be asking ourselves?"

# CHAPTER #16

## *A GAME OF WIT AND SKILL*

The Keltic Queen made excellent time despite the delay in rescuing survivors from the burnt-out boat. She now lay moored in the bay of Dara, having off-loaded her passengers and cargo earlier.

It was mid-morning with a hint of rain in the air. The town of Dara was buzzing with excitement as the Firemoon Tide was only days away. The Keltic Queen had been packed with tourists who were making their way into the shops and cafes.

Shandy Blu Gruaige walked with the rolling gait of an unsteady land-bound sailor. Tharill and Rutgar followed behind him by a few paces, smiling at his odd stride.

"I'd take the pitching deck of a heaving ship over this unforgiving, hard-packed ground any day," Shandy griped. "My back will ache before the day is out if I do much more walking." Spotting a bench, Shandy pointed to it and they strolled over.

"What are yer plans, my lads?" Shandy asked, plopping down on the bench with a thud. "Is Rory meeting you here on Dara? I know he usually sails back from the Faire with the horses."

"Oh, I forgot to tell you. I sent Rory to Councilor Feylan O'Shea's ship the *Mor Telyn*, to tell him that Rutgar would be with me," Tharill said, adding, "Reesa Burlong gave me the key to her family's cottage just up the hill from here. We'll go there and wait for Rutgar's uncle Madog ap Gruffydd who should be sailing with Councilor O'Shea."

"If the *Mor Telyn* set sail the same day we did, it will take them at least four more days to get here. Well, maybe three and half if there is a strong wind in 'er favor," Shandy said thoughtfully, tapping his pipe on the arm of the bench. "I will meet ye at the cottage after I check on Sea Pucca's refit. The shipyard is over yonder," Shandy continued using his pipe as a pointer. "But first I think I will set here a spell, get my land-legs and smoke my pipe."

After saying their good-byes, Tharill and Rutgar began to walk away, but stopped at the sound of Shandy calling after them. They looked and he motioned them to return. Putting a hand to one side of his mouth he said, just above a whisper, be on yer guard lads. Just because ye are back on Dara Island don't mean the prince is safe."

"Surely there would be no Spanians here," Tharill said, and gave Rutgar a sidelong glance.

"Then who killed the mighty dragon, Volcae, on Whidley Island if King Van Slauthe had nothing to do with it?" Shandy asked and took a draw from his pipe, expelling a puff of sweet smelling smoke.

"Therein lays the answer," Rutgar said.

"Think about it…" Shandy replied tapping the mouthpiece of his pipe to his forehead. "Do not sail close to the wind 'ere lads. Any blaggard could hoist 'is black flag and slit yer throat before ye could yank-yer-anchor."

"What?" Rutgar said, puzzled.

"Slit your throat," Tharill grimaced, "is all we need to understand."

"All right lads, go ahead and shove off," Shandy said, "I'll be up in an 'our or two."

"We'll watch the road for you," Tharill said and the lads walked away.

As Tharill and Rutgar walked through the busy streets packed with people who had come to watch the dragons during the Firemoon Tide, Rutgar stopped to read a *Dragon Watch 1814* poster:

*Fast Balloon Transport to Druml*
*See Shedding Dragons Up-Close*
*Fun & Educational for the whole family!*
*Lectures by renowned Ignispirologist*
*Professor Mortimar Burlong of Briton*

"I don't understand," Rutgar said. "What do people watch the dragons doing exactly? I thought the dragons were dormant during the Firemoon Tide to shed their scales."

"Well, they are, but they are not," Tharill paused, considering the best way to explain the scale shedding process. "What do you know about it?"

Rutgar pursed his lips in thought for a moment. "Let's see, I didn't know there would be a test on the subject or I would have studied."

Tharill gave out a hardy laugh. "Point taken, but I'd rather not start at *in the beginning there was light*, if you get my drift."

"Ok, Ok," Rutgar said. "According to the Foreign History book I read, the Firemoon Tide happens once every four years and causes the tides in the Celtic Islands area to rise by at least forty-feet."

"That high tide turns Druml, the south-end of Whidley, into an island of its own," Tharill said, adding, "and there is only about three feet difference at low tide, during the twelve day period. I believe it's nature's way of taking care of the dragons while they are shedding their scales. They are pretty much helpless during the shedding process."

"I read that they go blind, can't eat or even stand when they shed," Rutgar said thoughtfully.

As they got to the road that led up to the Burlong's cottage, a startled flock of birds sprang from the brush and charged into the sky, their little yellow wings making a whistling sound as they flew. Tharill and Rutgar stopped to watch for a moment and then continued on.

"As the dragons shed their eyelid scales," Tharill picked up the topic again, "they secrete a fluid causing their eyelids to mat together; to protect their eyeballs, I guess. But they can't see for about six days as the old scales drop off or get rubbed off and the new ones develop."

"I understand your grandfather is a Dragon Tender," Rutgar said, kicking a little stone side-long to Tharill.

Tharill kicked the stone back which became a mini game of football as they continued up the road. "Yes, my Grandfather Fergal is the Dragon Tender for Druml. He will be organizing the scaling during the Firemoon Tide. It is too bad you can't stay and help. It is great craic."

"Really?" Rutgar said, "What do you do?"

"We use large long-handled brushes to help loosen the dragon's back-scales. We clean their teeth, check their health, and doctor them if needed. The new hatchlings and draglings get measured to record their growth, as well."

Rutgar stopped suddenly and said, "Wait, did you say 'brush their teeth'? Why would you want to brush a dragon's teeth?"

"They like it," Tharill answered, straight-faced.

"You are joshing me, right?"

"It gets rid of the fire-mite parasites that live in their mouths. We use a mixture of soda-ash and snowberries," Tharill laughed. "The process also seems to calm them while helpers are brushing at the scales."

"What about the little fact that dragons blow flames?" Rutgar quipped, rather as a statement than a question.

"They can't blow when they are shedding. Another reason they are so defenseless during the shedding," Tharill said and kicked at the stone so hard and fast that Rutgar missed it.

"Score!" Tharill cheered, adding a little winner's dance.

"Dung!" Rutgar looked for another stone along the road.

"I would say that not being able to blow flames keeps them from blindly cooking each other by accident," Tharill joked

"That would be one way to control a dragon population," Rutgar laughed and turned at a sudden sound behind them.

"What is it?" Tharill asked, looking over his shoulder.

"I thought I heard something down the road behind us."

"Birds?" Tharill asked.

"It sounded more like voices," Rutgar answered, looking about. "Are there other cottages up this road?"

"I don't know. Maybe we should hurry up a little, just in case." Shandy's words of 'slit-yer-throat' ran through Tharill's mind.

"Agreed," Rutgar said, a slight nervous edge in his voice.

They picked up their pace, the small yellow cottage now insight. The road continued past Reesa's cottage, where two more cottages could be seen. No one seemed at home up there either.

Tharill found the key where Reesa said it would be and opened the front door of the cottage. Stepping inside, Rutgar closed the door behind them. Even though Reesa had said no one would be home, they stood in the shadows of the hallway listening for movement in the cottage. After several minutes of peering out through the windows they both began to relax.

Rutgar found the kitchen and started to look through the cabinets for something to eat.

"Find anything?" Tharill asked.

"No."

"Hopefully, Uncle Shandy will bring something from town." Tharill seated himself by a window that overlooked the road down to town. He could hear Rutgar in the kitchen opening cupboards looking for food.

"Hey, there are fruit trees in the back garden!" Rutgar announced, banging the back door as he went out.

"Sounds good to me," Tharill replied, leaving the comfort of the chair, in favor of feeding his growling belly.

They were delighted to find pears, apples, strawberries and blueberries in the garden. They sat on the circular bench of a shade tree contently stuffing their faces.

"I noticed a Ficheall board game in the cottage. Would you like to try your luck?" Tharill asked.

"No luck needed," Rutgar said. "It is *pure wit and skill* that will beat your gnart butt."

"You are on, Your-Most-Gnartness," Tharill said with a bow and returned to the cottage for the game.

Just then, Rutgar heard the sound of breaking glass coming from the front of the cottage. He jumped up and started for the cottage as Tharill came bounding through the back door catching the door with his hand to ease it shut.

"Go, go, go!" he mouthed at Rutgar pointing to a potting shed toward the back of the garden.

The back door of the cottage flew open seconds after Rutgar and Tharill had taken cover behind the locked potting shed. A tall heavily-mustached man with dark hair stepped through the doorway brandishing a pistol. He stood looking about for a few minutes and then went back inside the cottage.

"What do we do now?" Rutgar whispered.

"Run!"

Tharill led the way around the potting shed and towards the road leading back to town. They stopped suddenly when they saw two men standing in the road by the cottage.

"Uncle Shandy was right. You are not safe here. We need to go to Druml. We'll have to take the path by the cliffs and hurry to catch the last ferry to Whidley before the tide changes," Tharill whispered. Rutgar nodded and followed Tharill along a winding path that skirted the cliffs of Dara.

They quickly made their way along the path, only to stop for a moment to catch their breath. Tharill pushed some branches aside to expose the clear blue-green water below the cliffs.

"Those are the Cliffs of Druml," Tharill said, pointing across the channel to a spectacular rock face soaring several hundred feet up from the crashing waves at the water's edge.

"They are truly more magnificent than any painting I've ever seen of them," Rutgar marveled and then they continued down the trail.

It took nearly an hour to carefully weave their way along the little-used deer trail. When the ferry landing came into sight, they crouched behind some hedges, the last vestige of cover between them and the dock. There was a good sixty-foot of open space with nowhere to hide between their location and the dock.

Waiting at the dock was the eighty-foot Whidley-Dara ferry *Dun Laoghaire*. She was moored stern first into the slip so the dock could lower the loading ramp for carts and passengers. Cargo pallets were already being hoisted over the side into the hold.

"We're in time; the ferry has not started to board yet," Tharill said. "It will land us in Paraic. From there we can make our way down to Druml and stay at my grandfather's place. He may still be on Scotia for the dragon council meeting. But it will be okay to stay there."

"What about your Uncle Shandy?"

"I think he will guess where I am taking you."

"Or he may think we've been captured." Rutgar said.

"You're right, but we can't take the chance to go looking for him right now. He could be at the boat yard or any one of several pubs he likes to drink in." Tharill scanned the area and spotted a man with dark hair and bushy mustache leaning against a large barrel smoking a cigarillo. He appeared to be watching people as they lined up for the ferry.

"We've got company," Tharill said pointing to the man.

"He is not the only one," Rutgar replied indicating two other similar dressed, mustached men looking at carts and wagons waiting to board.

"What are we going to do? There is no way to get across this open space without being seen by one of those guys. Plus, I don't have any willets, do you?" Rutgar asked.

"Not enough to pay passage for both of us," Tharill answered, then snapped his finger in recollection and added, "but that won't matter if Caleb is the ferryman. He will let us cross for free. He is a close friend of Rory's."

A tarp-covered cart drawn by a small grey horse caught Tharill's attention as it clattered down the road toward the ferry. A large tan and white collie dog sat next to its master barking loudly.

"Be quiet Rusty! Sweet Dragon's Breath, would you just shut-up!" Colin O'Murchu repeatedly griped at his unrelenting and very vocal companion. When the dog noticed Tharill, it stood up and wagged its tail with great ferocity, slapping Colin in the face with each pass of its long white-tipped tail.

Grabbing hold of the animal's tail and searching the bushes, a delighted smile crossed Colin's face as he recognized that Rusty was barking at Tharill. Colin was about to shout out a greeting when Tharill held up a finger to his lips and ducked back behind the bush.

"Come on Rusty, I'd better give you a wee break before embarking the ferry," Colin said in a load voice and snapped the reins for the horse to move in Tharill's direction. Not waiting, Rusty jumped from the cart and ran into the bushes where Tharill and Rutgar hid.

"Boy am I glad to see you," Tharill said, relief and excitement reflected in his tone when Colin walked around the shrubs. "This is Prince Rutgar Van Slauthe," he added pointing to Rutgar.

"Glad to …uh… make your acquaintance, your Highness." Colin said with an attempt at a deep bow and sheepish smile.

"And who is this?" Rutgar asked scratching the dog behind an ear.

"His name is Rusty. He seems to like you,…uh…your highness" Colin answered.

"The Prince is in great danger from some men who have been following us," Tharill said.

Instinctively, Colin started to glance around and then thought better. "Where is Rory?" he asked

"He should be with Prince Rutgar's uncle on their way here from Scotia. But, it will be another three to three and a half days before they arrive. I want to take the Prince to Druml and hide him there until his uncle gets here," Tharill said. "Can you help us get on the ferry without anyone noticing?"

"I think I can move enough beehive crates around in my cart to fit both of you under the tarp," Colin said.

"Bees?" Rutgar said with concern.

"Don't worry. They are dormant right now and won't bother you as long as you don't disturb them."

"Bees," Rutgar repeated.

"Oh, your Princeliness can't be afraid of a few cute little fuzzy bees, now can he?" Tharill teased, his eyes coming alight with humor.

"I don't like bees," Rutgar said.

"Well, we won't mention that to them," Tharill said.

Colin made it appear as if he were looking for something while nonchalantly rearranging the back of his cart. Tharill and Rutgar climbed into the cart and Colin covered them with the tarp. Colin signaled Rusty to get into the cart and the dog obediently jumped onto the seat next to Colin.

The two men observing the dockside activity watched as Colin's cart rolled up to the ferry loading area. One of the two walked past the cart eyeing the tarp very closely, causing Rusty to bark and snap at him. The startled man side-stepped away from the dog and moved on.

The ferry loading went quickly and then two tug-rows towed the ship out into the current which would carry it north and then around to the backside of Dara Island.

When the docked passed from sight, Colin told Tharill that the two men had remained on the dock.

The crossing would take an hour or so to reach Whidley from Dara Island. Once in the town of Paraic, Colin would have to turn north to return home while Tharill and Rutgar would go south toward Druml. But, for now they relaxed on the deck of the ship, enjoyed Colin's company and ate the honey butter, biscuits and wine he offered them. Rusty begged for tidbits in that silent stare and wag of the tail that was hard to resist.

"Bad dog," Colin said, but gave Rusty a piece of his bread and then patted him on the head.

"So we are going to the *home* of your dragons?" Rutgar said. "The place they *all* live, the dragle caves and such?"

"Yes," Tharill said, a questioning look on his brow. "They won't bother you. They will sense the Dragon Tender in my blood."

"I understand they are very intelligent."

"I believe they are, why?"

"Do you think they remember being hunted by my family?"

"Well, I am sure the survivors do," Tharill replied. "Why? You weren't even born then."

"You say the dragons will sense the Dragon Tender blood in your family line. What is to say they won't sense the Van Slauthe *dragon hunter* blood in mine?"

# CHAPTER #17

## *BOUND FOR DRUML*

The current was strong and the ferry made good time rounding Dara Island. The port of Pariac was now visible and Rutgar leaned over the railing to get a better look. As he looked, he noticed boats putting out from port. "Why are those two large row boats coming at the ferry?" Rutgar whispered to Tharill, concern edging his voice.

"Oh, those are the tug-rows. As the ferry just rides the currents circling Dara Island, the tug-rows will pull us out of the current and then swing the ferry's bow around so it comes in stern first."

"And that draw bridge looking contraption on the pier?" Rutgar asked, his concern now replaced with curiosity.

"That is the embark/disembark ramp," Tharill said. "It works the same way when the ferry lands at Dara."

"Really? I hadn't noticed the draw bridge at the ferry dock on Dara."

"I guess it is a little hard to see what is going on from behind the bushes and then under a tarp." Tharill laughed and Rutgar nodded in agreement.

As the tug-rows approached, Tharill stood with his back against Colin's cart looking at Rutgar who was engrossed by what the tug-rows were doing. *I wonder if Rutgar is right about our dragons sensing the Van Slauthe blood line.*

"Tharill," Colin shouted. "Are you deaf? I've been calling you."

"What?" Tharill answered. "Sorry I didn't hear you. What is it?"

"You better go talk to Caleb before he gets too busy docking the ferry."

"Talk to Caleb about what?" Tharill asked, unable to think past Rutgar's concern over what he perceived might be the dragons' reaction to him.

"Getting a message to your Uncle Shandy. What in dragon's breath is wrong with you?" Colin barked.

"It's just something Rutgar said," Tharill answered. "I can't get it out of my head. Thanks for reminding me about Uncle Shandy." Tharill gave Colin a friendly smack on the back and left to go find Caleb.

By now the tug-rows had their ropes firmly tied to the ferry and began the strenuous task of pulling the ferry out of the main current and toward the ferry dock. The boat jerked as the ropes tightened and then gave and tightened again.

Colin rested his arms on the railing next to Rutgar. "You will be in the heart of dragon country by the end of the day. The Spanians surely won't follow you there. Surely not," Colin said gazing at the shoreline. Rutgar frowned.

"What if they have someone waiting on Whidley?" Rutgar asked.

"You and Tharill will ride in back under the tarp with the bees. The same way you rode onto the ferry."

"Bees," Rutgar growled. "I really do not like bees."

"They are all asleep, I tell you," Colin chuckled. "We will need to figure out a way to get you a Whidley Fever Patch for you, without documenting your arrival."

"How does the patch work?" Rutgar asked.

"Off-islanders usually start showing signs of Whidley Fever on day ten after arriving on the island. If they don't leave the island by day fourteen the fever can be fatal." The ferry jolted suddenly as the ropes from the tug-rows took up their slack. Colin continued, "The patch sticks to your skin and starts to change colors as your skin absorbs toxins in the air on Whidley."

"Where do I get a patch?"

"They are kept at the Off-islander Registration Office," Colin said. "But, if Spanians are on Whidley they will check there every time the Dara ferry docks. So you can't go there officially. We'll have to steal one."

"Hold that horse in place, you bloody fool!" Caleb snapped at a wagon driver who was not paying attention to his restless steed.

Tharill weaved his way through cargo, carts and passengers to the deck where Caleb stood. "Caleb," Tharill shouted. "Can I come up?"

"Hold on lad," Caleb threw the core of an apple he had just finished eating, hitting one of his crewmen in the back of the head. "Are you blind? Look at that bloody bow line! Get yer arse over there and get her coiled-up proper!"

Turning back in Tharill's direction he said, "Come on up lad."

"Tavish! Don't make me come down there!" Caleb yelled at apple-head and then turned his attention to Tharill. "What can I do for ya lad?"

But before he could answer, Caleb poked one of his callused index fingers at Tharill's still swollen and sore nose. "What happened there? Trip over yer quiver?"

"It's a long story," Tharill answered.

"Well, that there nose pretty much tells the long and short of it anyway. Don't it?" Caleb laughed, feigning a left hook to Tharill's jaw.

"Can you get a message to my Uncle Shandy?" Tharill moved past the subject of his bruised face. "And tell him I will be at my grandfather's cabin in Druml and to pick us up there as soon as he can?"

"Of course, lad," Caleb answered. "But it won't be till tomorrow."

"You can find him at the Dara Boatyard on the Sea Pucca."

"Where is Rory?" Caleb asked. "Rolling around on the cargo ship with the rest of the horse' arses?" He chuckled at his own joke.

"No, he should be sailing with my Uncle Rist and Aunt Maura."

"Do you want me to tell them where you are when they return?" Caleb asked, snatching up a belaying pin. "Duck," he told Tharill and lobbed the heavy wooden pin at Tavish, hitting the man square on the backside.

"Bloody hell, Cap," Tavish yelped. "I got 'er coiled!"

"Stowe it 'til we need it!" Caleb bellowed and turned back to Tharill. "How did he and the colt do?"

"What? Who?" Tharill was still startled from the missile Caleb had launched within inches of his head.

"Rory, Mounted Short-Bow? Where is your mind, lad?"

"Oh, yes he won." Tharill looked past Caleb and saw the dock coming into sight.

"I am surprised that bloody Saxon royalty didn't pay off the judges to rig the contest somehow. Bloody dragon murder mongers," Caleb spit out the last words.

"What?" Tharill was shaken from the brief tranquility that being so close to his home had brought.

"Everybody knows it was a Van Slauthe arrow pulled from Volcae," Caleb barked. "Two off-islanders from Saxony were beat up at the Fin-n-Fiddle two nights ago."

"The arrow had the Van Slauthe mark but that does not mean it was done by them," Tharill objected. "The Dragon Council and King Fios are working on the matter."

"They can politic all they want! We Whidlians will keep our dragons safe from those bloody trophy-hunting Saxons!" Caleb charged. "We will get all Saxons off Whidley and Dara islands. Dead or alive. No matter to us."

"Caleb that's a bit rash, don't ya think?" Tharill, astonished at Caleb's words, warily glanced back in Rutgar's direction. "They can't stay more than two weeks at a time anyway, because of Whidley fever."

Caleb made no comment at that. He only smirked and turned to check the progress of the tug-rows.

"Best be off, lad. It is time to turn-bow for docking. I'll get word to both your uncles." Caleb turned, and began to shout orders to his crew.

It appeared to Tharill that opinions on the dragon slayings had turned rather dark sense he left for the highland Faire. He stood silent for a moment as his sense of security drained away, along with the color in his face.

Colin clucked to his horse when the carts starting leaving the ferry. "Here we go," Colin said to no one in particular. Tucked safely under the tarp with the bees, Tharill and Rutgar kept very still and quiet as the wagon rolled across the ramp and onto the dock.

Rusty barked at a man approaching the wagon. Colin only smiled at the man.

"Good day, Colin. Your pa will be glad to get those bees." A tall man wearing the uniform of the Garda Síochána said.

"Aye," Colin casually replied with a wave before turning to his dog, "Rusty shut-up!" The dog took no notice and continued to bark and wag his tail. Colin turned back to the Garda. "He will at that," he said. "Is he in town, do you know?"

"He told me to tell you that he would meet you at Sullivan's Boarding House. He has a room reserved there for the both of you." The Garda shouted over the barking dog.

"Thanks, I will see to the horse and wagon and go over when I am through," Colin yelled above the noise of his dog. "Shut-up, Rusty! Sit down, you old flea bag!" The collie paid no attention and continued to bark his hellos to all passersby.

The wagon rolled past the dock area and the Off-islander Office. Colin turned the wagon into an alley between the general store and the wheelwright's shop. He stopped the wagon and jumped down, Rusty followed. Colin looked around to see if anyone was watching and then whispered over his shoulder, "We need to get a patch for Rutgar."

"Is the coast clear?" Tharill asked, pushing the flaps of the tarp apart to expose his face.

"Aye," Colin answered and Tharill shimmied his way from under the tarp and out of the back of the wagon.

"What about me?" Rutgar complained. "You aren't going to leave me here with these bees are you?"

"It would be better if you stayed hidden until we get to Druml," Colin said, "and don't be bothering my bees! They need their beauty sleep." Colin winked at Tharill in jest. Rutgar merely grunted his discontent.

Tharill and Colin left the alley and walked toward the Off-islander Office two buildings back down the street. "What is our plan?" Colin asked, as they walked.

"Let's see what is going on in the office and we'll go from there," Tharill answered as he glanced left and right to see who was on the street.

As they walked up the steps to the office the door opened and Garda Dahy O'Ceann emerged. "Hello Tharill! I didn't see you get off the ferry," Garda O'Ceann said shaking each lad's hand.

"I was hiding in Colin's wagon under the tarp with the bees," Tharill said displaying an ear to ear grin.

"Now, why would you be for hiding in Colin's wagon?" O'Ceann chided.

"Because I asked Colin to smuggle the crowned prince of Saxony on to Whidley," Tharill said, putting his hand on the garda's shoulder. "He is still in the wagon. Would you like to meet him?"

"Ha, ha, ha. Very funny, lads," O'Ceann shock his head in mild, if not slightly irritated, amusement. "How did you and Rory fare at the Highland Faire?"

"Rory won Mounted Short-bow and I took first in Distance, Moving Targets For Distance and second in Timed Shots," Tharill boasted, his pride beaming with each word.

All three turned toward the Fin-N-Fiddle across the street as the sounds of a fight erupted from inside the pub. Without another word O'Ceann raced down the steps and across the street toward the pub's front door.

O'Ceann reached the door just as it burst open and two men embraced in a punching bear-hug tangle of fists and legs collided with the garda causing all three to fall into the busy street. Startled cart and wagon drivers tried to maneuver their horses and vehicles around the struggling men. A woman screamed and a small dog ran out of the pub and chomped down on the pant leg of one of the skirmishing men.

Behind Colin the door of the Off-island Office popped open and the clerk ran out. "What's going on?" the thin, beak-nosed clerk cried.

"A fight!" Colin yelped. "And it has rolled out into the street. Come on, we've got to help Garda O'Ceann before they all get trampled!" Grabbing the clerk by the arm Colin pulled the reluctant clerk down the steps and out onto the chaotic street.

Tharill eased his way into the Off-Island office and leaned over the counter where he saw the patches. Each patch was numbered and not wanting to attract attention to a missing patch, he pulled one from the bottom of the stack and shoved it into his pocket.

Quickly making his way back outside, Tharill rushed down the steps and onto the street where the clerk sat on his backside, dazed from a blow to his face, with blood trickling from his nose. Traffic had stopped moving and a crowd gathered to watch the brawl. Tharill stopped to help the clerk stand up and then moved past the crowd where Garda O'Ceann had the two scrapping drunks by their shirt collars. The small terrier dog still tugged at one man's pant leg.

"Off to the hoosegow wit' the both of you!" O'Ceann barked and banged the two drunkards' heads together. He tried to shoo the little terrier away but the dog would not let go of the pant leg he had clung on to so diligently during the scuffle.

"Whose mutt is this?" O'Ceann yelled, looking about.

"He's mine, Garda O'Ceann," answered the man wearing the pants the dog had attached himself to.

"Well, if he don't let go, he'll be for spending the night wit' you!" O'Ceann growled.

"Oh, thanky, Garda. Thanky. Little Mac there would be lost wit' out me."

"So, be it," O'Ceann sighed and hustled the two men down the street with the little dog in tow hanging from his master's pant leg.

Colin stood off to the side, looked over at Tharill who gave him a thumbs-up sign and both headed in the direction of the alley where they had left the wagon.

The wagon rattled along the cobblestone streets of Pariac until it reached the town's edge where it bounced onto a dirt road. Colin's horse snorted at the dust raised by its hooves as it clopped down the road toward Atha Luain. It had not rained in the past few days and the area was unusually dry for the time of year.

It was late afternoon when they passed through the small village of Atha Luain and once again approached the water's edge. Colin stopped the wagon and jumped down, Rusty following at his heels.

"Wake up you lazy gnarts' arses!" Colin shouted and threw open the tarp flaps where Tharill and Rutgar were jolted from their slumber. "You better hurry and cross while it's still slack-tide. There is already over a foot of water on the road."

Rutgar stiffly climbed down from the wagon. He stood for a minute looking around. They were at the southern tip of Whidley where the island ended abruptly, like a dead end road. Yet the road itself continued down into and under the water for a quarter of a mile and then back up onto the dry land of Druml where the road disappeared through a stand of towering pine trees.

The water between the land masses was crystal clear and blue-green in color. Rutgar could see the submerged road under the gently rolling waves. He walked closer to the edge of the water while Tharill and Colin stood by the wagon talking.

From what Rutgar could see, there were great drop-offs on both sides of the sunken road. A chill went up his back. The road was just wide enough for a narrow cart to pass. Colin's wagon was obviously too wide to venture any further. That meant they would have to cross the expanse on foot.

"We best be away," Tharill said from the wagon and Rutgar turned to walk back to it.

"We will need to hurry to the other side during slack-tide. The current will grow too strong to cross in a matter of minutes after the tide shifts.

The three lads said their good-byes and made their well wishes before departing. Colin turned the wagon back to Pariac with Rusty barking at his side. Tharill and Rutgar made their way down the road and into the water. The water was cold, ankle deep, and without resistance for about the first two-hundred yards. Then the depth began to increase and Tharill could feel the tug of a current developing.

"We need to go faster," Tharill said, over his shoulder.

"Is that the start of the current I feel?" Rutgar asked.

"Yes," and without stopping Tharill added, "if it gets strong enough to knock you off of your feet, treat it like a rip-tide. Just swim for the island. Don't focus on swimming to where the road comes out."

Even as they rushed through the water, it grew deeper and the pull stronger.

The familiar sound of 'Whoosh-swish-whoosh, whoosh-swish-whoosh' caught Tharill's attention

"Oh, nooo! Not now!" Tharill griped.

"What the?" Rutgar turned to see a large dragon flying toward them.

"Dragon! Dragon!" Tharill grabbed Rutgar and pushed him down into the water. One of the dragon's enormous silver-blue wings struck the water as it flew over only a few feet above where Tharill and Rutgar kneeled in the water. The dragon raised his wings and extended his clawed feet as he turned his head to look back at the two. He then made a deep guttural sound which transformed into a loud screech that was answered by another dragon in the near distance.

"We've got to hurry!" Tharill gasped, choked by the water. He slipped when he tried to stand up causing him to go back under the water. The water pulled at him. Watery grappling hooks snagged at the tops of his boots and used his shirt as a submerged sail to take him away from the shallows and into the deep.

He bumped into Rutgar and the two grasped hands. Combining the strength of two into one, they charged on through the rushing current and rising tide. They forged their way toward life, leaving the chaos of the swirling water behind them.

Rutgar and then Tharill flopped down on the dry earth of Druml. Exhausted and coughing, too tired to move or even speak. They lay there quiet for several minutes. Each lost in their own thoughts of what had just happened.

Rutgar broke the silence, "That dragon turned and looked directly at me. He knows, doesn't he, he knows I am a Van Slauthe."

# CHAPTER #18

## *THE DRAGON TENDER'S COTTAGE*

"Come on," Tharill said, getting to his feet and extending his hand to Rutgar. "We need to get to my grandfather's cabin before dark."

Rutgar grasped Tharill's hand and quickly stood up. "That dragon looked directly at me. I am sure of it."

"I really doubt that," Tharill tried to sound reassuring as they began walking down the road. "That was Ci Lleaud of the Ean Corcra Dragle. He is well over one-hundred years old and losing his eyesight."

Rutgar rolled his eyes at the statement and continued to cautiously walk forward.

"I can't walk in these soaking-wet boots," Rutgar sat down on a large rock and began to remove his boots and socks. Tharill sat next to him and also removed his footwear.

"Truly, I do believe he is going blind," Tharill continued as the two began walking again. "Three weeks ago he flew so low over my uncle's boat, he nearly collided with the mast."

"Really..." Rutgar replied, with more than a hint of sarcasm in his tone.

"I was in the boat when he flew over. He scared the gnart dung out of me and I am no Van Slauthe!"

Rutgar smirked, "What about that squawking he did?"

"Oh, you will hear a lot of that."

Rutgar eyed Tharill, a quizzical look crossing his face, "why?"

"The dragons talk to each other a lot when they are with their dragles," Tharill noted Rutgar's change of facial expression from apprehension to curious. "Dragons are very social creatures and not as dumb as they are portrayed in the off-island history books."

A breeze picked up rustling the leaves in the trees and bending the grasses that bordered the well-traveled road. Rutgar sniffed the air, wrinkling his nose. "What is that pungent odor?"

Tharill took in a deep breath and looked into the sky as if to see the smell. "I don't smell anything."

"I guess that elbow shot to the nose, dunged-up your sense of smell," Rutgar smirked.

Tharill frowned and then walked to a growth of bright yellow-orange flowers. He bent over and inhaled. "I smell these," he said, turning back to look at Rutgar, still standing in the road.

"And you can't smell the stink?"

"No," Tharill paused in thought for just a moment and then, his eyes bright with recollection, said, "you are smelling the dragons," he laughed.

Startled, Rutgar looked about, seemingly close to panic. "Where? Where are they?"

"It is okay, Rutgar." Tharill put a reassuring hand on Rutgar's shoulder. "They won't hurt you." *At least I don't think they will,* Tharill said to himself.

"Where are they?" Rutgar demanded.

"Most likely by their dragle caves about two miles to the west."

"They stink so bad you can smell them two miles away?" Rutgar asked and then added, "Why didn't I smell the dragon before it got close enough to fly over us?"

193

Tharill scratched his head in thought. "It's not the dragons themselves; it's how they have marked their territory over the centuries. This is why off-islanders become sick after being on the island for more than a few days. The patch," Tharill said, indicating Rutgar's arm, "like yours will turn darker as poison is absorbed by your skin."

They continued to follow the road, the forest about them growing more dense. "I didn't notice the smell on Whidley," Rutgar said.

"Oh, it is there too." Tharill slapped at a large leggy mosquito that landed on his arm. "All three dragles reside in the Druml caves and their draglings are reared here. Their scent is everywhere and very powerful. That is probably why it is more noticeable here."

A blue-tailed fox trotted nervously across the road followed by four fuzzy little kits. Tharill and Rutgar stood quiet for a moment and watched them pass.

"Is it dragon scent that causes the sleeping sickness?" Rutgar sounded puzzled. "I thought it was something in Whidley's air."

"Centuries of dragons living on the island make it what it is. The scent is in the water, trees, plants and in the ground. They make the air the way it is. Does that make sense?"

"Yes, I think so."

The road curved around a very large knotted saben oak tree. Its acorns littered the road and Tharill stopped to gather a few. "These are great roasted."

Rutgar nodded and gathered some too, stuffing them in his pockets.

It was mid-afternoon when the two barefooted lads reached the dragon-Tender's cottage of Tharill's grandfather, Fergal O'Shannessey Gruaige.

White-washed stone with a tightly woven thatch roof the cottage was very cozy looking. Rutgar peered through one of the small square-framed, front windows, while Tharill opened the unlocked door.

"It needs to be aired out," Tharill said stepping into what he considered a musty and dank atmosphere.

Rutgar poked his head through the open doorway, but did not enter. "You grandfather lives in this little shack? I would have thought such a dignitary of the Dragon Council would be accommodated in a more fitting manner."

"No," Tharill laughed. "My grandfather has a house in Atha Luain. This cottage is just for his convenience while on Druml."

Tharill unlatched each window and propped them open with the sticks found on the window sills. There was only one room which served as the kitchen, dining, and sleeping areas.

The cooking hearth was equipped with a metal hanger holding a cooking pot and removable grill for placing frying pans or meat directly on the fire. Next to the hearth which served to heat the cottage as well, was a small counter with shelves above and below filled with cups, dishes, utensils and a few jars of preserves.

"Well," Tharill moaned, "It looks like roasted acorns and fruit preserves are all we have, unless we go catch some fish." When Rutgar made no reply, he turned around and saw Rutgar had not entered the cottage.

"Rutgar?"

"I'm out here."

"Come on in, Your Gracelessness! This is our castle until we can leave the island."

When Rutgar did not reply to the light-hearted jibe, Tharill went outside, where he found the prince standing stark still, staring at a four-foot tall, eight-foot long, hatchling. Neither creature nor prince moved. They just stood staring at each other. Rutgar with his hand on the hilt of his dagger and the hatchling's baby-new green and blue scales shimmering in the sunlight.

"Step back to me slowly," Tharill calmly announced, but Rutgar did not move.

The hatchling spread his six-foot wings and gently flapped them before folding them back to his side. Then it simply turned and walked away.

Rutgar let out a great huff of air and staggered slightly when he turned toward Tharill. "I thought I was a dead man."

"It was just a hatchling. He would not have hurt you," Tharill said sharply, betraying his annoyance at what he considered merely paranoia on Rutgar's part.

"I've heard stories-" Rutgar began to protest only to be cut short by Tharill.

"They eat fish! Fish, only fish! Get it through that crown-bound melon head of yours, Prince scaredy-gnart!"

"I was...er...am not scared!" Rutgar objected. "I am just cautious... by nature." He pushed past Tharill and entered the cottage. "How old was that...that foul-smelling lizard, anyway," Rutgar quipped over his shoulder.

Tharill let out a subdued snort of laughter and said, "he was a hatchling, less than a year old. If he lives past his first year it will be considered a dragling and given a name."

"What do you mean, *if*, he lives past his first year?" Rutgar questioned and glanced around the little cottage with curiosity glinting in his eyes.

"The mortality rate for hatchlings under a year old has increased the past twenty years from 27% to 50%. Sometimes even higher," Tharill said. "Let's roast the acorns. What do you say?"

Rutgar emptied his acorn filled pockets into a bowl that Tharill placed on the table. "Why do they die?"

Locating a stash of kindling in a cubby-hole next to the hearth, Tharill began to build a fire. "Their wings don't fully develop until they are about a year old, for one thing. So, if one were to venture out on the cliffs and fall it would be the end. But that is very rare." Tharill blew on the barely lit fire which burst into flames within a few breaths. "My grandfather believes the hatchlings are not developed enough to filter out new toxins that may be entering our region."

"Hand me that pan, would you?" Tharill motioned to a pan on one of the shelves.

"What do you mean by *toxins entering your region?*" Rutgar asked. Rutgar picked up the bowl of acorns. "Ready for these?" Tharill nodded and dumped the acorns he had gathered into the pan as well.

"Grandfather is not sure. But four years ago a ship anchored in Dara Harbor washed something thick and foamy out of its scuppers into the water. The grey foam was carried by the current around to the backside of Dara and drifted ashore on Druml." Tharill shook the pan to roast the acorns evenly.

Tharill pulled the pan from the fire and fingered the roasted nuts. "Ow, ow!" He blew on his fingers. "I think these are done."

Rutgar shook a tin he found and then opened it, "Tea biscuits!"

"This may turn out to be a tasty meal after all," Tharill smiled.

"So, what happened to the ship?" Rutgar revived the conversation.

"Nothing happened to the ship. It just sailed away," Tharill said doling out the acorns into separate bowls. "But, dead shamton started to wash-up on the shores by the hundreds."

"Shamton. Those are the fish the dragons eat, right?"

"When they are not roasting and eating people," Tharill teased and then sadness shadowed his face. "All of that year's hatchlings died within three weeks of the dead shamton washing ashore. Plus, two of the older dragons became very ill. Ci Lleuad was one of them."

"From eating the dead fish?" Rutgar's voice rang with remorse.

"No, they only eat live fish. But, the fish they ate must have been contaminated all the same."

"How did the hatchlings get a hold of the fish if they can't fly down to the beaches?" Rutgar asked.

"The dragonesses feed their young through regurgitation."

Rutgar cringed at the thought then said, "The hatchling I encountered today had one green eye and one blue eye. Is that common?"

"No," Tharill perked up at the news and slapped his leg. "Oh, grandfather will be so pleased! That must have been Aillen's hatchling."

"Who is Aillen?"

"She is a dragoness with one blue eye and one green eye. Her last hatchling was one of those that died."

"How did she end up with different colored eyes?" Rutgar asked.

"Dragon's do not interbreed at all. The female draglings always stay on the island and most of the young bulls leave."

"Where do they go?"

"They fly out to sea heading west."

"Are there islands out there?"

"Well there must be. Sometimes a bull dragon will come back years after it originally departed."

"That is fascinating," Rutgar said astonished.

"My grandfather said there is a record of a blue-eyed bull dragon flying in from the west and mating with several dragonesses. After which it just left again."

"When was that?"

"Close to seventy-five years ago. Only Aillen has the different eye colors. This will be the first hatchling of hers that has inherited her eye color." Tharill cracked another acorn and said, "Grandfather will be so pleased! I can't wait to tell him."

They finished their meager meal and did the washing up. When the evening became chilly Tharill closed the cottage windows and made himself comfortable in a padded rocking chair.

Rutgar lit some candles and eyed book titles stacked on a shelf. He was surprised at the variety of books. Most were in Whidley's native Gaelic, which Rutgar did not read or speak very well. He was pleased to find some books in Anglo-Saxon and settled on *The Vicar of Wakefield*, a novel he had heard of, but yet to read.

"Your grandfather has eclectic tastes in reading," Rutgar said but Tharill did not reply as he was already fast asleep in the chair.

Three row boats quietly eased through a series of gently rolling waves below the caves of the Éan Gorm Dragle. Each boat carried six men, ropes, pulleys, climbing gear and one heavy metal cage large enough to confine an average size hatchling.

The moon was very bright although shaded by thick low lying clouds. There were no lights lit aboard the ship *Hav Fuglen* and Commander Curro Delagarza stood silently peering through his Metius glass.

Below deck, Professor Burlong rubbed the knot on his head where he had been struck earlier. The room was dark and smelled of spices, tea and old wine barrels. "Olive?" he whispered.

"I am here dear," she answered from the crate where she sat.

"Are you alright?"

"Yes, dear," she said and made her way over to him. "I'm just a little cold."

The hatchling awoke to the sounds of intruders entering his cave. He was alone, his mother still out feeding near the northern tip of Whidley Island would not return until morning.

He heard a loud screeching come from another nearby cave. Then his cave burst into light as torches appeared at the opening along with several men holding them.

The little hatchling with one blue eye and one green eye backed up to the furthest corner of the cave as the men came closer.

# CHAPTER #19

## *IN SEARCH OF DRAGLINGS*

Rutgar woke to the sound of a loud screeching noise. In the darkness of the cabin he was momentarily puzzled by his surroundings but memories of the previous day's journey quickly took shape in his mind. "Tharill?" he whispered.

"Over here," Tharill answered from where he stood by an open window. Another long high pitched shrill rang out piercing the cold night air, again.

Rutgar padded barefoot to the window and stood next to Tharill, "what is making that noise?"

"It sounds like it is coming from the caves," Tharill said turning toward the cottage door. "Put your boots on. Let's go see what is going on."

"What caves?"

"The Ean Gorm dragle caves," Tharill said over his shoulder as he walked through the doorway and into the night. There were clouds in the sky blocking the nearly full-moon's silvery glow.

Rutgar pulled his socks on, shoved his feet into his boots, grabbed his jacket and ran out the door after Tharill who was almost out of sight.

"Wait, wait, wait!" Rutgar hissed as he ran. When he caught up to Tharill, he grabbed his shoulder to stop him. "Dragle caves?"

"Don't start that dung again!"

"What?" Rutgar scowled.

"The 'they are going to get me' dung."

"That's not fair," Rutgar snapped. You have been raised with these creatures. I grew up listening to old hunting stories and how fierce these dragons are. My great-uncle Boris Van Slauthe was killed by a dragon on one such hunt."

Tharill's expression softened and he said, "the bulls and dragonesses are still feeding north of Whidley and will not return before dawn. We can-" His words cut short by another loud, high-pitched, primordial scream.

"Whatever is screaming sounds terrified," Rutgar sighed.

"It's a hatchling, that I am sure," Tharill said. "Come on, we need to get down to those caves!"

The path down to the dragle caves was barely visible in the limited light of the night's cloudy sky. Leaving the wooded path, the two youths picked their way down the narrow cliff-side trail. At times there was no good footpath to follow and they climbed between rocks and under overhangs, which Tharill, like the draglings, knew by heart.

Rutgar tried to follow Tharill's footsteps, but stumbled and tripped over unseen objects several times. It took them over thirty minutes to reach the mouth of the first dragle caves. They stood quiet for a few moments in the darkness listening for sounds. But, all was silent in the area.

"Is this one big cave where the whole dragle lives?" Rutgar finally broke the silence.

"Yes, but there are several smaller caves like fingers where each dragoness lays her egg," Tharill answered, sniffing the air. "It smells of smoke and oil-cloth."

"Yes, there have been torches in here," Rutgar added.

As the moon's glow peeked down between clouds, its bright light splashed over three boats pushing off from the beach below the caves. Tharill and Rutgar stared down at the water shocked by the sight of the large metal cages in the departing boats.

"How many hatchlings were in these caves?" Rutgar asked

"According to Grandfather, there should be three," Tharill said.

"Three boats with three cages," Rutgar stated. "Are those cages big enough to hold a hatchling?"

"Yes, they are!" Tharill yelped. "We need to get down to the beach!"

"Is there a boat we can use to follow them in?"

"No, but we can light a signal fire down on the beach. Come on let's go!" Tharill said running from the cave, Rutgar close on his heels.

They tripped and staggered over unseen rocks and tree roots as they scampered down the steep path to the bottom. By the time they reached the beach both were breathless and gasping to take air into their lungs. Rutgar put his hand over a small but deep gash he received in one of his legs by a sharp rock or stick.

"There is the signal fire pit!" Tharill yelled pointing to a large stack of wood. He ran to the pit filled with wood and ready to light in case of a dragon emergency. The box of flint and small tinder was easy to find next to the stacked wood. Tharill had a good flame going in a matter of minutes.

It was only after the fire was burning strong that Tharill noticed Rutgar had what appeared to be a piece of cloth wrapped around his leg. "Are you okay?"

"I cut my leg on the way down. But, it is not bleeding as bad as it was before I wrapped it with a piece of my shirt," Rutgar answered from where he sat on a rock.

The clouds were clearing and the moon's light bathed the beach in a wash of silver and the water sparkled like liquid diamonds. Bobbing on the water out in the bay, Tharill could see the three row boats and scanning further he made out the shape of a large ship.

Tharill peered at the silhouette of the ship. He noted its strange shape, with its high narrow decks and an overall pear-shaped design. "Have you seen that type of vessel before, Rutgar?"

Rutgar stood up and hobbled to where Tharill was. "The foremast is set too far forward to be Saxon or Spanian."

"And look at the lateen type sail on the mizzen," Tharill added.

"I'd say it's a Noreg-built fluyt," Rutgar concluded.

"Whatever it is, the rowboats are heading toward it."

"When do you think the fire will be noticed?" Rutgar asked gazing back at the blaze.

"Someone from Dara will check for a fire every hour or so," Tharill sighed, "which may be too late to stop that ship from leaving with the hatchlings they stole."

They sat on the shore helplessly watching as the rowboats, towed a stern, and the ship faded from sight.

The dawn broke on a cool overcast morning. The wind was fair and the sea mildly choppy. Captain Shandy Blu Gruaige snapped his Metius glass closed with a loud clank. "Let 'em know we see the signal fire!" He roared over his shoulder.

One of the Sea Pucca's twenty-four, nine-pound cannons erupted in a blast of smoke and flame. The 120 foot frigate was well armed and boasted one of the finest sailing and fighting crews in the Celtic region, leading some to speculate that the Sea Pucca was more than just a privately owned ship.

Shandy Blu Gruaige, having departed from the Celtic Navy twenty years earlier under a scandal filled cloud involving an admiral's wife, never married. It was said he won the then derelict and un-seaworthy, Sea Pucca in a game of stone-throw on Scotia Island. Where he came up with the money for the extensive refit the ship immediately underwent at Diarmaid's Boatyard was a well of great speculation and gossip.

Even the color of the ship was considered unconventional by seafaring standards as her hull was a dark blue, masts and spars black with some of her sailing canvas rumored to be black, as well. Not to mention that only twelve of her gun ports were clearly framed and visible. The other twelve seemed to blend in with the hull and although there were also twelve swivel guns they were not displayed but stowed until needed. The Sea Pucca and her crew were a mysterious lot indeed to the local seafarers and all gave her a wide berth whenever encountered in the open sea.

"Prepare to launch the cutter," Capt. Shandy ordered. "I'm going ashore. Blade, hold 'er steady until I return and keep a good watch for other ships."

"Aye, Cap," Blade MacIntosh, Shandy's second in command answered, and shouted through a speaking trumpet, "Reduce sail and I want eyes up-top! Look lively there, look lively now!" At these orders the men climbed Sea Pucca's yardarms and burst into a well choreographed dance of rope acrobatic maneuvers and canvas furling. Scampering up to the top of the main and foremasts the look-outs steadied their spy glasses to scan the horizon for sails.

"Who is shooting at us?" Rutgar yelped as he belly flopped onto the sand.

"No one. They have spotted our signal fire and are answering!" Tharill's excitement was reflected in the stammer of his voice. He pulled a burning stick from the fire and waved it excitedly.

Rutgar brushed the sand from his clothes and walked closer to the water. "I see a row boat," he yelled back to Tharill. "It is coming this way."

Shandy's boat crunched to a stop on the sandy beach. Before he could rise from his seat, Tharill and Rutgar had jumped into the boat. "We need to go now!" Tharill insisted. "We need to find the Noreg fluyt that just sailed to the south!"

"Slow down lad," Shandy urged. He ordered his oarsmen to "Shove off and make haste to return to the ship. Pull hardy lads, pull hardy now!" Returning his attention to Tharill and Rutgar he said, "I got a message from Caleb the ferryman to meet you on Druml. What is going on?"

"They took three hatchlings!" Tharill cried.

"Who? What? Wait… start with why you left Dara," Shandy's confusion was visible on his face.

"Three men turned up at the Burlong's cottage and chased after us when we ran down the hill. We snuck onto the ferry under a tarp in Colin's wagon. Colin took us from Paraic to Atha Luain where we forded the low tide-water between Whidley and Druml."

"I met up with an odd-eyed hatchling," Rutgar interjected, his pale blue eyes glinted for a moment in morning sun.

"Odd eyed?" Shandy asked, puzzled.

"Aillen's hatchling. It has one blue eye and one green eye," Tharill chimed in.

"Your grandfather will be very pleased," Shandy said. "Now continue with your escape from the men on Dara Island. Where they Spanians?"

"Although they were dressed like Noregsmen, they spoke with Spanian accents," Rutgar said rubbing the make-shift bandage on his leg.

"Did they follow you from the transport we were on?"

"No," Tharill answered. "I believe they were waiting. Wouldn't you agree Rutgar?"

"Yes, I am sure they weren't on the ship," Rutgar added, "and there was another Noreg-dressed man checking everyone coming off of the ferry from Dara when we landed in Paraic."

"There was a Noreg fluyt anchored off of Dara until yesterday," Shandy said as the rowers shifted their oars just before the boat gently tapped against the side of the Sea Pucca. A boarding rope-ladder was cast over the side for the occupants to climb aboard and ropes lowered to bring the little bobbing boat aloft as well.

Rutgar faltered as he climbed the ladder almost sending him into the water below. Firm hands from sailors leaning over the rail grabbed at him, pulling him onto the Sea Pucca's deck.

"Are you alright, lad?" Shandy laid his hand on Rutgar's shoulder. "You look a little peckish."

"I cut my leg on a sharp rock or stick, coming down to the beach," Rutgar said indicating the bandage around his leg.

"That is not good. Are you wearing the Whidley sickness patch?" Shandy asked.

"Yes,"

"Let me see it,"

Rutgar removed his jacket to reveal the once beige colored patch was now a very dark blue. "How do you feel?" Shandy asked as Tharill stared at the patch, without saying a word.

"Kind of tired," Rutgar answered looking from Shandy to Tharill and then to the patch on his arm. "I take it this is not a good color."

"The wound on your leg has exposed you to a higher toxin level than normal," Shandy said with a sigh.

"So what do I do?"

"Drink!" Shandy said with a slap to Rutgar's back. "We need to flush the toxins out of you, my lad. Licorice tea and wine should work. I'll have Butters whip up a brew that will soon have you back on an even keel."

"Sail, ho!" yelled a voice from up in the rigging.

"Where away?" shouted Blade in response.

"South, South-east! Heading for the Weite Ozean," howled another voice.

"Cap?" Blade shouted.

"Spread 'er wings, lads! Let's see how our seabird flies!"

"Aye, aye, Cap!" Blade shouted back and then proceeded to bellow orders to the crew to lay on all sail. Grey sheets of heavy weather canvas dropped, ballooned out as they filled with wind while studding spars pushed even further out like an eagle extending its wings to the fullest. The Sea Pucca could truly fly on the water, her bow slicing through the waves as she went. Her newly cleaned copper bottom presented little resistance to the floating seaweed and kelp in the choppy water.

"Get some sleep lads and I'll wake you when we get close to the fluyt," Captain Shandy had told them after showing them to a cabin.

Tharill and Rutgar rested in a guest cabin having eaten their fill in the galley. "If I drink another drop of this tea, I am going to throw-up," Rutgar complained.

On deck crewmen wrestled with canvas and ropes while white caps exploded against the hull and the wind howled in the rigging. "Reduce sail and bring her head up into the wind," Shandy shouted to Blade.

"Aye, Cap!" Blade yelled back through the thickening sound of wind, rain and the water crashing across the deck.

"Life lines bow to stern, larboard and starboard," Shandy shouted above the thundering storm, from the quarter-deck. The ship leaned into a great wave which burst across the forecastle loosening the tie-downs of one of the nine-pound chaser guns causing it to roll wildly breaking the ropes that held it in place.

"Secure that gun!" Blade shouted and men scrambled to capture the wayward cannon without themselves being injured in the process.

Below deck Tharill and Rutgar swung helplessly in their hammocks. The force of each dip and roll of the ship kept them anchored in their bag-like beds. A time or two the waves hit the ship with such force it felt and sounded as if the ship had run aground. There was a single lamp in the little cabin and in the darkness the water could be heard periodically washing under the door and across the floor below them.

"You think we'll be okay?" Rutgar asked trying to subdue the nausea from the wine he'd consumed while wondering if it would really help or just get him drunk so he wouldn't care.

"My uncle is a good captain and this ship is one of the finest in build."

"What about the other ship and the hatchlings?"

"That I can't answer," Tharill said, his fingers gripping the sides of his hammock so tight he could no longer feel them.

The cabin lurched sideways with such violence that Rutgar's hammock was wrenched from its hooks and slung against the inner wall of the room. Tharill could only watch stunned and in that instant thought *we're capsizing!*

# CHAPTER #20

## *SURVIVING THE STORM*

The ship leaned perilously to starboard for what seemed an eternity to Tharill. When it did right itself, it immediately plunged forward throwing Rutgar and his hammock in another direction like a ragdoll. Water splashed about the cabin in mini tidal waves. Books, clothing, chairs and other items sloshed back and forth with such violence the legs of the secured cabin table snapped and the top flung clear.

Tharill managed to pull himself out of his cocoon-like sleeping bag and was instantly flung onto the watery floor as the ship slammed into what must have been another monster wave. A rampaging chair struck him in the back with such great force he screamed in pain.

*Where was Rutgar?* Tharill tried to stand and search the room in the dim light of a single swinging lantern, but was thrown back down by another violent jerk of the ship. The whole room shuddered and the frigate's structure wailed with a thousand groans and shrieks of pain as if its very bones were being fractured.

"Rutgar!" Tharill yelled over the roar of wind and rain outside of the struggling ship. "Where are you?" Unable to stand on the floor that convulsed beneath him without mercy, tossing the room's inhabitants and furnishings about, Tharill crawled on his hands and knees.

"Rutgar, where are you?" Tharill's words pleaded for an answer from his friend. He crawled toward the area where he thought Rutgar had been thrown. The room was small in size, but the crazy rocking and jolting of the floor made every inch covered by Tharill seem endless and filled with peril. Nails shot out of loosened boards, splinters darted about in all directions from breaking planks, and furniture flew across the room each time the ship slammed into another unyielding fist of the sea.

"Tharill," Rutgar groaned. "Help, me... I am wedged into a-" His words were cut short by the sound of a huge tree cracking and then folding under the pressure.

But, Tharill knew it was not a tree. It was the mizzenmast, the mast that towered above this section of the ship.

Then there was a series of high-pitched popping sounds like huge over tightened war-harp strings all snapping at once. *Was the noise the peak halyards, shrouds and back-stays which kept the mast in place letting go in succession?* The answer came when the great mast toppled downward and the crew could be heard scattering to get away from the falling timber.

To Tharill's surprise the cro'jack's large yardarm spiraled down to and through the quarter deck, impaling itself in the ceiling and then the floor of the guest quarters barely missing him. Rope, tackle and torn bits of sail whipped around the room as the rigging above deck pulled and yanked on the broken limb.

Tharill ducked into a corner, unable to reach Rutgar who was calling from the opposite side of the room. Sounds of what must have been hatchets, boarding axes and the crewmen wielding them pierced the noise of wind and waves.

"Hello, the cabin! Is anyone harmed, within?" a voice yelled down through the hole the yardarm was protruding from. "Hello, hello?" the impatient voice shouted.

"Help …. help!" Rutgar's distinct yet hoarse voice rang out. "Something has me wedged inside this locker. I can't budge it."

"Hold fast, lads! Help is on the way!" the voice from above shouted reassuringly.

Tharill tried a crablike crawl to make his way around the intruding obstructions without success. He found himself blocked by rigging and other debris in every direction. With each pitch and yaw of the convulsing ship, the mizzen wreckage shifted, making moving about the cabin treacherous.

Sounds of crewmen pounding and kicking could now be heard at the cabin's door. "The door is jammed shut!" a crewman bellowed.

"Tharill?" Shandy shouted from the other side of the cabin door.

"I'm here! We're here, uncle!" Tharill screamed.

"Are you lads injured?"

"No, I am not. But, Rutgar is trapped by the wreckage in here. Are you going to get the door opened?"

"Listen carefully, my lad," Shandy's voice echoed through the door and into the cabin. "The door is wedged shut. To open it would weaken the frame at this time and we need all the possible extra strength these walls can give 'er hull." Shandy paused for a moment. "Do you understand?"

"Yes, uncle," Tharill answered in a quivering voice. "Can you pull us out through the hole the yardarm made?"

"No, lad. The spar needs to stay in place for now, too. It has pierced the hull and is acting like somewhat of a cork at this point." Shandy broke off his conversation with Tharill to bark orders at a crewman.

Tharill's whole body began to shake, his breathing growing faster and more shallow. *Is the air growing thick? The room seems smaller!* He put his hands over his face and then suddenly slapped himself, hard. "I am alright. I am alright." He repeated the words over and over just under his breath.

"I need to go back on deck," Shandy shouted into the closed door.

Tharill again tried to calm himself. He had been in the cabin for awhile and the confined space had not bothered him. *Why now?* But, the answer was clear, *no way out*. If the ship were to founder, there would be no way out of this would-be *coffin* room. "Tharill!" hearing his name snapped him out of his gloomy introspection.

"Yes," he answered, barely audible over the noise of the storm topside and the wailing of the ships bones, skin and heart.

"Get your gnart-ass over here and help me out of this paddy-jack of a box!" Rutgar yelled, anger flaring in his tone.

"I can't!" Tharill cried out.

"Yes, you can!" Rutgar shot back.

"No, I can't..."

"Listen to me, Tharill. You can make your way over here. You can do it! I need your help to free myself."

Tharill got to his knees from where he sat and began to crawl. Ropes with tackle still attached, thrashed about him coming within inches of his head. Something hard slammed into his shoulder, ripping his shirt and gouging the skin of his forearm. But, he did not stop or even slow down, only continued to move closer to Rutgar's location.

He saw the broken tabletop wedged against a battered locker. "Rutgar?" He shouted and pounded on the side of the locker.

"Yes, Yes! Get me out of here, gnart-breath!"

Tharill cocked his head, the tightness of his chest vanished and a scant smile creased his cheeks. "Why yes, of course Your Most Dungness," he answered and looked around him for something to pry the table loose. Spotting a table leg still upright and attached to the floor, he managed to crawl over and break it free. With three hardy yanks on the thick wooden leg, the tabletop broke loose and Tharill shoved the heavy object out of the way.

The door of the locker sprang open and Rutgar tumbled out looking like an Azwan mummy, still tangled up in his hammock. "Hiding in the linen cupboard?" Tharill chided.

"No!" Rutgar retorted, "I was thrust in there when my hammock broke free and the door slammed shut, gnart-ass!"

"You alright?" Tharill asked, helping Rutgar out of his hammock canvas and ropes.

"Doch," Rutgar answered in his native, Saxon, language. Looking past Tharill, he saw for the first time what had plunged through the ceiling. "What the... Where did that thing come from?" Tilting his head sideways and looking at the sail cloth and dangling ropes he added, "Is that a yardarm?"

"I think the mizzen mast gave way," Tharill answered. "Uncle Shandy says it has punctured the hull and can't be removed yet."

Rutgar nodded in agreement, "I also heard that the door is jammed."

Tharill only nodded and closed his eyes tightly, taking in a deep breath. He once again found himself fighting off his inner most fear, *confined spaces*.

Although the ship did not seem to shudder as often or severe as it had been the last several hours, it was apparent the storm was not quite finished with this little bobby cork it had grasped firmly in its clutches. The room suddenly jolted sideways causing Tharill and Rutgar to slide along the soaked floor. Water began to pour in the hole in the ceiling again, where earlier cloth had been shoved around the spar in an attempt to somewhat stifle the flow of water into the ship.

"There is no way out!" Tharill suddenly yelped, startling Rutgar.

"What?"

"There is no way out! We're stuck in here!" Tharill repeated and began trembling; his breathing became short and raspy. His mind raced along with his pulse and he felt as if his heart was going to explode from his chest.

213

"Tharill," Rutgar said in a calm, reassuring tone. "We will be alright, friend. Whatever happens we'll go through it together. Together, do you hear me?"

"Yes, yes," Tharill felt Rutgar's hand on his shoulder and closed his eyes repeating: *Calm down, calm down. I'm alright, I'm alright.* "I don't do well in small spaces, sometimes," he said.

"Well, then we are even, I don't like heights."

A bottle of wine rolled toward them and Rutgar grabbed it. "What do ya say?"

From a distance, in the early morning light, the weather worn ship appeared to have just come from a battle, with the mizzen mast snapped in two at the upper-tree and the foremast sprung with sail and rigging swaying in the gentle breeze. Crewmen with monkey like coordination hurriedly scampered up and down masts and out on yardarms. Others on deck busied themselves with holystones, paint, saws, nails and other needed items to rush the *Sea Pucca* back into seagoing and fighting shape.

The cabin door thumped against the inside wall when it was finally shoved open in the early dawn hours. Tharill and Rutgar leaned against salvaged pillows across from each other on one of the only semi dry lockers, the empty wine bottle resting at Tharill's feet.

"Wake up, you lazy land lubbers!" Shandy roared from the open doorway. "What, do you think you are on holiday? Get up! There is breakfast to be et!" Before leaving he also said," What in dragon's breath did you do to my guest cabin! Look at this mess!" At this Shandy roared with laughter and tromped down the hall.

How the cook, Butters, managed to get the galley fire going in all of this dampness gave Tharill a whole new sense of respect for the man. Plus, Butters had whipped up a breakfast fit for a king or prince, as if nothing had happened the night before. Shandy sat with the youths, watching them gobble down eggs, potatoes, gnart-bacon, biscuits slathered with butter and snowberry preserves. They also sucked down the hot coffee like cold milk.

"Slow down lads," Shandy laughed. "You'll burn yer inners clean through with all that hot coffee."

"This is great! Thank you!" Rutgar exclaimed.

"Yes, thank you so much, Uncle," Tharill muffled in agreement, his cheeks bulging like those of an engorged hamster.

First Mate Blade MacIntosh appeared in the galley doorway and knocked on the wall, as there was no door. Shandy looked up and motioned Blade to come in. "Butters, fetch Mr. Blade a cup of tea," Captain Shandy ordered.

"Thanky, Cap. But I need to speak with you, in private," Blade said glancing at Butters

Tharill and Rutgar began to rise, but Blade motioned them to sit. "This may very well involve you, Prince Van Slauthe."

"Don't mean ye can't have a cup of tea," Shandy insisted.

"I get the hint," Butters growled, adding "I'll keep watch in the hall, for ye." Mumbling as he went into the hall, "it don't count that I've been with skipper for nay on twenty-five year...no..it's 'out wit' ye Butters, out wit' ye' fine t'anks I git."

"The preventers on the back-stays to the mizzen were cut. That is why she gave way." Blade said, concern creasing his brow.

"I knew that something was amiss!" Shandy slammed his fist onto the table causing the cups to bounce and splash their contents. "She had a complete refit! New rigging, lumber, caulking and the lot."

"What does this mean?" Tharill asked

"Sabotage!" Shandy bellowed.

Butters could be heard grumbling something from out in the hall. But no one inquired to what he'd said.

"We picked up thirteen new crew on Dara," Blade said. "It has to be one of them."

"Well, the blaggard didn't try to sink us. O'course he'd go down too," Shandy surmised.

"There is your launch and the other boats, escape can be made on one of those," Blade suggested.

"Aye, but sabotaging the mizzen seems more like an act to delay rather than destroy," Shandy calculated. "Although that yardarm piercing the hull is rather bad luck."

"Do you think they will try to take me from your ship?" Rutgar asked.

"Not bloody likely!" Blade assured. "They can try, but they won't do."

Shandy took his pipe from his vest pocket, tapped it on the table and brushed the old tobacco onto the floor.

"For dung's sake, Cap!" Butters hurried in and began to tidy up where the tobacco had fallen from the pipe. "There is a dust bin right next to the table," he grumbled. "Clean, cook, clean and what thanks do I get?" he continued to mutter.

"Butters, go ask the purser for the ship's roster," Shandy ordered and began to fill his pipe from a pouch of tobacco. At that order, Butters marched out of the room making growling sounds.

The sound of someone running down the hall in the galley's direction came to an abrupt halt and was replaced by the thud of a collision and, "Oh, I am so sorry, Mr. Butters!" A young voice rang out and then the sound of running resumed. All at the table watched as a young lad barged into the galley, gasping for breath.

"Sail spotted to the north, north-west, sir!" the tall, lanky boy of about fourteen with curly red hair, and large, olive-green eyes gasped out. "Lookout says he thinks it's the Noreg fluyt."

Getting to his feet, Shandy told Blade he wanted a report from both the head carpenter and the sailing master, as soon as possible. "You lads are welcome to come on deck. Just watch yourself to stay out of the way of repairs, unless someone asks ye to help."

Up on deck, Shandy slid his telescope glass from its case and extended it to its fullest. He lifted the glass to his right eye and peered through the lens. "Well, yank-my-anchor! She took quite a beating in that storm," he gleefully reported to Blade. "Here take a gander," he said, passing the telescope to Blade.

"Make all sail for that fluyt!" Shandy yelled. "We'll have her by midday or I'll know why."

"Captain?" the lanky, red-headed lad said in a soft voice.

Shandy turned to see the youth standing at the stairs of the quarter deck, piece of paper in his outstretched hand. "Speak up lad," Shandy roared noticing the paper in the young man's hand. "Come on up here. Is that the list I asked for?"

"aye, sir," the red-headed lad said, quickly withdrawing his hand and stepping back when Shandy grabbed the paper.

"Yer McAffrey's boy, aren't ye?" Shandy asked, with a bit of a growl in his voice.

"Aye....sir," the lad stammered in return, standing straight, eyes darting from left to right.

"How old are ye?"

"Fourteen, I think."

"When did yer Pa sign you on?" Shandy questioned.

"On Dara, I helped work on the ship's refit," the toothy boy smiled.

"Good lad, now back to your station," Shandy said, took a quick look at the list and then whistled to Blade waving him to come to the quarterdeck.

"Aye, Cap?"

"Look at the names added to the roster on Dara," Shandy said handing Blade the log.

Blade stared at one of the names entered on the list. "How can this be?" Blade murmured and shot a look of disbelief at his captain. "How can this be?" he repeated. "And how could I not have noticed him while making my rounds on the ship?" he added, shaking his head.

Shandy tapped his pipe on the rail and said, "Well, this does change things a bit, don't it?"

# CHAPTER #21

## *A SEA OF DISCONTENT*

"We're gaining on 'er, Skip!" A voice from the top of one of the masts rang out.

"We'll soon have the blaggard within range of our bow-chasers!" Another excited crewman yelled as cheers were shouted around the ship by other crewmen.

The wind was strong and in *Sea Pucca's* favor. The frigate glided across the water like a leaf blown by the wind. Displaced waves sprayed up from both sides of her bluff bow, along the ship's hull and vanished into the transom's wake.

The other ship attempting to evade the *Sea Pucca* was not fairing so well. Badly damaged by the storm, it limped along with sprung masts and shredded canvas for sails. Shandy squinted as he looked through his Metius glass, unable to make out the ship's name painted on its stern, he snapped it closed in frustration.

"Have you found him?" Shandy asked, without removing his gaze from the fleeing ship's direction.

"Who?" Blade asked.

"You know who," Shandy barked and then let out a great chuckle.

"Oh, that who," Blade frowned. "I spotted him earlier on the gun deck but did not approach him." At that he raised his own telescope lens and took measure of the distance between the two vessels.

"Do you think he is the saboteur?" Shandy asked bluntly.

"I hope not, but if he is … I'll clap him in irons and have him thrown in the holding room like anyone else," Blade stated flatly.

"I leave the matter of what to do with this person in your capable hands. Watch your lee, though, I'd hate to see ye get broadsided by him." At that, Shandy flipped his scope open again, peered through, and roared, "Prepare the bow-chasers!"

"Aye, Cap!" Blade saluted and shouted to his gun crew. "You heard the captain, lads! Load those guns! Our prey is close at hand!"

"Fire!" Blade shouted and two shots rang out filling the forecastle with smoke and the smell of spent gun powder. The cannon balls splashed into the water just shy of the other ship's stern.

"Up four degrees," Blade said sighting along one of the gun barrels. The gun crew quickly made the vertical corrections and he tapped the fuse of the gun in front of him with slow match and it exploded with fire and smoke again. The ball shot straight and true, blasting through a set of fancy gilded stern windows of the frenzied ship.

Blade could see the fluyt crew working desperately to hoist new canvas and jury-rig masts to hold them once the new sails filled with the increasing wind.

"Hav Fuglen," Shandy muttered and lowered his spy glass.

"What Cap?" Blade asked.

"It's the name of the ship. Ever come across 'er before?"

"No, but the name is Noreg. It means Sea Bird."

"She'll be for having 'er wings clipped today!" Shandy roared with excited laughter and clapped Blade on the back so hard the first mate had to take a step forward to maintain his balance.

"Sail ho, sail ho," Rang a voice from somewhere high up in the rigging.

"For dung-sake, what now?" Shandy shouted in surprise. "Where away?"

"Four points to starboard," the nameless voice yelled back.

Shandy crossed to the other side of the deck where he put the glass to his eye again and was puzzled by what he saw. The approaching naval ship fired a shot, but not at the *Sea Pucca* or the *Hav Fuglen*. It appeared to be only a signal shot to get Shandy's attention. Then a series of signal flags began flying on the ship.

Tharill and Rutgar ran to the bow from the quarter deck, where they had been standing. "Who are they?" Tharill asked Blade, anxiously. Blade only shrugged his shoulders.

"Well, yank-my-anchor," Shandy growled. "Reduce sail, and make for that bloody ship over yonder!"

"What?" Tharill said incredulously. "But, the fluyt will get away! What about the hatchlings?"

"Sorry lad, it's one of King Fios' ships. I can't refuse to meet with it," Shandy walked away and barked out more orders to his crew, anger clearly raging in his tone.

"Should I have the cutter lowered and send a crew to follow the *Hav Fuglen*?" Blade asked.

"Aye, give them extra sails and tell them to stay out of gun range," Shandy replied. "Make sure they have a week's worth of provisions and tell them we will rendezvous at that small island west of here."

"Creggan Island?" Blade asked.

"Aye, it has nice tall trees for timber and would be a good place to carry out repairs. Hopefully, the fluyt will go there. If not, at least we'll have a good idea what harbor she is bound for on the continent by the direction she takes after we stop pursuit."

"Uncle," Tharill said as soon as Blade left to take care of the cutter's crew and stores. "Can Rutgar and I go with the cutter crew to follow the fluyt?"

Rutgar stood silent at Tharill's side. Although he said nothing, his eyes had a pleading expression that tugged at Shandy's heart. "No lads, I can't let you go." His voice was soft and understanding. "I would much rather bag that bird than meet with a king's messenger boy. But, I sail at the King Fios' pleasure and must give way if summoned by one of his ships."

"I understand," Tharill tried to sound appeased.

"The foolish sots probably got lost in the storm and just want us to point them south," Shandy laughed. "I am sure whatever it is will not take long and we can head out after our cutter."

Prince Rutgar's eyes widened as he leaned closer to Tharill and whispered, "Lost? No ship in our navy would ever have such an issue."

Tharill burst out in laughter, "Come on let's see if we can help ready the cutter."

It was mid-morning by the time a barge from the King's ship crossed to the waiting *Sea Pucca*. Rutgar and Tharill had gone below to help clean up their cabin.

Shandy smiled when he saw the face of the man emerging from the barge now tied off to the *Sea Pucca*. "Captain Finbar Flannagáin! What in the paddy-jack brings you out this way?" Shandy smiled, extending his hand to welcome the newcomer aboard.

"Good to see you too, old friend," the Celtic Naval officer said vigorously shaking Shandy's hand. "I am happy to find you this quickly!"

"Find me?" Shandy asked. "You were looking for me? How did you know I was out this way? I didn't even know I would be out this way until last night."

"No, I thought you were still at Dara Island. That is where I was heading when we got caught in the storm," Captain

Flannagáin said. "Listen my friend, I have some troubling news and orders from the King to relay to you."

"Come, maybe the news will be better swallowed over a cup of tea or tot of rum." Shandy gestured for his friend to precede him down the stairs and toward the captain's cabin. As they passed the galley Shandy shouted, "Bring us a fresh pot of tea, bottle of my best rum, and something sweet to nibble."

"Aye, Cap," Butters' voice rang out.

Shandy moved the maps from his table when Butters entered the room with a large serving tray. He poured tea with rum and served scones with butter to both captains. Butters closed the door behind him when he left.

Captain Flannagáin set his cup down and pulled a large envelope from his breast pocket. "It seems we are going to war with Saxony," He said and handed the sealed envelope to Shandy.

"What? Why would..." Shandy tore the envelope open and started to read. As if jolted from his seat, he jumped up almost over-turning the table and ran from the room leaving Flannagáin perplexed.

"Rutgar!" Captain Shandy shouted, barging into the guest cabin.

Startled by the sudden out-burst of his name, Rutgar swung around, broom in-hand, causing his elbow to strike Tharill in the face.

"Oh, my nose!" Tharill cried and fell back into a chair, both hands cupping his nose as blood began to trickle down his chin. "Not again," he moaned.

"I'm so sorry," Rutgar exclaimed, dropping the broom.

"Rutgar!" Shandy repeated, grabbing the lad by the shoulder. "Your father believes you have been abducted by someone in King Fios' Court and is at this very moment declaring war against the Celtic Islands."

Rutgar stood staring at Shandy, "What?"

"I sent Rory to tell Rutgar's uncle that he would be with me and to come to Dara Island," Tharill called out from where he sat, his hands cupping his injured nose.

"Well, he failed to do so-" Shandy barked.

"A war?" Rutgar said, staring at Shandy

"Something must have happened to Rory. He knew how important it was to get a message to your family," Tharill said, his words muffled by a handkerchief Rutgar had handed him to cover his bleeding nose. "Where is my brother?"

"Come with me to my cabin, lads," Shandy said helping Tharill to his feet. "Hopefully, Captain Flannagáin will have some answers for us."

"Where is Rory? Where is Rory?" Tharill repeated, his heart started to pound in his chest. His breath caught in his throat as though he were choking on a piece of food. Tharill's mind began to fill and race with the memories of when his father went missing. Panic rose up the back of his neck and thundered into his mind.

"They were all found murdered," Flannagáin said. "I am sorry Your Highness."

"And my uncle, Madog ap Gruffydd?"Rutgar asked without missing a step passing back and forth in Shandy's cabin.

"It was Councilors Madog ap Gruffydd and Feylan O'Shea who found the bodies of the crew when they arrived at the ship." Flannagáin adjusted himself in his chair to better meet the intense questioning gaze of the Prince. "Among the dead was a body wearing Castle Garda uniform. Sheriff Tearjoy said he did not recognize the dead man as one of his Gardaí."

What about my brother?" Tharill pleaded, a muffled, nasal twang in his voice due to the gauze now stuffed up his nostrils.

"I am sorry, but as I've already said, there was no sign of your brother. Only an abandoned boot on the dock that Councilor Fergal Gruaige, your grand-father, identified as the same type of boot your brother may have been wearing. But, that is all I know, lad and that is just the scuttle-butt around the fleet," Flannagáin sympathized.

"I don't understand why King Van Slauthe would believe anyone in the Fios Royal Court would want to hurt the Prince?" Shandy questioned tapping more tobacco into his pipe.

"In reprisal for the poaching of dragons by the Saxons?" Flannagáin suggested.

"This whole thing makes no sense," Prince Rutgar said. "Saxony signed the Dragon Protection Treaty along with the other nations. Why would any Saxony citizen risk imprisonment for dragon trophies?"

"No one would take dragon hatchlings as trophies, yet they are on that ship we were chasing sure as gnarts have tusks," Tharill said.

"And that is no Saxon ship," Shandy puffed through his pipe smoke. "That ship is a Noreg fluyt and Noreg has no history hunting dragons at all."

"They signed the treaty, too," Flannagáin added, sipping his tea.

"Let's step back a pace and map this out from the beginning as we know it," Shandy said pointing his pipe at Tharill. "Go ahead lad, when was the first indication that something was amiss with the dragons on Whidley?"

"My brother and I found a downed balloon transport in Uncle Rist's pasture where Rory picked up an arrow that was filled with a green colored solution. Rory cut himself on the arrow and it made him very sick. We took him to the old druid Urmi Landfor and he treated Rory, discovering that the liquid was a very potent sleeping draft. Just the few drops almost caused Rory to die."

"Were there any markings on the balloon," Flannagáin asked. "and what about the transport crew?"

"It was one of the Celtic Moon Transport Company's inland balloons. The captain's name was ..." Tharill squinted and looked down at the floor. "Mossey ... Mosley ..."

"Moseby?" Shandy asked.

"That's it, Moseby," Tharill said. "Do you know him?"

"That scurvy-faced, son-of-a-gnart's-ass," Shandy growled. "Aye! I know the blaggard, well. I don't know what he may have been up to, but I'd bet my last gold willet, it was no good."

"Why did he say he was in the area?" Flannagáin asked.

"He said he was showing his passenger some property that was for sale. But, off-islanders can't buy property on Whidley and I told him so," Tharill answered and added, "and he should know that."

"Passenger?" Shandy inquired

"A tall man dressed in black with a long red sash tied around his waist," Tharill said.

"Red sash, you say?" Shandy asked and without waiting for an answer added, "was he also wearing a large black hat with a red band?"

"Why, yes, I believe he was at that," Tharill said in surprise. "Another man familiar to you?"

"Delagarza?" Flannagáin posed to Shandy

"It sounds like him," Shandy said and took a long draw from his pipe.

"Who is Delagarza?" Rutgar asked.

"Blade's brother-in-law and a high ranking commander in the Spanian Military," Shandy said and rose from his chair to walk to the cabin door. Opening it, he called to a crewmember standing in the hall. "Send for Blade to come to my cabin and tell Butters to bring us more hot tea and another bottle of rum. We are definitely going to need the rum."

"Aye, Cap," the crewman answered.

"Curro Delagarza looking at property on Whidley?" Blade puzzled, lifted an eyebrow. "I've not known him to be interested in any property outside of Noreg or Spana, for that matter. Plus, everyone knows only Whidley natives can purchase land on the island."

"Noreg?" Rutgar asked.

"Yes, his father is Spanian but his and my wife's mother is Noregn," Blade said.

"I did not know you were married, Blade," Flannagáin said.

"We have unfortunately been a long time estranged from one-another."

"I see," Flannagáin said.

"He has recently found that his oldest son is a new member of our crew," Shandy added.

Blade shot Shandy a slight look of reproach and said, "Well, the lad is using his grandmother's surname and I didn't pick up on it until we were out to sea."

"Why would your son do that?" Rutgar asked

The question appeared to catch Blade off guard and he stammered, "He … he must have … I mean … I am …,"

"He may very well be our saboteur," Shandy interjected.

A streak of pain flashed over Blade's face as visible as a shooting star across the sky on a clear night. "Hopefully, not, but it might well play in with the Noregn ship, and Curro being seen on Whidley Island," Blade conceded.

"Do you think Delagarza might be on the Hav Fuglen?" Shandy asked

"The timing is right," Blade answered.

"Ok, but what does all of that have to do with me?" Rutgar asked to no one particular.

"Pitting Saxony against the Celtic Islands, would take King Van Slauthe's military focus off of his border dispute with Spana for awhile," Flannagáin suggested.

"But, why take the hatchlings?" Tharill asked, the blood flow from his nose now staunched. "And where in the dragon's breath is my brother?"

"I do not know where the hatchlings come into play with this whole situation but the possibility of Delagarza being on that fluyt we sent our men to follow changes things." Shandy said.

"I have a swift little cutter you are welcome to, if you want to send another crew to follow the fluyt," Flannagáin offered. "It can bear four swivel guns and eighteen-crew."

"Aye, that would be grand," Shandy said and turned to Blade. "Take extra shot, boarding axes and your best fighting men."

Blade stood to leave and Tharill jumped to his feet, "I am going too."

"Tharill," Shandy began to object.

"Uncle Shandy, the answer to where my brother is may be on that ship. I have to go."

"Then go lad," Shandy said and stood to escort Captain Flannagáin and the others to his barge. Grabbing his long, thick boat-cloak from a hook by the door he handed it to Tharill. "This will keep you warm and dry but Blade will keep you alive, so do everything he tells you to do."

"I will Uncle."

"What about me?" Rutgar complained.

"You lad, need to stop a war, before it begins!" Shandy answered.

The afternoon sun was bright and the sea rippled with soft waves from a northerly breeze. Shandy stood in deep thought as he watched the cutter sail out of sight. He was uneasy about letting Tharill go, but trusted Blade to take care of his nephew.

"Where do you think Rory is?" Rutgar asked.

"I don't know, but I hope he is alive, where ever he is," Shandy answered, his tone melancholy, and took another deep draw from his pipe.

Badar Al-Nassir peered at the two large ships that would cross his ship's wake by early evening.

"Who are they?" Badar asked, holding the Metius glass steady with both hands.

"Two Celtic Islands ships," Fozan replied. "One appears to be Celtic Islands Navy and the other a civilian of some type."

"It has too many gun ports to be private. I would believe it to be a privateer rather than civilian."

"You, have a point," Fozan said. "What are they doing out here? Do you think we should be concerned about them? They do appear to be traveling together."

"No, they are on a north by north-east tack. We are sailing north-west," Badar said.

"If the wind holds, we should be at Creggan Island by noon tomorrow," Fozan surmised. "What do you think?"

"I agree," Badar answered.

# CHAPTER #22

## *CREGGAN ISLAND*

Rory groaned in pain as the woman dabbed at the deep wound in his shoulder, with a wet cloth. It had been several days since a bullet ripped through his shoulder with such force he was flung backwards into the water off pier #12. He would have surely drowned if Badar al-Nassir had not plucked him from the cold water.

"Where am I?" Rory asked trying to focus his eyes to the dim cabin light.

"On the *Kwaitia*," A soft voice answered.

"*Kwaitia*?" Rory said and turned his head for a better view of the person sitting next to him. "Reesa? Reesa, is it really you?"

She pressed her hand on his and said, "Welcome back to the land of the living."

"My shoulder hurts really bad."

"You've been shot. The bullet went through your shoulder."

"Shot? Why? By who?"

"Do you remember anything about the night you went to pier #12?"

"No, why would I go to pier #12?"

"I don't know. But, it must have been important."

Rory tried to sit up, but quickly laid back down wincing in pain. "What ship is this?"

"It is Fozan's ship," Reesa said patting Rory's brow with a damp cloth. "We are headed to Creggan Island. It was Fozan and Badar who pulled you from the water."

Blade's cutter slid easily onto the moonlit sandy beach. Several men jumped out and pulled it further out of the water, while others unwrapped pistols from their protective water proof oil-cloth wrappings. Few words were spoken, each man already knew their part to play in this game of search and observe or as a last resort, search and destroy.

The cutter was carefully camouflaged in a stand of nearby shrubs before the band of well armed men ventured from the beach into the green wooded inner-island terrain.

"It smells like rain," whispered a large bulk of a sailor with one of the four swivel guns from the cutter strapped to his back.

"Aye," answered his mate, treading close behind with two small boxes of cannon shot, slightly swaying under an oar shouldered between himself and another.

"And we know what that can lead to in these here parts," another added.

Creggan Island, the northern most island of the Celtic Islands realm, where the weather was known to turn from a light rain into a blinding snow blizzard in just a matter of hours, had once been home to the Cancregga dragle of dragons. The beautiful, all be it vicious, dragons had been hunted to extinction decades ago for their silver-blue, fur covered scales.

Blade heard a rustling of branches ahead of him and signaled his men to stop and take cover. The men silently slipped from the path and into the surrounding vegetation. Voices could be heard in the distance and Blade quietly moved in their direction.

"Where are they?" an unseen man asked.

"How the bloody dragon's breath should I know!" another voice snapped in reply.

Leaving the cover of the trees, Blade sighed and walked onto the path where the two men stood griping at each other. Startled by the intrusion, the taller of the two men pulled a long knife from his belt.

"Belay, that weapon!" Blade commanded.

"Mister Blade!" The tall knife-man cried.

"Mister Blade," the other, a man with long dark, braided hair and beard, repeated. "How did you find us?"

"My deaf grandmother on Scotia could hear you two, blithering ejits going at it!"

"Sorry, Mister Blade," Tall-man said and sheathed his knife. "We saw your boat come in and Mister Duffy sent us to collect you."

"Well then, lead on McDuff," Blade said with a wave of his hand and a whistle to summon his crew from their hiding places

"Oh Sir, my name is McDougall, not McDuff," Tall-man said, looking slightly bewildered.

"Never mind," Blade said with a grin. "Lead on anyway."

"Mister Blade must have you confused with one of the new men we took on at Dara," Braided-man whispered to his tall ship-mate.

"Aye, that would explain it," McDougall replied. "And it being dark and all."

Blade shook hands with Lieutenant Orin Duffy and glanced around the small encampment. "You've done well in your choice of positions here on the back side of this hill."

"Thank-you, Mister Blade," Duffy answered with delight. "I have a look-out on top the hill with a view of the whole island and surrounding waters. That's how we first spotted you."

"Is the Hav Fuglen here, also?" Blade asked, anticipation showing on his face.

"Aye," Duffy grinned. "Captain Shandy was correct. They are around the north-side of the island in a little inlet."

"Any signs of our draglings?" Tharill asked, having stood silent listening to the exchange as long as he could bear.

"No," Duffy said with a frown.

"Could they have off-loaded the dragons without you seeing them?" Blade asked. "Any other ships in the area?"

"No, it was almost dawn when we landed and as we were only a half-day behind them. I don't see when they would have had time to unload them without us seeing it," Duffy continued. "As for any ships in the area, we have seen only your cutter."

"Very well," Blade said. "We've brought four swivels, 200 pounds of shot, powder, extra weapons, provisions, and sixteen more able bodied fighting men,

"What is happening with the *Sea Pucca*?" Duffy asked. "Where is she bound and when will she come for us?"

"That whole situation is, as captain Shandy says, *best discussed over a strong cup of tea*," Blade said with a pat on Duffy's back.

The far northeast area of the Weite Ozean was well known for its rough waters and changing winds. Although, the Saxon Navy had larger, double and even triple-decked man-of-war ships, compared to the smaller Celtic ships, the playing field was more level now as the turbulent water would only allow for the upper gun-ports to be usable.

Also in the Celtic Navy's favor was the weather-gauge. The Celtic Navy had the advantage of the strong north-easterly winds, giving them more maneuverability than the lumbering Saxon ships. Both navies were drawing closer to each other, cannons poised, sharpshooters high-up in the rigging and boarding parties readied.

It was into this intense scene the *Sea Pucca* and Captain Flannagáin's ships sailed into. Up on *Sea Pucca's* signal mast flew several flags which translated into a request for a parley. While Captain Flannagáin's ship set a course for the Celtic Navy ships *Sea Pucca* veered in the direction of what Prince Rutgar said was King Van Slauthe's flagship.

Possibly not understanding the signals from the *Sea Pucca*, a 74-gun Saxon man-of-war let loose a thunderous volley of cannon shots which blew bursts of flame and clouds of smoke across the water. Rutgar screamed out in pain before being slammed onto the deck.

Tharill could see his breath in the chilled morning air. The glow of the rising sun was bright, but not warming. *The hatchlings will not last long in this cold,* he thought and blew on his hands, rubbing them together. He found the smell of the air was depressing. It was dragonless. Although there were plenty of other creatures and birds about the small island, having once been home to a thriving species of dragons, it was tantamount to being lifeless, as far as Tharill was concerned.

"Cup of tea?" Blade asked, startling Tharill from his thoughts. "Here, this will warm your hands and innards," Blade said holding a metal cup in his outstretched hand.

"Thank you, if you don't mind me asking," Tharill said, "which one is your son?" he asked, indicating in the direction of the *Sea Pucca's* crew who were lining up for breakfast.

"I am sorry to say," Blade said lowering his head and toeing at the ground with his booted foot. "I have been informed he disappeared shortly after the boat landed."

"Then they may know we are here and already be lying in wait for us."

"Aye,"

"Does your son dislike you enough to watch you die?" Tharill bit the end of the sentence off just as he said it; instantly regretting having said words. "Oh, Mister Blade, I did not mean to…"

"It's alright lad," Blade cut him short and took a sip of his steaming tea. "I don't know him well enough to know if he would or would not *want to see me dead*." The two walked to a nearby log and sat down. "It has been over eight years since I've seen my wife and son. So, you see I almost did not even recognize him when he was pointed out to me on the ship."

Tharill was unsure if Blade wanted him to ask questions or just listen. But, when Blade said no more, Tharill decided to ask, "Why have you not seen them?"

Blade seemed to be relieved at the question. "Oh, it is all political, actually. My wife is Countess Kjersti of the royal Kvale family. Her mother married Prince Joaquin Garcia Delagarza of Spana as part of a treaty between Noreg and Spana. When the border dispute between Saxony and Spana broke out ten years ago Noreg stayed neutral but my mother-in-law stayed loyal to her husband's family."

"Well that sounds complicated," Tharill said.

"Aye, it is." Blade sighed with a half-laugh, "As you know King Fios sided with Saxony."

"And who is declaring war on us, but Saxony. When all fingers should be pointing at Spana!" Tharill said through gritted teeth.

"Hopefully, that will change when *Sea Pucca* intercepts the Saxon Navy."

"If it makes it in time."

Duffy ran over with shaving soap dripping from his cheek. "Mister Blade, one of the lookouts reports a ship bearing in from the southwest."

"Is it ours?"

"Definitely not, the lookout said he was not familiar with the ship's build," Duffy said, wiping at his face with a cloth. "I've sent others to investigate."

"Very well, Mister Duffy. How long until they make land," Blade asked striding back to camp.

"Two hours or more,"

"Bring me my charts," Blade shouted to a crewman holding his cup out to the cook to be refilled. "Have everyone eat up a good breakfast and gather their weapons. We must prepare to defend ourselves, in case this ship sends a landing party to this side of the island." The camp came alive with scurried yet seemingly well-ordered activity of crewmen hurrying here and there.

When the drawing of the island and surrounding water was rolled out, Blade tapped his finger on the locations where he wanted the cannons set, sharp-shooters placed and rough barricades built. "We don't know if this approaching ship is friend or foe. Once we have dealt with it, we can move on to our plan for rescuing your baby dragons." The last comment was directed at Tharill.

"It is an Azwani baghlah ship," a crewman relayed upon returning from the lookouts' position.

"A what?" Duffy posed as a statement of astonishment rather than a question. "What is an Azwani ship doing in these waters?"

"We crossed paths with a west bound baghlah before leaving the *Sea Pucca*," Blade said and scratched at his day old beard. "And this ship appearing here can't be a coincidence."

"Should it not have beaten us here, in that case?" Tharill asked.

"Not necessarily," Blade said. "We packed on all the sail our cutter could bear and the baghlah we saw did not seem to be in much of a hurry." Blade walked to his tent and retrieved his telescope from within and motioned Tharill to follow. "Come with me and let us take a gander at what this ship is about."

The two walked to a narrow bluff that overlooked the south side of the island's shoreline. They crouched down in the brush and Blade peered through the Metius. He saw a small row boat containing three men pull away from the baghlah.

"Well, they are definitely not an invasion party," Blade said and handed Tharill the scope.

Tharill stared through the lens for a few seconds and then changed his position to view the boat from a different angle. "It's Fozan!" he cheered handing Blade the telescope.

"Who?" Blade asked and lifted the glass to his eye.

"He and his brother were at the Faire on Scotia."

"What is he doing here?"

"I don't know," Tharill said jumping to his feet. "But, I'm going to find out!"

"Wait!" Blade rose from his crouching position and grabbed Tharill's arm. "Are you sure you can trust him?"

"Do gnarts have tusks?" was all he said before making his way down to the beach; Blade following a short distance behind him. *Sea Pucca's* sharp-shooters watching them as the small boat landed and two men got out.

"Tharill, my friend!" Fozan shouted. "I was not expecting to find you here."

"Me neither," Tharill said as the two shook hands. "This is lieutenant Blade MacIntosh, second in command of my uncle's ship the *Sea Pucca*."

"Greetings," Fozan said and raised his fist to his heart while taking a slight bow.

"Tharill has spoken fondly of you," Blade said eyeing the Azwani closely. "What brings you to Creggan Island?"

"His brother," Fozan said, indicating Tharill.

"Rory?" The relief in Tharill's voice was profound and he began to pound Fozan with questions. "You have had contact with him? Is he alright? Where is he?"

Fozan raised his hands and said, "Be of good cheer, my friend. Your brother is on our ship and in good hands with Miss Burlong." Then putting his hand on Tharill's shoulder he continued. "He was shot and fell from a pier at the Scotia dock-yard. Badar and I were about to row out to our ship when it happened and we plucked him from the water."

"Sweet dragon's breath," Tharill said in a shaken and trembling voice. "Thank you, thank you. With all my heart, thank you. I must go to him."

"But, why did you come here?" Blade interrupted.

"Badar followed the men and heard them talking about plans to come to this island. We thought this is where Rory had planned to come."

"No, he was supposed to tell Rutgar's uncle that Rutgar was safe with me and to meet us on Dara Island." Tharill said with deep concern sounding in his voice.

"Oh, I see."

"King Van Slauthe has declared war on the Celtic Islands because no one was notified that Rutgar was safe," Tharill said.

"Shall we set sail for Saxony, then?" Fozan asked.

Tharill said no and relayed the current hatchling dilemma and how Rutgar was already on his way to correct the misunderstanding between King Van Slauthe and King Fios.

"Let's return to the camp so I can show you how the situation currently stands here on the island," Blade said and gestured for Tharill and Fozan to head in that direction.

"I'll send my men back to bring Badar to shore and tell Miss Burlong and your brother that you are here," Fozan said and shouted something in Azwani to his men standing by the row boat. They pushed the boat back out into the water and began rowing back to the baghlah.

First Blade showed Fozan the map of the island and then took him and Tharill to a large out cropping of rocks on top of a steep hill overlooking the other side of the island where the Spana encampment was located.

"They have started moving the hatchlings from the ship to the island," Tharill said pointing at two boats with a cage in each heading for the shore. "It is too cold here. They will die if left out in the open tonight." His face colored with a deep sense of concern and he turned to Blade. "We have to do something and do it before it gets much colder or there will be no hatchlings alive to rescue."

Blade took in a deep breath, sighed in thought and brought his telescope to his eye. "There has to be well over a hundred crew on the ship plus at least another thirty or so in the encampment below," he calculated. "How many men do you have on your ship, Fozan?"

"I have thirty-seven, not counting Badar or myself."

"We can't take both the ship and the encampment," Blade said shaking his head. "We need to have all the dragons in the same place for one thing," He added. "We will also need a diversion to keep the ship crew distracted while we overtake their encampment.

"We can take care of that. My brother and I will burn it to the water line!" Fozan answered slamming his fist to his chest. "It would be an honor!"

"Tharill, can the dragons be removed from their cages?" Blade asked. "They would be easier to transport to Fozan's ship. Possibly only tie them up so they don't run away."

"But, won't they burn us with fire?" Fozan voiced his concern for his crew and ship.

"Oh, they are just hatchlings," Tharill said. "They don't have any flame yet. Their scales aren't even fully formed so they can't even retain their own body heat. That is why it is so important to get them out of the cold."

"Can you transport the dragons in your ship back to Whidley?"

"Yes, I only have the three horses in the cargo hold," Fozan said.

One of the *Sea Pucca's* crewmen approached Blade and with a sheepish look on his face, whispered something in his ear. "Really? Just now?" Blade asked and promptly turned about without a word and strode down the hill in the direction of the *Sea Pucca's* camp.

"May I ask the matter?" Fozan voiced to the crewman.

"Mr. Blade's son has just walked back into the camp," The crewman answered, tapped the side of his nose twice and hurried to follow Lieutenant Blade back down the hill.

With a quick glance back toward the Spana encampment, Tharill asked, "What do you think? Should we go back to the camp, too?" Fozan made a 'why not' gesture with his hands and Tharill nodded in agreement.

Blade went into his tent and then summoned someone to bring his son to him. A tall lad with a hawk-like nose, high cheek bones, firm chin and large inquisitive brown eyes was led to Blade's tent where he entered alone. Several *Sea Pucca* crewmen, Tharill and Fozan approached the tent but did not attempt to enter. Mr. Duffy walked over to the tent and looked as if he were about to say something to the men, but then stood silent listening as well.

Suddenly, the tent flap flew open and Blade shouted, "Orin! Orin Duffy! Come at once!" The flap quickly closing once again. Duffy quickly ran to the front of the tent and entered. Within minutes, Blade poked his head out again and called for Tharill and Fozan to enter, which they did.

"This is my son, Joaquin Milo MacIntosh," Blade said to Tharill and Fozan. "He has informed me that there are prisoners on Delagarza's ship who must also be rescued. So, burning it is out of the question until they are freed."

"Pardon me sir," Duffy said sheepishly.

"Speak up man!" Blade snapped.

Duffy swallowed and then said, "No disrespect sir, but can we trust what the lad says. He did sabotage our ship and endangered the lives of everyone aboard."

Softening, Blade answered, "That is a very good question."

"May I answer?" Joaquin said stepping forward. "I am truly sorry for that," he said to all. "I had no choice. My uncle Curro is holding my mother and little sister captive."

"Your mother....and sister?" Blade asked, stunned. "What sister? Never mind. Does he have other hostages?"

"Yes," Joaquin continued. "There is a professor and his wife in the room next to mother's and there is someone else. I don't know who he is, but we should save him too. He is just clinging to life after the unending torture he has been going through."

"And you have no idea who this captive is?" Blade asked, but Joaquin just shook his head.

"I did sneak on to the ship to check on mother," Joaquin said. "My best friend, Hector is guarding her quarters and will help us. But, we must act quickly; the Spanian armada is expected anytime."

The group of men moved out to the map table and began making plans for the combined rescues. Badar joined the discussion when he arrived from his ship. A dense fog that had begun to roll in from the ocean would work well into their plan of attack on both the ship and the encampment.

"Timing is everything," Blade said.

"Badar and I will distract the men on shore," Fozan said.

"Tharill, twenty crewmen and I will free the dragons," Duffy added.

"As soon as the ground attack begins, Joaquin, the rest of the crew and I will board the ship and retrieve the captives," Blade said in conclusion. "This thick fog will benefit us all greatly." The group of men exchanged words of encouragement, shook hands and left the tent.

Down on the beach three horses were unloaded from the boat which had ferried them from the ship. A man and woman led the skittish and stomping animals up the beach. Tharill walked toward them with Fozan and Badar looking at the familiar horses. Then he realized he knew the man and woman as well. He ran over to them startling the horses as he drew the man and woman close to him.

"Ouch! Sweet dragon's breath, Tharill!" Rory cried out in pain. "You trying to break my ribs as well?"

"Are you alright?" Tharill pulled back to look at his brother from head to toe. "You've been shot? Should you be out like this?"

"Do gnarts have tusks?" Rory answered. "Besides, I have my nurse with me."

"So, I see," Tharill said noticing that he still had his arm around Reesa, who looked slightly embarrassed at all of the attention. "I am so glad to see you!" Tharill blurted out before he could catch himself.

"And I you," she answered, her large blue eyes glinting with moisture.

"Did you bring the fire balls?" Badar asked Rory.

"Yes, they are wrapped in the tarp as you asked."

"Fire ball?" Tharill asked.

"Remember the mounted whirling-fire demonstration Fozan and I did at the Faire?" Badar asked, making a twirling motion with his hand over his head.

"Oh, yes! That will surely distract the Spanians while we free the dragons," Tharill laughed at the recollection of how startled the spectators were when Fozan and Badar rode there wonderfully decorated horses onto the exhibition field whirling two ropes in each hand with balls of fire on the ends. How they did not hit themselves, their horses, each other or any of the obstacles they galloped around was truly amazing to him.

"It is time," Blade said to Duffy and shook his hand. The crew was already pushing their boats into the water and climbing in. "As soon as we hear your signal we will board the ship. Give us twenty-minutes from when we push off to get out to the far side of the ship."

"Two shots from the swivel cannons," Duffy confirmed the signal. "And we will make sure to aim short until you've signaled that your mission was successful."

"How do you plan to get the dragons to Fozan's ship?" Blade asked Tharill.

"Free them from their cages and hopefully get them to follow me."

"Are you serious?" Reesa asked. "They won't follow you Tharill."

"Then we'll have to drive them to the beach,"

"Like cattle?" Reesa snorted with laughter. Her face instantly overcome with crimson coloring. "You mean like herding ducks?" Innocent laughter bursting from within her and spreading to the others.

"Stop!" Rory pleaded. "It hurts to laugh!" This made the others laugh even harder.

"Fozan," Reesa said, trying to regain her composure. "Please have one of your men bring two baskets of the dried fish from your ship. I bet the hatchlings are very hungry by now."

"Feed them?" Duffy asked, very skeptical. "Don't they bite?"

"Like Nile crocodiles, I hear," Fozan laughed over his shoulder from where he stood talking to one of his men.

"Do they bite? Really. Tell me the truth," Duffy asked, genuinely concerned.

"They can, but it would be more like a huge goose pinch than a bite," Tharill tried to sound reassuring.

"They don't have any teeth yet," Reesa said. "You'll be fine, Mr. Duffy, truly."

"Geese can bite pretty hard…" Duffy grumbled.

# CHAPTER #23

## *WHEN DRAGONS CRY*

The fog was thick, cold and grey. It had quickly rolled in from the east, engulfed Delagarza's ship, swept onto the beach, through his encampment and up over the steep hills behind him. He stamped his boots on the ground trying to warm his feet. It was only around 3 o'clock in the afternoon but it felt like early evening. There was something in the air. He took in a deep breath and held it for a moment. It was a musky smell. He inhaled again and walked to where one of the dragon cages sat.

"¿Como estas?" He said to the trembling hatchling. "Oh, I guess you do not speak Spanian. Do you, little fire monster?" Sniffing the air again, he said, "it is you stinky creatures I smell." Out of the corner of his eye, he caught sight of a flash and then the sound of a loud boom. *Cannon fire.*

"Nos van a atacar! Delagarza yelled to the men near him guarding the cages, pulled his sword from its sheath and a flintlock pistol from his belt. He heard a high pitched screaming 'lil-lil-lil-lil' and the sound of hoof beats thundering in from three directions.

243

He prepared himself to fight the mounted intruders and shouted orders for his men to repeal the invaders.

But what he saw instead was a blaze of whirling fireballs on top of some type of glittering beast. The vision of the creature caused him to step back in shock. Men around him began to abandon their posts, running away in terror screaming, "El Diablo! El Diablo!"

Two more fire-wielding animals stormed through the camp. Delagarza shaded his eyes to cut the glare of the flames from his vision and saw that the demon creatures were actually men on horses twirling balls of fire on the ends of ropes or chains. The horses they rode were adorned in some type of sparkling paint and long flowing fabric.

"Son sólo hombres a caballos!" Delagarza shouted over and over. But, his men saw what they considered devils and not merely men on horses. Most of his crew was already out of sight.

Tharill could hear Fozan and Badar screaming their Azwani war-cry. From where he and Reesa crouched in the shadows, he could also see Rory riding into the campsite whirling the blazing fireballs around his head. Even though he knew who and what they were, the sight still made him gasp in awe at the spectacle horse and rider presented.

Bull reared up and spun around causing the fireballs to leave long streaks of thin flames encircling both horse and rider. Tharill cringed at the thought of the long sparkling fabric that draped the horse catching fire and burning both Bull and Rory alive.

"Oh, my!" Reesa cried and gripped Tharill's arm. "He is going to catch himself on fire!"

"No, they'll be fine," Tharill tried to assured her. But there was an obvious lack of conviction in his voice. "Come on. Let's go free our dragons!"

The air was not only filled with the Azwani battle cries and smoke from the fireballs, but the hatchlings were now alternating between wailing and making high pitched screaming sounds.

Tharill and Reesa skirted the camp and made their way to the cages. "I'll unlock the cages," Tharill said. "You start enticing them to the beach with the fish." Reesa nodded and pulled some fish from one of the baskets.

As Tharill opened the doors, Reesa tossed fish to the frightened hatchlings and began walking toward the beach dropping more fish as she did. The hungry draglings immediately started to follow Reesa gobbling up the fish as she tossed them. Two very skittish hatchlings had to be dragged from their cages by their tails. But, once with the other hatchlings they followed like little scaly sheep.

Blade heard the cannon fire from shore but signaled his men to wait a while longer before boarding Delagarza's ship. He could hear the sound of men leaving the ship to help their companions on shore. When the last boat departed, Blade and his crew boarded the boat with little resistance.

Joaquin lead the group down into the hold of the ship where they broke down the doors of three rooms. The first held Urmi Landfor, Professor Burlong, and his wife. In the second room they found a severely beaten Rastom Razmadze who appeared close to death. Duffy was shocked by what had obviously been an unrelenting and savage beating.

Blade entered the third room with his son, where he saw a very beautiful, slim, dark-haired woman sitting by the stern window of the cabin. On her lap sat a large white cat, at her side a packed bag and coat. Joaquin strode over to his mother and kissed her on the cheek. She brushed his bangs from his face and whispered something to him that made his smile. Gracefully getting to her feet she walked to the door where Blade stood stiff and pale with emotion.

245

"Hello, Mr. MacIntosh," she said, raising her hand for him to kiss, which he did and bowed at the same time.

"It has been a long time Countess," Blade said, his voice cracking and still holding her hand which she did not pull away.

"Come here, Rhona," She called to a young girl sitting quietly in a chair holding a stuffed bunny close to her chest. Blade turned and looked at the girl. His face flushed and he choked back his tears. The child of about eight years of age rose and walked to her mother, shyly clinging to her stuffed toy.

"Rhona, this is your father, Mr. MacIntosh," Countess Consuela Delagarza Macintosh said in a soft reassuring voice. "Say hello."

"Hello," The girl said quickly and then pulled her bunny close to her face.

Blade knelt in front of the little dark haired beauty, a child version but exact image of the woman standing next to her. "Hello, my dear," Blade said, tears now streaming down his face. Upon seeing this, the little girl pulled a handkerchief from her sleeve and offered it to him.

"Thank you," he said and returned his gaze to the Countess. "You named her after my mother."

"Just as we talked about doing," Consuela answered; taking the handkerchief their daughter offered and wiped the tears from Blades face. "Naming our first daughter after your mother," she continued.

"Why didn't you send for me?" Blade asked pulling her in close to him. "I would have come for you."

"And that is why," Consuela said, lying her head on his shoulder. "I did not tell you. My brother would have killed you."

"Well, he might have tried," Blade said and kissed her again.

Hector poked his head through the open door and said, "Tenemos que irnos ahora!"

"Si," Joaquin answered, "we need to leave now!" And picked up his little sister.

Blade escorted his wife from the room shouting, "Let's go! Let's go!" to the remaining *Sea Pucca* crew.

Lieutenant Duffy led his raiders, a mixture of *Sea Pucca* and *Kwaitia* crewmen out from the trees and onto the beach where the boats from the *Hav Fuglen,* filled with heavily armed men, were now landing.

The Azwani men began screaming their high-pitched war cry, "Lil-lil-lil-lil-lil-lil" and wielding their long curved swords as they ran toward the men jumping from the boats. The *Sea Pucca* crew ran out onto the beach brandishing boarding axes, swords and pikes. They too yelled and hooted as they ran at the enemy.

Delagarza had just lost the blood trail of an injured fire-wielding men on horseback, he had been following, when he heard the loud clash of metal on metal and screams coming from the north beach head. He started to run in that direction but then checked himself, instead turning back to the area where the cages were.

When he got there he discovered the cages were empty. Looking around the ground he found dragon and boot prints. Delagarza called out to his men, but none answered. *They must be fighting at the north beach.* As the fog was still thick, he had to crouch down every so often to make sure he was still heading in the right direction, although he was certain the tracks would lead him to the south beach of the island.

In a small clearing just before reaching the beach, Tharill stopped and looked about. "This will be a good place to keep the hatchlings while we wait for the boats."

"Yes," Reesa agreed. "These trees and those bushes will make excellent boundaries to help me keep my little herd of scaled-sheep together."

"I think a group of sheep are called a 'flock'," Tharill laughed.

"They are a herd if they have scales," Reesa joked back.

"I'll signal the boats to come in and pick us up," Tharill said. "Do you think you can keep these little smoke-puffers here until I get back?"

"As long as I don't run out of fish!" Reesa said with an obvious lack of conviction.

Tharill returned from the beach to find the hatchlings and Reesa gone.

"Reesa?" He yelled. "Reesa where did you go?" He grinned at the thought of her chasing after her herd of hatchlings like *Little Bo Peep*. But, the grin left his face as soon as he saw Delagarza approach pushing Reesa in front of him, a knife at her throat.

"Stop or she is dead!" Delagarza barked, his face red with anger.

Fozan, Badar and Rory brought their panting and sweaty horses to abrupt stops when they got to the beach. Fozan was bent over in his saddle, a bullet wound to his shoulder.

"Dismount!" Delagarza commanded. "Dismount now!"

Rory instantly pulled a pistol from his belt, cocked the hammer and pointed it at Delagarza.

Tharill seeing this, pleaded, "Rory, do as he says! Please!"

"Rory? Rory Gruaige?" Delagarza questioned. "I thought we had done away with you!"

Rory moved his horse closer and Delagarza put more pressure on the knife he held at Reesa's throat. "Dismount! Now!" Delagarza ordered.

Rory stepped down from Bull's saddle, maintaining eye contact with Delagarza. Badar helped his wounded brother off of his horse and sat him down on a nearby log.

"What do you want?" Rory questioned.

Delagarza looked Rory directly in the eye and said, "For you to be dead and stay dead." Tharill shuddered at the intense hatred in Delagarza's voice.

Blade's row boats softly thudded against the side of the baghlah. *Kwaitia's* crew helped the passengers up into the ship and settled them in the guest cabins. Blade then went to the cargo hold and saw that the hatchlings and horses had not been loaded yet. So, he took his telescope to the bow and peered through it toward the beach. At first he could not see anything due to the thick fog and stood peering into the telescope for several moments. He was about to give up when a mild breeze brushed some of the fog aside and saw what was happening on shore.

"Shite!"

"What is it?" Joaquin asked stepping up beside him.

"Look," Blade said, handing Joaquin the telescope. "Curro has captured our raiding party."

"We will now return to the encampment and put those smelly little creatures back in their cages." Delagarza yelled out, amusement ringing in his voice. "Then I will deal with my brother-in-law," he added and shoved Reesa to the ground. Turning to his crew, which had reassembled on the south beach, he shouted orders for them to round up the dragons, take control of the horses and bring the prisoners back to the encampment.

Crewmen kicked and hit the little dragons with sticks trying to get them to head back to the cages but they kept scattering and started making screeching noises so loud that Delagarza threatened to start shooting them if Tharill and the others did not help contain them.

"Quietly, now," Blade said, just above a whisper to his men as the three row boats approached the shore. But, it was not the noise of rowing or men talking that he had heard. He raised his hand for the boats to stop and he listened. They all listened. It was the sound of massive amounts of air being displaced by wings of birds. *No, not birds.* But, what? They sat in their boats which rocked silently on the waves of the incoming tide.

Rory latched the last door of the hatchling cages and said, "I'm sorry little ones. We will find a way to get you back home. Dragon's Honor." One of Delagarza's men began ushering him in the direction of the other prisoners when Rory stopped mid-stride, hearing something. The sound of rushing wind. He turned back and looked at the hatchlings when they all started making a high pitched squealing noise. The guard prodded him on with the poke of a musket barrel in his back. "Alright, alright," Rory exclaimed, the jab being close to his wounded shoulder.

Delagarza cocked his pistol, "I'm going to kill those smelly, screeching little creatures right now! I don't care why they want them so badly back in Spana!" He roared, walking out of his tent. But, he stopped just outside of the tent, something was amiss. The smell of the hatchlings was now over powering and their incessant screaming was almost deafening.

The first large bull dragon dove into the camp from the air landing on all four feet. He opened his mouth and blew a long hot flame catching several startled Delagarza crewmen that were instantly burnt to bones before they knew what happened.

Large adult dragons were flying into the camp and spraying fire everywhere they looked. A young bull dragon flew over a tent and grabbed the top with its claws, pulling it from the ground, stakes and all sending men running for their lives. Dragons were attacking everything that moved except the frightened horses that were running toward the beach.

The *Sea Pucca* crewman yelled to their Azwani allies to lie down and not move; which they did, in spite of the natural urge to run from such danger.

As the dragonesses came, fury raging in their deep billowing calls to their young, they grabbed at the cages bending the metal and ripping the wood apart to release their offspring. As each hatchling was freed a dragoness would tenderly grasp it in her clawed feet and fly away. But, not the bull dragons, they appeared to be resolute on the destruction of the entire camp.

Tharill ran through the chaos with Reesa in tow. When a bull dragon swooped down on them, as if to blow flame, Tharill threw himself on top of Reesa. But, the dragon pulled up at the last moment and flew away.

Tharill lifted himself off of Reesa. "Are you alright?" He gasped, pulling her close to him. "I don't know what I would do if anything happened to you."

"No, I am fine," She stammered and then he kissed her. He kissed her with all of the passion he did not even know existed.

"Oh, I am so sorry!" He cried. "I don't know what came over me!"

Reesa blinked her eyes as if confused about what had just happened. Tharill released her and sat back for an instant looking at her. *Is she puzzled over the near dragon attack or my kiss?* "I'd better go find the others and make sure they are alright." He finally said.

"Oh, we are just fine," Rory said, approaching from the bushes.

"But, you two appear to be better," Fozan laughed, holding a cloth to his injured shoulder.

Tharill and Reesa looked at each other and blushed with laughter.

"Let's get out of here before Delagarza, if he is still alive, can organize what is left of his crew." Fozan said in an attempt to hurry everyone to safety.

Blade and his men waited in their boats off shore and out of the carnage until all of the dragons had flown away. Blade surveyed the beach with his telescope, when he saw Tharill, Reesa and the others with horses in tow come out into the open where he gave the order to once again begin rowing.

"We need to sail away as soon as possible." Fozan said. "We can't go up against Delagarza's well armed ship and hope to come out unscathed."

"Sunk or burned to the water line is more like it," Badar stated. "He means us dead, to say the least. You should have set that ship alight when you were on it."

As soon as the horses were secured in the hold, Fozan gave the order to make sail and just in time as the *Hav Fuglen* was spotted rounding the south side of the island. The *Hav Fuglen's* gun ports were open and the cannons run out.

The *Kwaitia's* sails sprung to life like a great white peacock spreading his tail feathers. The triangle shaped canvas filled with wind and the ship began gliding southward. At her best she could sail at 9 knots but she was also somewhat unwieldy; whereas the *Hav Fuglen* could bear twice the canvas and was rather agile for a ship her size.

The first shot from the *Hav Fuglen* sent a ball through one of *Kwaitia's* large ornate stern windows. The next was lower. "They are going for our rudder!" Fozan yelled. He was right as that is exactly what the next round of shots did. Without steerage the ship was bound to just go wherever the wind blew it.

"What do we do now?" Tharill yelled.

"What can we do?" Badar responded, his face tight with anger.

Fozan ordered his flag to be lowered, to acknowledge an offer of surrender. But, when the *Hav Fuglen* drew near, it let go a full broad side of cannon fire decimating rigging, sail, the deck and injuring many of *Kwaitia's* crew.

"He plans to sink us?" Fozan yelled to Blade. "With his own sister, nephew and niece on board?"

Blade did not answer but climbed up the mizzen mast with a sharp-shooting rifle slung over his back. He took aim at who he believed to be Delagarza and pulled the trigger. But the next broadside took out the mizzen mast sending it and Blade into the water below with a great splash. Blade sprung to the surface of the water gasping for air. Seeing this, Joaquin jumped into the water.

He swam to his father and helped him hold onto the floating mast. The water around the two reverberated with the sound of cannon fire. But, it sounded as if it were coming from another direction.

"It's the *Sea Pucca*!" Tharill shouted and threw a rope to Joaquin and his father.

"I knew he'd come," Blade moaned, blood flowing from a wound on his forehead.

And the *Sea Pucca* did come. Guns a blazing! The *Hav Fuglen* came about and made a hasty retreat in the direction of Spana. The *Sea Pucca* did not peruse but rather went directly to the aid of the floundering *Kwaitia*.

# CHAPTER #24

## *A SCHEME OF MISDIRECTION REVEALED*

Dinner in the great cabin in the *Sea Pucca* was very festive that evening. Repairs to the *Kwaitia* were well underway and the tone was relaxed and joyful. Fozan and Badar had just bid their farewells to return to their ship when the door to the cabin re-opened. The men rose to welcome the women back as they had departed earlier to put Rhona to bed and do a last check on Rastom Razmadze's bandages and comfort for the night.

"How is Rastom faring, tonight?" Rutgar asked Mrs. Burlong who had been tending to the unconscious, man since he was brought aboard.

"He is a strong man," she answered as her husband took her hand to escort her to her chair. "I believe it is his strength of mind that is keeping him alive with so many broken bones and deeply bruised internal organs. I have done all I can as a nurse, he will need to see a doctor as soon as possible."

"For just that reason, we are headed to the closest port," Shandy assured her.

"Why would they do that to him?" Reesa asked, taking a seat between Tharill and Rory. "He did not know where you were," she indicated to the prince.

"It was more than just about me," Rutgar said. "I am sure he was questioned about Saxony's defenses and military strengths," Rutgar rubbed his hands together, his face shaded with anger. "He would have taken that information to his Death Kingdom rather than tell."

"Well, it was you," Shandy chuckled, pointing his pipe in Rutgar's direction, "who was about to go to the Death Kingdom when we approached your father's flagship!" Shandy slapped his knee and began to roar in laughter.

"What?" Reesa asked, visibly shocked by Shandy's jocular attitude after just discussing Rastom's grave injuries.

"I beg ye pardon miss for veering off course a mite. But, the lad was standing on the bow sprit waving his hands to get the attention of someone on the Saxon ship," Shandy said without sounding defensive in anyway. "I tackled him as soon as I saw him standing there, just as someone from his father's ship took a shot, barely missing him."

"Why would anyone on King Van Slauthe's ship shoot at you?" Reesa asked Rutgar.

"My hair," Rutgar said pointing to his still orange-red hair color.

"You look like a Scotia-carrot!" Shandy burst out in laughter again, but this time laughter filled the room as everyone else in the room joined in, including Rutgar. The irony that Rutgar's change of hair color played in keeping him safe during his time in the Celtic Islands would later almost result in fatal consequences from his own people was overwhelmingly viewed as rather funny although serious in nature.

After the amusement died down and the glasses were refilled with wine, Countess Consuela changed the subject. "Did you know the dragons would come for their offspring?" she asked to no one in particular.

Professor Burlong shook his head and asked Tharill. "Did you?"

"No, it had not occurred to me, either. But, we should have guessed something like that was up when we came across that ship burnt to the waterline during our balloon crossing," Tharill answered.

"Remember the piece of wood brought up from the water?" Tharill asked Shandy.

"Aye and it had dragon flame burns on it," Shandy said filling his pipe.

"That must have been their first attempt at taking a dragling." Reesa surmised.

"I think Volcae was their first attempt at taking a dragon," Urmi said.

"But, they killed Volcae," Rory said.

"I don't think they meant to," Urmi offered. "Volcae had been injured in a fight with a bull from the Ean Dubh dragle a few months earlier and was missing some scales. Unfortunately the arrow filled with enishlafen pierced his heart. Killing him."

"Enishlafen is a potent sedative," Tharill explained to the rest of the group.

"I received a mere prick of a broken arrow containing the liquid and it almost killed me," Rory said and shuddered at the thought, as if suddenly chilled.

"I was walking on the road to Paraic when I came across a group of men dressed in the Noreg style but distinctly speaking in Spanian," Urmi said. "And they forced me to go with them."

"That must be where we saw your satchel," Tharill said.

"Oh, speaking of the satchel," Shandy said and snapped his fingers. "You can pick it up at the bee Tender Malacai's cottage. He reported that he'd found it to the sheriff."

"The men were dressed in Noreg clothing, you say?" Reesa asked

"Yes indeed," Urmi nodded his head.

"The ship we were held on was Noreg, but the crew mostly spoke Spanian," Urmi said.

"By using the cover of the Noreg flag they were able to move about freely in Celtic waters," Shandy offered.

"Noreg has always maintained an uneasy neutrality in the Saxony-Spana border dispute," Blade said and picked up the wine bottle to offer refills for everyone.

"As you know," Countess Consuela reminded the group. "There are many members of the Noreg royalty who are married into the Spana royal family, like my parents are."

"So do you think they were complicit in this scheme to pit Celtic Islands Kingdom against our longtime allies, Noreg?" Shandy asked Blade.

"If pressed by Spana," Blade answered pouring wine into Professor Burlong's glass. "I don't know that they would have had much of a choice. Noreg has no military to speak of and relies on Spana for most of their textile imports."

The discussion was abruptly interrupted by the sound of loud thundering booms in the distance. Shandy and Blade smiled at each other and raised their glasses in a toast.

"Is it a storm?" Countess Consuela inquired.

"No, my dear," Blade answered sitting back down and grasping her hand. "That is the sound of the Celtic and Saxon navies chasing down the Spana armada that was to meet up with Delagarza's ship at Creggan Island.

"I don't understand," Olive Burlong said. "Where is the Spana armada bound for?"

"After speaking with my father and King Fios," Rutgar began, "it became clear that the king of Spana was behind a conspiracy of misdirection on the dragon killings and the attempts to kidnap me."

"Why did they want the hatchlings, though?" Reesa asked.

"Spana's chief alchemist wants to do experiments on the hatchlings," Urmi said.

"Magic?" Tharill grunted. "There is nothing magical about dragons!"

"No, not magic. Alchemy," Urmi corrected. "Many alchemists have long asserted that if fresh dragon's blood could be

257

mixed with various minerals it could be instantly dried to make the most powerful gun powder known to man."

"That is a load of gnart-dung!" Rory objected, shocking the others with his loud response. "Pardon me," he said. "But, don't you think someone would have tried all of those experiments long ago?"

"Yes, such experiments were conducted by Spana alchemists decades ago when dragon hunting was still legal, but to no avail," Urmi said. "Science is a work in progress and new things are being discovered every day."

"Well, the only thing I desire to discover this evening is a nice dry bed!" Rory said.

"I do agree, my lad," Shandy said, and gulped down the last of his wine.

Professor and Mrs. Burlong got to their feet as did Reesa and began to bid their goodnights to everyone.

Blade helped his wife to her feet and told her, "I will escort you to our room my dear, but I cannot stay. It is close to my watch so I must go on deck after I say my goodnights to you and kiss our daughter." The Countess simply smiled and nodded her head in understanding.

"Well, my lad," Shandy said walking to the cabin door with Tharill. "We should be back at Whidley Island in time for you to make the Firemoon Tide.

"Great!" Tharill laughed, "Just what I want to do after this relaxing holiday, brush scales off a bunch of blind, cranky, dragons! I simply can't wait."

On the very southern edge of Whidley Island, on the peninsula/island of Druml, in the caves where the Ean Gorm dragle live, purring sounds of content hatchlings cuddled with their mothers could be heard. All was well at the home of the Whidley Island dragons once again.

Watch for

Tharill's next adventure

## *In Search of Dragons*

To be released in 2017

## *About the author*

Catriona was born dyslexic at a time when little was known about the condition. Learning to read was very difficult and led to a troubled childhood continuing into her teens and on through her young adult years.

When her son became school age and was diagnosed with dyslexia things began to make sense. She now embraces the *creative* side of dyslexia and lets 'spell check' and her 'editor' take care of the finer points.

MacRury describes herself as *a figment of her own imagination* and those who know her best will agree. She lives on an island in the Pacific Northwest of the USA. But, she makes regular trips to Ireland and Wales to draw inspiration for her writing.

The dog depicted in this novel is based on her own collie, Rusty. He is her constant companion and every bit as *talkative* in real life as in fiction.